MW01232666

The Hard Luck Klub

For Kathy
All the best,

***Other Five Star Titles
by Doug Allyn:***

Welcome to Wolf Country

The Hard Luck Klub

Stories by Doug Allyn

Five Star • Waterville, Maine

Copyright © 2002 by Doug Allyn
Introduction copyright © 2002 by Doug Allyn

All stories reprinted by permission of the author.

"Roadkill," copyright © 1996 by Doug Allyn. First published in
Ellery Queen's Mystery Magazine, May 1996.
"The Sultans of Soul," copyright © 1993 by Doug Allyn. First
published in *Ellery Queen's Mystery Magazine*, March 1993.
"The Taxi Dancer," copyright © 1998 by Doug Allyn. First
published in *Alfred Hitchcock's Mystery Magazine*, November 1998.
"Sleeper," copyright © 1991 by Doug Allyn. First published in
Ellery Queen's Mystery Magazine, May 1991.
"The Hessian," copyright © 2000 by Doug Allyn. First
published in *Murder Most Confederate*, edited by
Martin H. Greenberg.
"Déjà vu," copyright © 1988 by Doug Allyn. First published in
Alfred Hitchcock's Mystery Magazine, June 1988.
"Candles in the Rain," copyright © 1992 by Doug Allyn. First
published in *Ellery Queen's Mystery Magazine*, November 1992.
"The Bad Boyz Klub," copyright © 1999 by Doug Allyn. First
published in *Diagnosis Dead*, edited by Jonathan Kellerman.

All rights reserved.

This collection is a work of fiction. Names, characters, places,
and incidents are either the product of the author's
imagination, or, if real, used fictitiously.

Five Star First Edition Mystery Series.
First printing

Published in 2002 in conjunction with
Tekno Books and Ed Gorman.

Set in 11 pt. Plantin by Al Chase.

Printed in the United States on permanent paper.

Library of Congress Cataloging-in-Publication Data
Allyn, Douglas.
    The hard luck klub : stories / by Doug Allyn.
        p. cm.—(Five Star first edition mystery series)
    ISBN 0-7862-4332-5 (hc : alk. paper)
    1. Detective and mystery stories, American.   I. Title: Hard
luck klub.   II. Title.   III. Series.
    PS3551.L49 H37 2002
    813'.54—dc21   2002029974

The Hard Luck Klub

Table of Contents

Introduction

Writing about Heroes is easy. Superman, Batman, Beowulf. The tough part is inventing a villain ferocious enough to pose a threat.

Writing about losers is a lot more fun. Not criminals, necessarily, although a few of the characters in this collection qualify.

The people in these stories are men and women (and one dog) who have made big mistakes in their lives. Like you and me.

They know what losing feels like.

And they don't want to do it any more.

Facing tough situations, they're determined to win, no matter what. Which makes them far braver than Heroes.

And a lot more interesting.

DA

Roadkill

The dead dog on the shoulder of the road twitched. Only a reflex, David thought, even as he touched his Jeep's brakes and switched on its flashers. He pulled off onto the shoulder of the highway and slowed to a halt a few yards from the dog's body. Big dog, brindle fur. Boxer, maybe? Or a Staff? It was so battered and bloody he couldn't even be sure of the breed. Or whether it was one of his patients. He considered getting a hypo of Socomb, sodium phenobarbital, out of his bag on the off chance the animal was still suffering, but decided against it. The movement he'd noticed was probably windblast from a passing car. The dog certainly wasn't moving now.

Some moron leaned on his horn as he blew past at eighty per. Traffic on the State Road four-lane was always fast and furious. Commuters from Algoma or points north hurrying to or from factory jobs in Saginaw. He waited for a break in traffic before climbing out of the Jeep and trudging up to the dog, automatically cataloguing its injuries. A godawful mess. Belly ripped open, purplish tangle of entrails oozing out onto the gravel, shoulder battered, possibly broken, and blood flowing freely from a dozen different lacerations. Not quite dead yet, there were still faint, feathery spasms of respiration. But it would only be a matter of minutes now. Maybe less. It looked like it had been hit and run over by some hotshot who probably hadn't even checked his rear view mirror to see what it was.

What it was, was a pit bull, female, four to six years old. David didn't recognize the dog, and he was fairly sure he would have remembered. The breed wasn't common in this

11

part of the state and they were remarkably hardy. He seldom saw them in his veterinary practice.

The dog was wearing an ordinary leather collar, not one of the spiked monstrosities the macho clowns who favor this breed seem to prefer. David knelt beside the dog, slid his fingers along the collar, feeling for a name tag or license so he could inform its owner what happened—

She bit him! Her jaws clamped onto his forearm like a vise, holding him immobile. Sweet Jesus! He froze, unable to move. He could already feel his right hand chilling, going numb, and so far she was only maintaining her hold. She hadn't savaged the arm, or even clamped down on it full force, yet. She was just holding him, to keep from being hurt. But Pits have jaws like metal shears. Dying or not, if she bit down much harder, she could break his wrist. Or sever it.

He shifted his position slightly, trying to read her eyes. They were clouded with pain, but not glazed. She was conscious, or at least partly so. He could feel the faint whisper of her breath on his upper arm. She was terribly injured. Not quite dead, though. But his arm was going to be, and soon, if she didn't let it go. If he'd brought the damned hypo, he'd have put her down on the spot. Death would've been nearly instantaneous, especially for a dog in her condition. But without it, trying to pull free or struggle with her was risky business. Any movement that caused her pain might well cost him his arm.

And so he knelt and began talking to her. Quietly, he tried to explain the situation. That he hadn't meant to hurt her, he'd only stopped to help. That he was the only veterinarian in thirty miles and wouldn't be nearly as useful with only one arm. She didn't seem impressed. He tried stroking her head with his free hand but she growled, or seemed to. It was hard to be sure considering she had a mouthful of his wrist.

He talked nonstop for nearly five minutes, to no effect. Her jaws remained tightly clamped. Maybe she'd forgotten she was holding him, or why. His right hand was totally numb now, and his lower back was on fire from crouching over her. The stench of blood and offal and road dust in his nostrils was beginning to make his stomach churn . . . And then she released him.

Just like that. She relaxed her hold on his wrist, and let him go. And lowered her head to the dirt. To die. He rose stiffly, massaging his bruised wrist, staring down at her. She hadn't broken the skin, but his fingers were sizzling with the fiery pinpricks of returning circulation. And his eyes were stinging, too, for no particular reason he could fathom. God knows, he'd seen animals die before. It came with the territory. Some of them, he'd known quite well. Still . . .

A car rocketed past at maximum speed, shaking him with its windblast, horn blaring.

"Asshole!" he yelled, shaking his fist at the driver. And the universe. The hell with this! He stripped off his leather jacket, then his shirt. He made a loop out of the shirtsleeve, slipped it over the dog's muzzle and tied her jaws closed, apologizing all the while. Then he slid her onto his jacket, picked her up and sprinted for his Jeep.

At the clinic, he barreled through the front door, yelling for his assistant, Bettina, as he charged past the startled patrons in the waiting room, blood streaming from the maimed animal cradled in his arms. In his surgery, he gently lowered the dog to the stainless steel operating table. Still alive. Barely.

"Give her atropine intramuscular, skip the Acepromazine," he barked as Bettina, his veterinary tech, trailed him into the small operating room. "She's already in shock. Give her a light dose of sodium pentothal and get a tracheal tube in her. Oxygen, nitrous oxide, and halothane."

"Respiratory monitor?"

"Not now. Her breathing's the least of our problems. I'll check her intestines for lacerations. You start cleaning up the gashes on her torso and throat so we can see what the hell we're into here."

"You'd better scrub," she said. He almost bit her head off. But she was right, of course. No point in suturing the body cavity closed only to have the dog die of infection later. Hell, she was probably going to die on the table anyway.

But she didn't. Bettina anesthetized her without incident. The dog was too weak now to offer even token resistance. The intestines protruding from the gash in her belly looked grim, but they weren't damaged. David cleaned off the road dirt, rinsed the wound with tetracycline in saline, then gently prodded the bowels back into the abdominal cavity and began suturing the gash closed.

"What happened to her?" Bettina asked.

"She got run over," David snapped. "What does it look like?"

"That's my point," Bettina said calmly, unruffled. "Look at these lesions. No car did this."

David glanced up from his stitching for a moment, and paused. She was right. The pit bull's shoulders and throat were crisscrossed with puncture wounds, dozens of them.

"How deep?" he asked.

"Two to three centimeters. They're obviously bites, David, but look at the span between the canines. Something very big did this. And why so many? I've seen dogs that have been torn up in fights. I've never seen anything like this."

"I've seen it once," David said grimly. "In my last year of vet school at Michigan State. The state police busted a dog fighting ring south of Saginaw. Arrested over a hundred

14

people, seized three dozen dogs, picked up nearly sixty grand in illegal bets. Most of the dogs were pits or Staffordshires, a few Rottweilers. Some of the dogs who'd fought in the ring looked like this one. Or worse. We had to destroy most of them."

"Destroy them? Why?"

"It wouldn't have been safe to place them with families. Pit Bulls as a breed aren't much more aggressive than any other, but dogs that have been blooded in the arena are like loaded guns afterward. They may seem docile, even friendly. Until some kid accidentally pokes Fido in the eye or something else trips his trigger. And then they're instant fighting machines, all reflexes and fangs and jaws and no compunctions about chewing people up. They've been bred for battle, and they're pretty damned good at it. Personally, I think people ought to be licensed to own them, the same way you need a license for pistols or a powerboat."

"Hey!" somebody yelled from the waiting room.

"Be with you in a minute," Bettina called. "We've had an emergency."

"How many people are waiting?" David asked.

"Not as many as there were when you came charging in with this godawful piece of meat. There's still a trail of blood—"

"Hey!"

"Go ahead, pacify the natives," David said. "I'll be finished here in a few minutes."

David was neatly tying off the final stitch in a shallow gash in the pit's shoulder when the dog's eyes blinked open. He knew she was still unconscious, the anesthetic machine was still pumping a mix of nitrous oxide and halothane into her lungs, but somehow her eyes seemed alert, as though she was aware of what was happening. David gently touched her bloodied brow a moment, and her eyes closed again.

"David?" Bettina said, sticking her head around the corner of the door, "I think you'd better step out here. A gentleman, and I use the term loosely, claims we have his dog here. A pit bull bitch? I suggested he come back later, but he's quite insistent."

"No problem. Why don't you take over here. Give her oxygen for a few minutes, then room air. I'd like to meet the *gentleman* who owns this particular lady, anyway. What's he look like?"

"Tall. You'll have no trouble spotting him," Bettina said dryly. "Trust me."

David stepped through to the waiting room counter. And stopped. Dead. The man at the counter towered over him. David was five eleven, but the Viking type facing him was nearly a foot taller, maybe more, dressed in faded work clothes. He was fortyish, thinning sandy hair, and gray eyes. His long narrow face had been permanently reddened by the wind, but even more striking were his scars. His face was marked with three deep vertical gashes, livid as warpaint. Love bites. From having a chainsaw blade buck back into your face. A savage, ugly mark. And not all that uncommon in this part of the state.

"You the doc?" His voice was gravel, and David could smell whiskey from across the counter.

"I'm Dr. Westbrook," David acknowledged. "And you are . . . ?"

"Kaipainen," he grunted. "People call me Ox. Somebody seen you pickin' up my dog. A brindle pit bull bitch? You got her?"

"I found a dog by the side of the road. She's in pretty bad shape."

"So you just brung her in, fixed her up, and now I suppose

I owe you a whole lotta money, right? Pretty slick. You had no right to take my dog."

"Maybe not," David admitted. "But right now I'm more interested in how she got into the condition she's in."

"What condition? I thought she got hit by a car."

"She was hit, all right. But she's also been thoroughly chewed up. As bad as I've ever seen. What do you use this dog for, Mr. . . . . Ox?"

"Use her for? She's my dog, that's all. She tracks some, looks out for my place when I'm workin'. What the hell business is that of yours?"

"I'm making it my business. She's been badly mauled. I think she's been fighting."

"Yah, well, she runs loose a lot, in the swamp. Maybe she tangled with a boar 'coon or somethin'. Or when she got hit—"

"No. Her injuries weren't caused by a car, or any animal she'd likely meet in the swamp. What happened to her?"

"How the hell do I know? She got loose, is all. Look, it won't do you no good to try to hold me up, Doc, I ain't got no money. So just gimme my dog and I'll get outa here."

"I'm afraid not. Not today. She can't be moved yet."

"Dammit, she's my dog and I'm takin' her."

"You try to move her now and she'll be dead before you get her to your car."

"Ain't got no car. I'll carry her careful—"

"Forget it," David said flatly. "You're not taking her. For one thing, I don't know that she actually *is* your dog."

"I just told you she was."

"Sorry, but that's not good enough. I'll have to see some proof. Why don't you come back when you're sober and we'll talk about whose dog she is. And what happened to her."

"Look you little wimp, I don't wanna hurt you, but I ain't lettin' nobody steal my dog. You'd best step aside . . ."

A police car roared into the clinic parking lot, lights flashing, and pulled up in front. The effect on Kaipainen was instantaneous. He seemed to shrink before David's eyes. The drunken rage faded like mist, and he was blinking and swallowing like a child who knows he's going to be beaten. He backed away from the counter, looked around the waiting room, then carefully sat down in one of the plastic chairs. And folded his huge hands in his lap.

Sheriff Stan Wolinski sauntered in, square as a block of concrete in his gray summer uniform. He glanced at Kaipainen, then nodded to the only patron who hadn't already fled, a tiny, silver-haired sparrow of a woman in a flowered dress, holding her cat.

"Miz Hitchworth," Wolinski nodded, touching the brim of his uniform cap. "You causin' trouble again?"

"I certainly am not!" she snapped. "Mr. Kaipainen came stomping in here yelling, and he's been drinking—"

"Yes, ma'am," Wolinski said, cutting her off with a smile. "I imagine he has. Doc, you and Ox got some kind of problem here?"

"I'm . . . not sure," David said, eyeing the subdued giant, who was all but cowering in the chair. "I ah, picked up an injured dog by the road this morning and did surgery on her. Mr. Kaipainen here claims the dog is his—"

"She is my dog," Ox interjected. "Ask anybody."

"Okay, Ox," Wolinski said mildly. "Chill out, I'll take care of things. So, Ox owes you a big bill, does he, Doc?"

"I'd like to be paid, of course," David said evenly, "but that's not the point. The dog will die if she's moved now."

"But if she's his dog, that's his lookout, isn't it?"

"I don't know that she's his dog. And under the circumstances, I'm not going to release her today. To Mr. Kaipainen or anyone else."

Wolinski eyed him a moment, then shrugged and turned to face Kaipainen. "How you been, Ox? Haven't seen you around lately."

"I been workin' over to Oscoda at the pallet plant there. Stackin' and cleanin' up."

"Kind of a long walk, isn't it?"

"I hitch. Most days I get rides. I never hitchhike on ten, though. I know that ain't legal."

"That's right," Wolinski said. "It's not. Tell you what, Ox, why don't you go home now, let me sort this thing out for you."

"But he's got my dog—"

"I know, and I promise you'll get her back. When she's better, I'll have the doc here deliver her personally so you won't have to walk back to town. That sound fair?"

"I don't know, Stan," Kaipainen said, swallowing. "She's all I got—"

"Look, Ox," Wolinski said, kneeling beside the Viking's chair, "do you remember Yvonne LeClair, the girl I used to go with back in high school?"

"Yeah, I remember Yvonne."

"Well, the doc here, he moved up here from Lansing a few years back, and ah, he and Yvonne got married. So you see, I'm not a big fan of his, you understand? And I won't let him do you wrong, Ox. You just trust me, okay? You go on home now." He rose and dusted off his knee. Kaipainen rose too, towering over Wolinski. And then stalked out without a word.

"My God, Stan," David marveled. "He's absolutely terrified of you. What on earth did you ever do to him?"

"Put him in jail once," Wolinski said simply. "Picked him up drunk, tossed him in the tank. He about went crazy in there. Tore the place up, tore himself up. I should have known better than to lock him in. So now he's afraid of me. And it's not something I'm proud of. Which is why you really are going to deliver his dog to him as soon as possible."

"No," David said. "It's not that simple."

"Look, Doc, if you're worried about your bill, Ox hasn't got doodley squat anyway. There's no point in trying to hold him up."

"It's not about the money. His dog's been ripped from one end to the other. I think she's been fighting. In a ring."

"Dogfighting, you mean? Are you sure?"

"The only time I've ever seen dogs chewed up the way this one was, they'd been fought."

"I don't know," Wolinski said doubtfully. "Ox lives out in the middle of noplace and I know that dog runs loose. Maybe she tangled with a 'coon or a bobcat—"

"No, from the bite patterns it was definitely another dog. A big one. You see, when dogs mix it up, they don't normally fight to the death. They battle long enough to decide who's stronger and then the loser lights out, end of story. Pit bulls are different, of course, because they were bred for fighting, but if they're losing, and believe me, this dog lost big time, they'll still run as a last resort. Unless they're somewhere where they can't get away. Like in a ring, for instance."

"I can't see it, Doc. For one thing, I haven't heard a thing about a dog ring. I'm not saying we've got a crime-free county. Two bikers from Pontiac are runnin' a crank lab over on the west end somewhere, some locals grow reefer in the state forest and a few cars have disappeared from the village. Hell, some kids even broke into my tool shed. But it's all small stuff. A dogfighting ring would involve a lot of people and a lot of money. There's no way I wouldn't hear about it. But even if there was one, Ox wouldn't be involved."

"Why not?"

"Hell, you met him. He's not your average social butterfly. He didn't mix with folks much before he bounced that saw off his face, avoids 'em altogether now. Doesn't drive. Can't read, for that matter. Lives alone out on Elkhart Road, traps some, probably poaches, works when he needs money for things he can't barter pelts for. He's just not the organized crime type, you know? Now, if you told me Ox was fightin' people for money, I might buy that. But his dog? Nah. Not likely."

"Then why does he have a pit bull?"

"As I recall, he found her runnin' loose a few years back. She was just a stray. Like him. Tell you what; I'll make a deal with you. I promise I'll keep a sharp lookout for any sign of your dogfighting ring, okay? But meanwhile, since a man's still innocent until proven guilty in this county, you give Ox his dog back as soon as she's fit to travel. Fair enough?"

"I guess," David said.

"Good. Oh, and Doc? The next time you see a roadkilled dog? Do me a favor and just let it be, okay? Ox Kaipainen thinks the world of that dog and he's nobody to mess with. For your sake, I surely do hope she makes a good recovery. And a quick one."

"Yeah." David nodded. "So do I."

And she did. Incredibly, when David checked on the dog a few hours after the anesthetic wore off, the bowlegged little bruiser was on her feet in the cage. She was weaving, and swathed in enough bandages to pass for a mummy's pup, but she was up. And from the fire in her eyes, she was game for a rematch with any and all comers. Bring 'em on.

David pulled a chair up beside her cage and talked to her for a full ten minutes before he even considered opening the cage door to check her wounds. No point in pushing his luck. The lady was no more sociable than her master and David's

21

arm still ached where she'd latched onto him. Over the next few days, she gentled down enough to tolerate his attentions, though she never really warmed to him. Still, they achieved an acceptable level of coexistence, civil, if not friendly. The only problem was, Kaipainen hadn't mentioned the dog's name, and it wasn't on her collar. So David called her Roadkill.

By the end of the following week, he could no longer justify keeping the dog on any medical grounds. She was still moving stiffly due to the contusions on her shoulder where she was struck, but the gashes in her back and belly were closed with no sign of infection.

So he swallowed his misgivings, loaded Roadkill into a travel cage in the back of his Jeep, and followed the crude map Bettina jotted for him. Elkart Road trailed off into the bottomlands east of Algoma, low swampy ground, not good for much but ducks, frogs, and muskrats.

And poachers. When David pulled into the overgrown yard near Kaipainen's small cabin, Ox was dressing out a dead deer. The buck was hanging from a branch of a large pine, spreadeagled and eviscerated. Ox was peeling off its hide, rolling the skin down from an incision in the animal's throat. He straightened slowly, still holding the bloody skinning knife, as David climbed out of he Jeep.

"Doc," Ox said, nodding. "Wasn't expecting you."

"I can see that," David said. "That buck's out of season, Mr. Kaipainen. Suppose I'd been the law?"

"What if you was? I found this one dead in the road. Musta been kilt by a truck."

"Not unless the truck shot it behind the ear with a small calibre weapon. I can see the bullet hole from here."

Ox glanced at the deer, then back at David. "Maybe you can. Look, Stan don't care much if a man takes meat illegal, if it's just to feed himself or his own. Long as he don't get to sellin' it, you know? You gonna rat me out to the D.N.R.?"

"What you eat and how you get it is your business, Mr. Kaipainen, I just came to bring your dog back."

"She okay?"

"She's doing very well, considering," David said, opening the cage door and carefully lifting Roadkill out. The dog limped directly to Ox, then sat obediently at his feet. The giant knelt slowly beside her and let her lick the blood off his hands. When he glanced up at David his eyes were swimming.

"She looks good," he rasped, swallowing. "I thought she might be, you know, scarred." He gestured toward his own face with the skinning knife.

"No," David said. "She's got a remarkable constitution. I doubt the scars will show at all in a year or so. Maybe a line on her belly where her fur is thin. No more than that. You'll need to change her bandages. I'll show you how to do that and give you some antibiotic ointment for her."

"No," Ox said, "I don't think I can do that."

"Do what? Change her bandages? Why not? You obviously don't go woozy at the sight of blood."

"It ain't that. Look, when I seen you that day in your office, I thought you was . . ."

"Trying to rip you off?"

"Somethin' like that, I guess. But I've talked to a few guys around town about you. They say you're okay, pretty much straight up. That you pick up stray animals sometimes, just to help 'em if you can. Somebody told me you even got a three-legged cat with one eye."

"That's right. Her name's Franken Kat."

"What the hell good is a three-legged cat?"

"She's a fair mouser. Can't catch anything but they take

one look at her and decide to change area codes."

"But why do you still have her? Didn't her owner want her back lookin' like she does?"

"Actually, we never found her owner, so I kept her. Why?"

"See, that's the thing. I ain't sure I can take Pekka back."

"What did you call her?"

Kaipainen repeated the name, but David still couldn't make sense of it. "Are you saying that in English?"

"Nah, it's Finn. Like me. So, how much do I owe you for fixin' her up?"

"I'm not sure you owe me anything, Mr. Kaipainen."

"Ox. My front name's Osmo, but people just call me Ox. Kinda fits me, you know?"

"Okay, Ox, the way I see it, you didn't bring your dog to me and you didn't authorize any treatment. I did it on my own. So, technically speaking, you don't owe me a dime."

"That ain't right. Hell, look at her. If you hadn't sewed her up she woulda died. But . . . see, I ain't got much. I don't own this place, don't even know who does. I'm on my own, you know? Free. Always have been. But I don't take no charity. And if I take her back without payin' you nothin,' that's what it'd be."

"Wait a minute, are you saying you don't want her back?"

"It ain't that I don't want her. I just can't take her like this."

"Fine, then I'll take her," David said. "She's mine, right?"

Ox nodded, frowning.

"Good. I like this dog a lot. Unfortunately, I've got a three legged cat, and strange animals coming in and out of the clinic all day. I think she'd be better off with room to run. Someplace in the country, maybe. Like . . . here. Mr. Kaipainen, I wonder if you could help me out by taking a stray dog off my hands. Not charity, you understand. You'd be doing me a big favor. She needs care, though. Maybe you ought to think about it."

Ox eyed him a moment, reading him. He shook his massive head slowly. "That's the other thing people said about you. That you're more'n a little crazy. Okay, Doc, you put it that way, I guess I can make room for a stray dog around here. Why don't you show me about her bandages?"

David knelt beside Roadkill and untaped the corners of the oily gauze draped over her shoulders. Ox winced at the savage tapestry of bite marks.

"Whoa," he said softly, "no wonder you thought I mighta been fightin' her. This is real ugly."

"The sheriff thought she might have tangled with a raccoon," David offered.

"Naw, no 'coon did this. Dogs. Big 'uns. Wolf size, I'd say."

"You think it might have been a wolf?"

"Ain't been no wolves in this part of the state for sixty years, Doc. 'Sides, the space between the front teeth . . . Where did you find her?"

"On State Road, just east of town. There are no farms nearby that have big dogs that I know of."

"Ain't nothin' around there," Ox acknowledged, massaging Roadkill's brow with his massive thumb. "Nothin' but state land around there, mostly swamp . . ." His voice trailed off.

"What is it?"

"Nothin'," Ox said. "Just thinkin'. How often do I change the bandages?"

"Actually, she's healing so quickly I think you can leave her shoulders uncovered now. Just apply the ointment once a day, and don't let her get too active. She's still stitched together like a rag doll. I'll stop by in a week or so to take her stitches out."

"Naw, no need for you to come all the way out here. You've gone to trouble enough. I'll bring her by your office," Ox said absently. "Tell you what, why don't you give me a bill. Write down how much I owe you."

"There's no need for that, I've already—"

"Just do it, okay? It don't have to be official, you know, with everything listed. Make it like a I.O.U. Use that little pad you got in your pocket there. And one other thing. Can you tell me where you found her? Exactly, I mean?"

David hesitated. There was an odd light in Kaipainen's eyes, an angry intensity. "Yes," he said at last, "I think so."

But Ox didn't bring Roadkill back. Two days later, as David was closing his office, Stan Wolinski stalked into the waiting room carrying a small plastic bag. He laid it carefully on the counter. "You recognize this, Doc?"

David swiveled the bag to read the single scrap of paper it held. "It's a bill," he said. "I gave it to Ox Kaipainen a few days ago."

"When, exactly?"

"Wednesday afternoon. Why?"

"Five hundred and seventy bucks? A little steep, isn't it?"

"Actually, it's low, but it doesn't matter. I never expected to see a dime of it anyway. How did you get it?"

"If you didn't expect to collect, why did you give it to him?"

"He asked me to. Look, what's—?"

"He asked you?" Wolinski echoed, not bothering to conceal his disbelief. "For a bill? Why would he do that?"

"How the hell do I know? In case you haven't noticed, the gentleman's a couple of sandwiches shy of a picnic. I took the dog out to him but he said he couldn't take her back. Didn't want to be obligated."

"So you gave him a bill?"

"No, I gave him the dog. She was his, and just looking around that place I knew he couldn't afford fifty bucks, to say nothing of five hundred. But as I was leaving, he asked me to write him a bill, so I did."

"A bill he couldn't pay."

"Lots of my clients can't pay their bills, especially the ones I pick up by the side of the road. It's no big deal. So what's the problem? Is Ox in some kind of trouble over this bill?"

"I don't know," Wolinski said. "Did you make any threats when you gave it to him? Like maybe you'd take his dog back if he didn't pay? Anything like that?"

"Threaten Ox? Are you nuts? He had a . . ." David hesitated.

"Had what? What were you going to say?"

"Nothing. Not until you tell me what this is all about."

"Look, Doc, you don't make the rules, I do. And I'm telling you to finish what you were going to say."

"Sorry. Not without a lawyer present."

"A lawyer? Why would you think you need a lawyer?"

"I don't know, but it always works on TV when people don't want to answer questions. So how about it? What's going on?"

"Nothing," Wolinski sighed. "It's over. Ox Kaipainen's dead. Suicide, looks like."

"Suicide? But . . . I don't understand. Why?"

"Who knows why anybody does a thing like that. He didn't leave a note; couldn't write. God knows Ox wasn't wrapped any too tight."

"How did it happen?"

"Buddy of his found him in his cabin. Looks like he shot himself in the head. Weapon was in his hand, a .22 Colt Woodsman pistol, long barrel. Poachers favor 'em. Real accurate. Especially when you're shooting at yourself. So, what were you going to say about Ox?"

"It doesn't matter now. He was skinning out a deer when I dropped off his dog and he had a bloody knife in his hand. Under the circumstances, I didn't make any heavy threats about a bill I didn't expect him to pay anyway."

"Maybe you didn't expect him to pay it, but I wonder how he felt about it? He'd always been on his own, you know? Maybe he shouldn't have been. When he drank, he could be a real handful. I've scuffled with him more'n once over the years. But he wasn't mean, really. Mostly he kept to himself, livin' off the land like a . . . natural man, I guess. Maybe the idea of owing an unpayable debt was more than he could handle."

Wolinski picked up the plastic evidence bag. "Who knows what a guy like that was thinking? Growin' up around here I knew a lot of guys like Ox. Woodsmen. Cedar savages, we called 'em. Not many left, anymore. And now, one less and it's a damned shame. I've got his dog in the car. Do you want her or should I take her to the pound?"

"No, I'll take her, for now anyway. She still needs some care."

"You sure?" Wolinski said sourly. "There's nobody to bill anymore, you know."

"She was roadkill when I found her, remember? I guess she definitely is now."

After Wolinski left, David led Roadkill into the clinic, put her up on the table, and removed most of her sutures. She offered no resistance. Twitched a time or two when a stitch pulled coming out, but didn't growl at him or even glare. The dog seemed as numbed by what had happened as David felt. Or perhaps generations of fighting to the death in pits as a diversion for subhumans unfit to share the same planet with her had made her skin less sensitive. If not her heart.

As he worked on the dog, snipping the Braunamid sutures and carefully threading them out of the wounds with tweezers, his thoughts kept returning to Ox, and their last conversation. Had the big man given him some hint of what he felt or what he'd planned? Or had he just missed it? Overlooked it because Ox didn't seem much brighter than some of the animals David treated.

No. It just wouldn't compute. Kaipainen hadn't seemed at all depressed. Quite the opposite, in fact. It wasn't so much what he said, as the look in his eyes.

After Ox had examined the bite wounds on Roadkill's shoulders, he'd said . . . that they were wolf size. But there weren't any wolves in this part of the state. Hadn't been for sixty years. And then he'd asked David for a bill . . . But, damn it, he hadn't seemed upset about it. It was almost as though he'd thought of a way to pay it. But that made no sense either. He'd only looked at the bite marks, then insisted on getting a bill. And then he'd asked David exactly where he'd found Roadkill. It made no sense at all.

David applied fresh ointment to the wounds and decided to leave the stitches in the deep gash in her belly for a few more days. He set the dog on the floor, then fumbled through his office junk drawer and came up with a County map. He traced State Road east of Algoma with his fingertip. He'd found her right about . . . there. Roughly six miles from the village. Kaipainen's cabin was probably a mile or so south of the spot where Roadkill was struck, with a farm and some small holdings in between.

David knew the farm, a small dairy operation owned by an old timer named Jase Papineau. He'd inoculated his cows, and once he'd handled a difficult calving there. Jase had a pair of border collies, but they couldn't have caused the wounds on Roadkill. She'd have eaten them for lunch. Besides, Jase was salt of the earth. No reason to think anything was out of line there.

The small holdings were forty and sixty acre patches of unimproved hunting land. No one lived on them and since they bordered Kaipainen's place, he would have been familiar with them. Hell, he probably poached on them.

So why would he think he could pay his bill if he knew where Roadkill had been struck? David frowned at the map. State Road was a four-lane highway and the dog was hit on the side farthest from Kaipainen's place. The north side. So perhaps she'd been crossing it coming back from somewhere. But there was nothing north of the road. Sixty thousand acres of state forest. Had Roadkill been ranging in there? And tangled with . . . What?

It didn't add up. David decided to call it a night. He locked up the clinic, lifted Roadkill into the Jeep's passenger seat, and headed home. It was after six, but thanks to the wonders of daylight savings time, the sun was still well above the hills west of Algoma, painting the farm buildings and forested bluffs of the rural countryside with purple shadows.

State Road was a river of steel, jammed with commuters. David settled into the right lane, musing as he drove.

Roughly halfway home he passed the spot where he'd rescued Roadkill. He pulled off the road, waited for a break in the traffic, then gunned the Jeep across the four-lane in an illegal U-turn, and parked on the shoulder of the road as close to the spot as he could guesstimate.

He scanned the area. There was nothing unusual about it. To the north, rolling, timbered bottomlands, mostly swamp. You'd need a tank to get through it. But Ox had definitely been curious about this spot, so . . . As David climbed out of the Jeep, Roadkill vaulted across the seat past him, and took off, trotting in her lame, herky jerky gait directly into the swamp.

"Roadkill!" She didn't even slow. Hell, why should she? It wasn't her name. Damn! He sprinted after her but she disappeared into the woods before he could run her down.

The brush at the edge of the wooded tangle was literally a wall of poplars and jack pines interspersed with tag alders, a trash tree that thrived in the sodden ground. David thrashed through the tangle of brush and ground cover into a more open area. He glimpsed Roadkill off to his right, moving at a steady, uneven trot. He slogged after her. His shoes were already soaked but at least the water was down this time of year, no more than ankle deep most places. The tricky part was just staying on his feet over the uneven ground.

And keeping the dog in sight. She was setting a good pace, but he was sure she'd fade quickly. The only question was whether her stamina would give out before she'd torn open her stitches. Damn it! What the hell did she think—he tripped over a hummock, and went down hard, face first into a stand of alders.

He rose to his knees, slightly dazed, and looked around. He was all right, a scrape along his cheek. No problem. Lucky he'd fallen where he had. There was a sharpened stake only inches . . . No, it wasn't a stake, just a sapling, severed near the base by a machete or an ax. As he glanced around he noticed other signs that someone had been through here before, carving a rude, barely visible path. Or at least one barely visible to people. To a dog, it probably looked like a forest freeway.

There was a familiar rusty stain on a clump of grass beside him. He tested it with his fingertips and they came away with a powdery residue. Dried blood. There were dribs and drabs of it on the grass all along the path. Roadkill must have come out this way after she'd been chewed up. And now she was following her own blood trail back, to . . . Whatever.

But she hadn't cut this crude path out. Someone else had. Ox? Maybe. A woodsman who could kill a deer with a .22 pistol could certainly follow a blood trail as well, marked as this one.

David glanced at his watch as he rose stiffly to his feet. Nearly seven. Two hours of daylight, less than that in the deep woods where the sunlight dies early. He had to find the dog and soon, or they'd both be lost in here, and the idea of a night in the swamps with something that could chew up a full grown pit bull like an hors d'oeuvre had no appeal at all.

He plunged after the dog, moving more cautiously now, wary of his footing. He couldn't hope to outrun her in here, but her strength would have to fade soon.

Or maybe not. He'd plodded on a good half hour without catching sight of Roadkill again. At least the going was getting easier. The ground had been slowly rising as he marched, fewer holes and hummocks, higher and drier. And then he came to the reason why. A slow moving creek meandered out of the woods. It didn't look deep, probably no more than chest high on a man, but it was ten or twelve feet wide. Roadkill had apparently just plunged in and paddled across. He could see her muddy tracks on the far bank. David spotted a fallen tree roughly forty yards to the east. He detoured down to it, clambered across the stream on it, then worked his way back to the trail.

Walking was almost pleasant now. The trees were taller and more widely spaced. Mature poplars and spruce shaded out the sun and thinned the ground cover beneath their canopy. There were even clearings, or would have been if they hadn't been clogged with head high alders and ferns and reeds . . . And then he found Roadkill.

She was sitting on a hummock at the edge of a clearing, her sides heaving, tongue lolling, utterly exhausted. He talked to her gently as he approached her, but she made no move to run. She'd gone as far as she could, and then stopped, out of gas.

He knelt beside her, ran his hands over her flanks and checked her stitches. Still solid. She'd pulled a couple of gashes open on her shoulders, but not all the way. They'd probably close again on their own. No major damage done. Thank God for small favors.

He rose slowly and took stock of his situation. The sun was nearing treetop level on the horizon. They still had an hour or so of daylight to find their way back. The path was clear enough at this point, as though . . . it had been heavily used. As he scanned his surroundings, David realized that the grass around him had been trampled, ferns broken, in a rough circle. And the whole area was spattered with rust spots. Dried blood.

Sweet Jesus, this is where it happened. Roadkill hadn't stopped here because she was spent, she'd stopped because she'd arrived at her destination. She'd been here before, fought here, and now her savage heart had brought her back for a rematch. She was resting, waiting for her opponent to show again.

But why here? There were no rocks or deadfalls in the area where a wolf could fort up, it was just a clearing, with tag alders and ferns and . . . reefer. In the mix of foliage ahead, every third plant was marijuana, mature plants with the tell-tale erose leaves and stalks as tall as a man. This was no whimsical patch seeded by some happy go lucky pothead, it was a serious growing operation, carefully camouflaged in the depths of the state forest. There were easily sixty to seventy plants in the clearing, possibly more, and God only knew how many more clearings like this one there were concealed back here. And for all David knew, they could have tigers guarding this place.

33

Time to go. He reached down for Roadkill, but she stiffened and growled. But the warning snarl wasn't for him. She was staring at something on the far side of the clearing. And then David saw it too. The ferns were moving. Something big was coming toward them. Moving fast.

Roadkill staggered to her feet to face the threat but David wasn't waiting. He scooped up the dog and ran, sprinting back down the path as fast as he could travel. Which wasn't very. Between Roadkill's sixty pounds and the brush snagging his clothes, the best he could manage was a reeling stagger. Still, he was covering ground. He could hear shouting behind him, and a raspy wasp-buzz as something whistled past his head and thwacked into a tree beside the trail. A bullet? No, there'd been no shot . . . Pellet gun. Like the one he used to inject aggressive bulls or elk. Not a boy's BB gun, a serious, high pressure air rifle. Lethal if they struck a man. And they fired .22 caliber pellets. The same size as the slug that had killed Ox.

The voices grew fainter, and for a minute David thought they might be giving up. But then Roadkill started growling and squirming in his arms, as though she sensed a danger he couldn't see. He risked a glance over his shoulder, and caught a glimpse of them.

Rottweilers. Two of them, about sixty yards behind him, coming on hard and fast. A hundred and forty pounds apiece, hurtling through the brush like black and tan demons. Silently. No barking. They'd been well trained.

Seconds. That's all he had now. If they caught him, he was done. He had no illusions about fighting off a pair of trained attack dogs. If he dropped Roadkill, he might be able to make it up a tree in the . . . confusion. Because she'd fight them, injured or not. She'd die fighting them. And he couldn't let that happen. He only had one ghost of a chance . . . So he kept on running, desperately wrestling with the fiery little bull who wanted nothing more than to break free and give battle.

And then they hit it. David broke out of the brush at the creek. He didn't hesitate. He threw Roadkill in the general direction of the far bank and plunged in after her. He found his footing in the middle of the creek, then turned to face his attackers. And not a moment too soon. The first Rott hurtled out of the trees like a missile and leapt at David's head, all fangs and snarling fury.

As the dog pounced, David dropped to his knees below the surface of the water, clawing desperately for purchase as the dog came down on him. He grabbed a foreleg and pulled it under. The Rottweiler thrashed, snapping at him, but only for a second. It got a lungful of water and instantly forgot its attack, forgot everything but frantically trying to fight its way to the surface for air. He let it go, and burst out of the water himself, just in time to take the full force of the second Rott's attack.

The dog struck him shoulder high, knocking him off his feet. It whirled on him, churning the water to foam as it clawed furiously toward him. And then its eyes widened, and it spun back to its rear as Roadkill clamped onto its hindquarters with her iron jaws.

David grabbed a fistful of the Rott's pelt at the shoulder and thrust him under with Roadkill still clamped on his rear end. The water had the same effect on both dogs. They struggled to the surface gagging and gasping for air. David pushed the Rott away from him toward the opposite shore where its companion was still trying to claw its way up the bank. He grabbed Roadkill, clambered out of the water, and staggered off down the trail.

Behind him, he could hear the Rotts hacking and gagging as they coughed up a fair amount of creek water. Great dogs,

Rottweilers. Loyal, intelligent, and no more aggressive than they're trained to be. But they can't hold their breath underwater. Only a very few retrievers can manage that particular trick. The two attack dogs were done, for the moment. And apparently their masters had counted on them to finish the job. David could hear no other sounds of pursuit.

The rest of the run was a nightmare, reeling through the woods in the gathering dusk, desperately trying to stay on the path and hold the dog struggling in his arms. Somewhere along the run, Roadkill settled down, panting with exhaustion. David knew exactly how she felt. He wasn't far from collapse himself.

The sunlight was rapidly waning and he knew if they didn't get clear of the woods before dark, they'd never get out at all.

But, somehow, they did. As the light gradually faded into shadows, it took every ounce of his stamina and concentration to keep putting one foot ahead of the other and to stay on the crude trace of a path. So that when he suddenly broke through a tangle of brush and found himself standing on the edge of the highway, only a dozen yards from his Jeep and the steady stream of traffic beyond it, he was stunned.

He sank slowly to his knees, gasping, exhausted. Only Roadkill's squirming to get free kept him from passing out altogether. If he let her go, she could die in traffic in a heartbeat. So he struggled to hold onto her, and to his consciousness. And realized they were coming for him.

A pickup truck pulled out of a forest trail a half mile back down the road, and began rumbling toward him along the shoulder with its lights out.

Christ, no wonder they hadn't followed him. They didn't have to! They knew roughly where the damned path came out. They just took some back road out, found his Jeep and waited for him to show up!

David lunged to his feet and staggered toward the Jeep. The pickup was gaining speed now, the passenger window was down and he could see the muzzle of the pellet rifle centering on him.

He ducked around the Jeep and yanked open the driver's door. A slug ricocheted off the roll bar only inches from his head. He tossed Roadkill onto the passenger's seat, vaulted behind the wheel and fired up the Jeep. The truck was almost on him, veering up on the edge of the freeway to come alongside for a point blank shot. No time to run for it.

He jammed the gearshift into reverse and floored the accelerator. The Jeep backed into the pickup, striking it just ahead of the passenger door. The impact spun the Jeep around, nearly upending it. The pickup caromed off and skidded out onto the highway. David caught only a glimpse of a bearded face in the window before a flatbed truck loaded with steel beams slammed into the pickup cab at seventy miles an hour, and rolled over it, crushing the truck beneath it, and dragging it along in a maelstrom of sparks and rending metal that howled like the end of the world.

David glanced up when the patrol car pulled into the clinic lot, but didn't bother to answer the door. The blinds were drawn and the "closed" sign was in place. Stan Wolinski came in anyway.

"Doc?"

"I'm back here."

Wolinski strolled through to the operating room. David had Roadkill up on the table, swabbing out the gashes that had reopened on her shoulders.

"How's she doin'?" Wolinski asked.

"Better than I am," David said, fingering the rubber neck

brace they'd given him in the emergency room. "This dog's got the damnedest constitution I've ever seen. I don't think you could kill her with an H-bomb."

"You look a little rough, though," Wolinski agreed. "The guy drivin' that flatbed got off with only bruises. The pair in the pickup are both dead. Real dead. It took the fire department nearly an hour just to cut their bodies out of the wreck. I've seen 'possums flattened in truck stop driveways that looked better."

"Who were they?"

"Couple of gang bangers from Detroit. Survivalist types. Figured they were gonna finance their new world order by growin' reefer up here in the great outdoors. You were right about that gun they were usin'. It was an air rifle, a Shamal, .22 caliber. I got a feeling when the medical examiner does the autopsy on Ox, he'll find the slug in him was from their gun, not his own."

"They fired at me without hesitating," David said. "They probably did the same thing when he showed up at their patch. Then hauled his body back to his place and arranged things to look like suicide. I feel partly responsible, though. If I hadn't given Ox that damned bill, he wouldn't have backtracked his dog—"

"You don't know that," Wolinski said, cutting him off. "Ox roamed all through that swamp, poaching. He probably would have come across them eventually. Or someone else would have. Those guys were ex-cons with a long record of violence. They were an accident waiting to happen. And, God bless him, maybe Ox was, too."

"Maybe he was," David conceded. "It still bothers me, though."

"A lot of things seem to bother you, Doc. So what are you going to do about the dog?"

"Actually, I was hoping you could help me out with her."

"Me?"

"Sure. Pit bulls are terrific dogs, but they're not your average mom and pop house pet. They're more like . . . power tools, or even weapons. They're great to have around, as long as you treat 'em with respect. They've been bred for tenacity and fighting spirit for centuries, and that heritage doesn't evaporate just because you teach the dog to sit up or fetch your slippers."

"Granted, but what's that got to do with me?"

"For one thing, you're a man who's used to treating weapons with respect. And didn't you mention that you'd had trouble with vandals on your place? I guarantee this lady would put an end to that. Besides, if it wasn't for her, those two loonies would still be on the loose. I figure you owe her one."

The sheriff eyed the dog on the table doubtfully. She returned his stare, unintimidated. "What's her name?"

"I'm not sure," David admitted. "Ox mentioned it, but it was in Finnish and I didn't understand. I've been calling her Roadkill."

"What the hell kind of name is that?"

"An appropriate one," David said. "If you take her, you can name her anything you like."

"No, I don't think so," Stan said. "The name kind of suits her if you think about it. It'll do, I guess. Roadkill."

The dog cocked her head slightly, as though she was trying to understand what Stan was saying.

"Roadkill," Stan repeated. And this time her tail twitched. It was only a twitch, definitely not a wag. But it was a start.

The Sultans of Soul

Papa Henry's Hickory Hut serves the best barbeque in the city of Detroit, bar none. Ribs to die for. The Hut is just a storefront diner, booths along one wall, a scarred Formica counter and backless chrome stools. Ah, but behind the counter, shielded by a spattered Plexiglas screen, is an honest to Jesus barbeque pit. You can watch your order revolve on the rotisserie, kissed by flames and hickory smoke, while homebaked hoecakes warm on the grill. High cholesterol? Probably. But since the Hut's on the rough side of Eight Mile, keeping your veins intact is a more pressing worry than having them clogged.

I'd ordered a late breakfast at Papa's, and was sipping coffee, waiting, when a white Cadillac limo ghosted to the curb out front. The chauffeur, a uniformed black the size of a small building, popped an umbrella against the April drizzle, and opened the back door. An elderly black gentleman eased slowly out. The chauffeur watched, wooden, offering no help.

The old man looked exotic, like a Nigerian diplomat. An orange patterned kente-cloth cap, a Kuppenheimer's continental-cut black suit, hand-tailored to a tee. He had cafe au lait skin, a spray of coppery freckles across the bridge of his nose, a metallic gray Malcolm X goatee. Dark, intense hawk's eyes.

He'd have stood six feet plus upright, but he was pain-hunched into a question mark, using a silver-headed bamboo cane for support. I guessed him to be fiftyish. Fifty isn't old for most people. It was for this guy.

He moved like he'd been wounded at Gettysburg. Step,

40

lean, step, lean. The gait was familiar. Sickle cell anemia, very late in the game. I grew up around it down home. This old man had lasted longer than most. But it was coming for him now. And he was coming for me, sizing me up all the way. I was easy enough to spot. As usual, I was the only white face in the Hut.

It took him a month to limp the dozen paces back to my booth. He stopped in front of my table, leaning on the cane, wobbly as a foundered horse. "You'd be Axton, right? From the detective agency up the street?" he asked, his voice a low rasp. Black velvet.

"Yes, sir. Something I can do for you?"

"For openers, you can speak up. I don't hear too well. My name's Mack. Varnell Mack."

"R. B. Axton," I said, offering my hand. He ignored it. "Would you care to sit down, Mr. Mack?"

"No thanks, too damn hard to get up again, and I won't be here long. I'm into a few things around Detroit, mostly real estate, own some rental units. Willis Tyrone, the guy that owns them pawn shops down in the ward? Willis tells me you're good at collectin' money folks ain't altogether sure they owe."

"I make collections sometimes," I said cautiously, "but I don't do evictions."

"Neither do I," Mack said, "that's the problem." A spasm took his breath for a moment. His knuckles locked on the cane and a faint sheen of moisture beaded on his forehead. "I believe I will sit down after all," he said, swallowing. He drew a silk handkerchief from his breast pocket, flicked the dust off the bench across from me, then casually replaced the hand-kerchief in his pocket with a flip of his wrist. A perfect fleur-de-lis. I was impressed. I can barely manage to knot a necktie.

"See, I had this old gentleman livin' in one of my buildin's," Mack said, easing into the booth. "Used to be a helluva singer 'round Detroit back in the fifties, early sixties, even cut a few records. Horace DeWitt. Ever hear of him?"

"Can't say I have, but I'm not from Detroit originally."

"Knew that the minute you opened your mouth. Where you from, boy? Alabama?"

"No, sir, Mississippi. A little town called Noxapater."

"They teach you to call blacks 'sir' down there, did they?"

"They taught me to be polite to my elders," I said evenly. "And to watch my mouth around strangers. You were saying about Mr. DeWitt?"

"I used to write tunes, sing backup in Horace's group. Called ourselves the Sultans of Soul."

"No kidding? I remember the group. From when I was a kid, down home. I've still got one of your songs on an oldies tape. 'Motor City' . . . something?"

" 'Motor City Mama.' I wrote that one. Our last single. Cracked the top twenty on the race charts in sixty-one. Never made no money off it, record company folded right after, but it got us a name so we could make a few bucks doin' shows. Then things petered out, the group busted up. I went into real estate, did all right for myself. Helped out Horace some, last few years, with rent and such. He had a stroke a few months back, had to move to a rest home. One of them welfare places. I offered to help, but he wouldn't take it. He's flat busted, cain't even afford a TV in his room."

"Sorry to hear it," I said.

"Maybe you shouldn't be," Mack said. "Might be somethin' in it for you. Thing is, I still hear 'Motor City Mama' on the radio sometimes. So I figure somebody must owe the Sultans some money. I want you to collect it."

"Collect it?" I echoed.

"That's what you do, ain't it?"

"I, ahm . . . Look, Mr. Mack, what I do is skip-traces mostly. People who light out owing other people money. I hunt 'em up, talk 'em into doin' the right thing."

"So?"

"So, for openers, who do you expect me to collect from?"

"That's your problem. If I knew who owed Horace, I wouldn't hafta hire you. I'd see to it myself."

"You can't be serious."

"Boy, I never joke about money."

"All right then, straight up. Even if I could find somebody who'd admit to owing the Sultans some royalties or whatever, it probably wouldn't amount to beans. And I don't work cheap."

"Two-fifty a day, Willis told me," Mack said, snaking an envelope out of an inner pocket, tossing it on the table. "Here's a week in advance. Fifteen hundred. You need more, my number's on the envelope. But I expect to see some results."

I left the envelope where it was. "Mr. Mack, I really don't think I can help you. I wouldn't even know where to start."

"Willis gave me your card," Mack said, using the cane to lever himself to his feet. "R. B. Axton, private investigations. That makes you some kinda detective, right?"

"Yes, sir, but—"

"So maybe you oughta try earnin' your fee. Investigate or whatever. Look, I know it'd be cheaper to just lay the damn money on Horace. He won't take it. He was a dynamite singer once. And people are still listenin' to his music. He shouldn't oughta go out broke like this. It ain't right."

"No, sir," I said, "I suppose it isn't."

"All right then," he said grimly. "You find out who owes

the Sultans some money. And you get it. How much don't matter, but you get Horace somethin', understand?"

I picked up the envelope, intending to give it back to him. But I didn't. There was something in his eyes. Dark fire. Anger perhaps, and pain. It cost him a lot just to walk in here. More than money. I put the envelope in my pocket. "I'll look into it," I said. "I can't promise anything."

"Banks don't cash promises anyway," Mack said, turning, and limping slowly toward the door. Step, lean, step, lean. "Call me when you got somethin'."

"Yes, sir," I said. He didn't look back.

Finding a place to start looking wasn't all that tough. The cassette tray in my car. I did have the Sultans of Soul on tape. "Motor City Mama." There was no information on the cassette itself. It was a bootleg compilation from Rock 'n Soul Recollections, on south Livernois.

R&S isn't the usual secondhand record shop with records piled around like orphaned children. The shop is a renovated theater, complete with bulletproof box office, which, considering its location, is probably prudent. The walls are crammed floor to ceiling with poster art, larger-than-life shots of Michigan music monsters, Smokey Robinson, Bob Seger, The Temps, Stevie Wonder. The bins are immaculate, every last 45 lovingly encased in cellophane, cross-referenced and catalogued like Egyptian antiquities.

All this regimentation is a reflection of the owner/ manager, Cal, a wizened little guy with a watermelon paunch and a tam permanently attached to his oversized pate. I don't recall his last name, if I ever heard it, but he knows mine. Not just because I'm a good customer, but because he remembers everything about everything. He knows every record he has in stock, and probably every record he's *ever* had in stock.

On the downside, he's compulsive, wears the same outfit

every day: green slacks, frayed white shirt, navy cardigan clinched with a safety pin. His hands look like lizard-skin gloves because he washes them forty times a day. Still, if I wanted to know about the Sultans, Cal was the person to ask.

"You've got to be kidding," he said.

"Hey, I should think you'd be flattered. I thought you knew everything about those old groups."

"I do know about their records," he said, irritated. "The Sultans cut three forty-fives and one album, all out of print. But as to who owns the rights to their music now? Hell, there were a million penny-ante record labels back then, and the royalty rights were swapped around like baseball cards. Most of the forty-fives were cut in fly-by-night studios owned by the mob—"

"Whoa up. Mob? You mean organized crime?"

"Absolutely. In the fifties and early sixties radio play was still segregated. Damn few stations would air black music, so the only market for it was jukeboxes. And most of the jukes and vending machines in Detroit were mob controlled."

"Terrific."

"The bottom line is, if you want to find somebody who might owe the Sultans a few bucks, you're probably looking for some smalltime hood who once owned a few jukes and a two-bit recording studio and went out of the record business before you were born."

"But I still hear 'Motor City Mama' on the radio sometimes."

"Local deejays play it because of the title, but Detroit's probably the only town in the country where it's aired. Wanna try muscling a few nickels out of Wheelz or WRIF?"

"Fat chance. What label did the Sultans record for?"

"That at least I can tell you," he said, flipping through a stack of albums. "None of their stuff has been reissued, even on a collection. The Sultans just weren't big enough . . . Here we go, the Sultans of Soul, 'Motor City Mama.' "

He passed me the album. The cover photo was a blurred action shot, four black guys in gold lamé jackets doing splits behind the lead singer, a beefy stud with conked hair. Mack appeared to be the tall guy on the left, but the picture had faded. So had Mack. I flipped the album over. "Black Catz?" I read. "What can you tell me about it?"

"Not much," Cal said. "It was a local label, defunct since . . ." He frowned, then shook his head slowly, his face gradually creasing into a ghost of a smile.

"I knew it," I said. "You do know something, right?"

"Nothing that'll help you, I'm afraid," he said. "But I did come across a Black Catz reissue recently. Not the Sultans though. Millie Jump and the Jacks."

"Never heard of them."

"Maybe you don't remember the Jacks, but you should remember Millicent. Soul singer who had a few hits in the sixties, then tried Hollywood and bombed? The Jacks was her original group, until she dumped 'em to marry the label owner and use his money to go solo."

"Wait a minute, you mean Millicent's husband, Sol Katz, was the original owner of Black Catz?"

"That's right," Cal said. "You know him?"

"I not only know him, I've worked for him."

"Worked for Sol?" Cal said, squinting at me from beneath his tam. "Doing what? Kneecaps with a baseball bat?"

"Actually I didn't exactly work for Sol. His daughter, Desiree, was an opening act for Was Not Was at the Auburn Hills Palace. I was her bodyguard."

"I would have thought Sol had bodyguards to spare."

"He wanted somebody who knew the local music scene. Most of his guys are from L.A."

"And it didn't bother you, working for a hood?"

"I—heard rumors about Sol, but in this business you hear smoke about everybody. Hell, half the guys in the biz *pretend* to be hoods just to spook the competition."

"Sol Katz isn't pretending, Ax, he's the real thing. His old man was an enforcer for the Purple Gang back in the thirties. Sol took to the family business like *The Godfather Part II*."

"I thought he was from L.A.?"

"He went out there awhile after the Purples ran him out of Detroit for marrying Millie. Having a black mistress in those days was one thing, but marriage? Not in his set. Besides, Millie figured she was ready for the bright lights. She was a fair singer, but never quite good enough to make it big, even with Sol's money. How's the daughter, whatsername, Desiree?"

"About the same, not bad, not gangbusters. I think Millie and Sol want her to make it more than she wants it herself. They've got her cutting an album of classic soul stuff out at the Studio Seven complex. What label was the reissue on?"

"Studio Seven, which means Sol may still own the rights to the Black Catz library. Including the Sultans. Lucky you. You going to try to collect?"

"That's what I'm being paid for."

"Hope you're getting enough to cover hospitalization. By the way, who is paying you? I thought the Sultans were all playing harps these days."

"They nearly are. Horace DeWitt, the lead singer, is in a rest home and the guy who hired me, Varnell Mack, looks like an AWOL from intensive care."

"I probably have them mixed up with another group. There were so many in those days," he said softly, glancing around the displays, filled with CDs, albums, tapes. And raw talent. And Soul. "So many. You know, it might not matter much to world peace, but it'd be nice if you could squeeze a few bucks out of Sol for the Sultans. Just for the damn principle of the thing."

"Principles?" I said. "In this business?"

Actually, principle was all I had going for me. Mack hadn't given me as much as a faded IOU to work with. In the music biz, sometimes deals with very serious money involved are done with a handshake or a phone call. I occasionally get hired to collect on oral contracts, but usually folks know in their heart of hearts that they owe the money. This was different.

Technically, Sol Katz probably didn't owe the Sultans dime one. Hell, after all these years he might not even remember who they were. Whatever deal they'd had, they'd lived with it for nearly thirty years, so if Sol told me to take a hike, I'd walk. Assuming my knees were still functional. Still, I figured I had a small chance. Mobster or no, a guy who'd risk his neck to marry the woman he loved must have a heart, right?

Right. So why did I keep remembering every story I'd ever heard about the Purple Gang? Two-to-a-box coffins, the shooters at the St. Valentine's Day Massacre, the gang that pushed Capone out of Detroit . . .

I shook it off. Ancient history, all of it. Then again, so were the Sultans of Soul.

The Studio 7 building is a spanking new concrete castle just off Gratiot Avenue, in the equally new city of Eastpointe, nee East Detroit. The locals rechristened the town, trying to shed its Murder City East image.

Funny, it had never occurred to me what a fortress Sol's studio complex was. I'd called ahead to let Dési know I was coming, but I still had to identify myself to a uniformed guard at the parking lot gate when I drove in, and to a second guard at the front door, then get clearance from a body-by-steroids male receptionist to use the elevator. There was nothing unusual about the stiff security arrangements. In a town where gunslingers will hold you up in broad daylight to steal your car, paranoia is an entirely rational state of mind.

Still, knowing Sol was a born-to-the-purple mobster made all the guards and guns seem a lot more sinister. It was like finding out your lover and your best friend were once lovers. You can't help revising all previous data.

The recording studios are on the fourth floor of the complex. The rooms are carpeted floor to ceiling in earth-tone textured saxony, and subdivided into a half-dozen Plexiglas booths which separate the musicians and singers on the rare occasions when two people actually tape at the same time. Nowadays most tracks are cut solo to avoid crosstalk and achieve maximal clarity. State-of-the-art digital recording, as sterile as a test-tube conception. And even less fun.

Roddy Rothstein, Sol's head of security, was leaning against the wall outside the studio door. He looks like an aging surfer: bleached hair, china-blue eyes, a thin scar that droops his left eyelid. He was wearing jeans, snakeskin boots, and an L.A. Raiders jacket that didn't quite conceal the Browning nine millimeter in his shoulder holster. He gave me a hard, thousand-yard stare. Nothing personal. Roddy looks at everybody like a lizard eyeing a fly.

"Hey, Ax, what's doin'?"

"Small stuff. Is Mr. Katz in?"

"Everybody's in but me," Roddy grumbled. "The music biz. Life in the fast lane."

"Beats honest work," I said.

"How would you know? Go ahead, green light's on."

Even with Roddy's okay and the warning light in the hall showing green, I still eased the door open cautiously. At five hundred bucks an hour, you never barge into a studio. But it was okay. They were in the middle of a soundcheck. Desi was wearing headsets in a sound-isolation booth. Recording company promos always shave a decade or so off performers' ages, but in her Pistons T-shirt and bullet-riddled jeans, Desi really did look like a high-school dropout, dark, slender, drop-dead gorgeous. If she ever learns to sing as good as she looks . . . She gave me a grin and flipped me the fickle finger. I waved back.

Millie and Sol were chewing on the engineer about clarity. Interracial couples aren't unusual in Detroit, but Sol and Millie were an especially handsome pair. Sol, slender, dapper, with steel-grey hair, grey eyes, fashionably blase in a pearl-grey Armani jacket over a teal polo shirt. Millie was probably a few pounds heavier than in her Millicent days, but she wore it well. Voluptuous, in deceptively casual jogging togs that probably cost more than my car. Sol left the argument to give Millie the last word and strolled over. *The Godfather II*? Maybe. Maybe so.

"Axton," he nodded, "how are you doin'? Glad you dropped by. Desi was going to call you. She's going to do some charity shows for AIDS next month, Cleveland and Buffalo. I'd like you to handle security if you're free."

"I'll be free," I said. "If you still want me. This, ahem, this isn't a social call, Mr. Katz. It's business."

"What kind of business?" Millie said, waving the engineer back to his booth. I felt sorry for him. Millie can be a hard lady to be on the wrong side of. A tough woman in a tough trade.

"It's a bit complicated, but basically, somebody hired me to, uhm . . . to collect an old debt."

"What kind of debt?" Sol said evenly. "Who am I supposed to owe?"

"I'm not sure you owe anybody, Mr. Katz. Look, let me lay this thing on you straight up. Do you recall a group that recorded for you back in the early sixties called the Sultans of Soul?"

"The Sultans?" Millie echoed. "Sure. We did a few shows together at the Warfield and the Broadway Capitol."

"Do you remember Varnell Mack?" I asked.

She shot a sharp glance at Sol, then back at me. "I remember him. Tall, with a goatee?"

"He's not so tall now," I said. "To make a long story short, Mr. Mack says Horace DeWitt, the Sultans' lead singer, is down and out. In a rest home."

"I heard," Sol said coolly. "So?"

"So Mr. Mack is hoping you can see your way clear to . . . help Mr. DeWitt out. For auld lang syne."

"Just Horace?" Sol frowned. "Or would Varnell be wanting a taste, too?"

"No, sir, Mr. Mack seems to be doing quite well. New Caddy and a chauffeur, in fact."

"Good for him," Sol said evenly. "Did he say anything about my trying to contact him?"

"He didn't mention it. Why?"

"Nothing heavy," Millie put in, a shade too casually. "We've been thinking of calling Desi's new album *Motor City Mama,* so we need Varnell's permission to use the song. We had Roddy ask around, but nobody seemed to know what happened to him."

"He said he quit the business years ago, went into real estate," I said.

Sol shrugged. "Well, if all Mack wants is a few bucks for Horace, maybe we can work something out. Tell you what, Ax, bring Varnell by the club tonight. Tenish? We'll have a few drinks, talk it over."

"Fine by me. I'll have to check with Mr. Mack, of course."

"Do that, and get back to me. Meantime, if you don't mind, we're gettin' ready to roll tape."

"No problem. I'll be in touch. And thanks."

I stopped at the first 7-Eleven I came to and used the drive-by phone in the lot to call Varnell Mack. He answered on a car phone; I could hear the traffic noise in the background. I tried to tell him what I had, but he cut me off.

"Boy, I can't hear worth a damn over this thing. You got news for me?"

"Yes, sir."

"Then meet me at that rib joint down from your office. Twenty minutes?"

"I'll be there."

Mack's Cadillac limo was parked illegally in front of Papa Henry's, motor running. His chauffeur was behind the wheel, his huge hands tapping out rhythm to the thump of the Caddy's sound system. Mack was sitting in a front window booth facing the street. Not a spot I would have chosen, but then I don't need a cane to get around either. At least, not yet. I slid into the booth. Mack was warming his hands around a cup of tea. I gave him a quick rundown on what I'd turned up.

"Ol' Sol's still in the business and livin' fat city?" he said, showing a thin smile. "And still with Millie? I'll be damned. Who woulda figured it after all this time?"

"It hasn't really been so long," I said.

"Been a lifetime for some people," Mack said, glancing out the flyspecked window at the street. A posse car cruised slowly past, a blacked-out Monte Carlo low rider. Mack didn't notice it. He was looking beyond to . . . somewhere else.

"Millie remembered you," I said.

"A lotta woman, Millie. Smart, too. Smart enough to

marry money, and stick to it."

"Maybe it wasn't like that," I said.

"No?" the old man said, annoyed. "Know a lot about it, do you, boy? You married?"

"I was. Once."

"Once oughta be enough for people, one way or another. You know, Willis told me you were sharp, Axton, but I'll tell you the God's truth, when I laid that money on you, I thought I was kissin' it goodbye, I truly did. You did okay."

"I haven't actually done anything yet," I said.

"How do you figure?"

"You hired me to collect some money for the Sultans. Sol said be was willing to work something out about the rights to 'Motor City Mama.' He didn't actually say he'd pay or how much."

"Don't worry 'bout it." Mack smiled grimly. "The important thing is, he's willin' to talk. This ain't really about money, you know? It's about doin' the right thing. So whatever Sol's willin' to pay, it'll be enough." He used his cane to lever himself painfully out of the booth. "I'll pick you up here at nine-thirty."

"Right," I said absently. The posse car was coming by again, probably checking out Mack's Cadillac. I watched it pass, then realized what was bothering me wasn't the car, it was something above it, something glinting from the roof of the building across the street. For a split second I froze, half-expecting gunfire. But the flash was too bright to be metal. And it wasn't moving. Mack was eyeing me oddly.

"Anythin' wrong?"

"Nope," I said, "not a thing. I'll see you tonight." I waited in the booth while he limped out to the Caddy and climbed in. As the car drifted away from the curb, a man stood up on the roof of the building opposite. With a minicam. He photographed Mack's car as it made a left onto Eight Mile.

I slipped out the back door of Papa Henry's into the alley, trotted down to the end of the block, and walked quickly to the corner, keeping close to the building. The man on the roof was gone.

Damn! I sprinted across the street, dodging traffic, and dashed down the alley. A blue Honda Civic was parked in a turnout, halfway down. It had to be his. Nobody parks in an alley in this part of town.

I heard a clank of metal from above and flattened against the wall. Someone was coming down the fire escape, moving quickly. A slender black man in U of D sweats and granny glasses, toting a black canvas shoulder bag. I waited until he was halfway down the last set of firestairs, then stepped out, blocking the path to his car.

"Nice day for it," I said.

He froze. "For what?"

"Taking pictures. That's what you were doing, right? Of me and the man I was with?"

He hesitated a split second, then shrugged. "If you walk away from me right now, maybe you can stay out of this thing."

"What thing?"

"An official Metro narcotics investigation."

"Narcotics investigation? Of who? Me? Papa Henry? You'll have to do better than that."

"I'm warning you, you're interfering in—"

"Save the smoke," I interrupted. "If you're a cop, show me some tin, and I'm gone."

"Fair enough," he said coolly. He unzipped the canvas bag, took out a packet, and flipped it toward me. I half-turned to catch it, and he vaulted the rail and hit the ground running. He only had me by two steps and the bag on his shoulder must have slowed him, but he was still too fast for me.

"Heeelllp!" he shouted as we pounded down the alley. "The maaan! The maaan!"

It worked. I broke off the chase a few feet from the alley mouth. There was no way a white guy could chase a black man down Eight Mile without attracting an unfriendly crowd, and we both knew it.

He cut a hard right when he hit the street and disappeared. I turned and trotted back to his car.

The packet he'd tossed at me was useless, a brochure for camera film from a shop on Woodward. I considered breaking into the car, but decided against it. For openers, I wasn't certain it was his car. But I was fairly sure that he'd been filming Mack and me. We were the only ones sitting in the windows; he'd photographed the Caddy as it pulled away, and stopped shooting when it was gone.

A narcotics investigation? Possible. God knows, there are enough of 'em in this town. But if he was a cop, why not just show me some ID? Or a .38? No narc would work an alley off Eight Mile unarmed. And if he wasn't a cop, then what was he?

I was getting an uneasy sense of blundering through a roomful of spiderwebs. The only reason I could think of for someone to film me talking to Mack was that one of us was being set up for something. I've ticked off a few folks over the years, but none I could think of who'd bother with a cameraman. Not in a town where you can buy a hit for fifty bucks. Or less.

That left Mack. Was he mixed up in the drug scene? Maybe, though the drug trade'd be a rough game for somebody who can barely walk. Besides, he hadn't asked me to do anything illegal. He hired me to collect money for the Sultans from persons unknown.

Or had he? All I really knew about Mack was what he told me. Millie remembered him, and Sol too. From the old days. This whole thing kept coming back to that. The old days. And the Sultans of Soul.

And Horace DeWitt. And since in a way I was actually working for DeWitt, maybe it was time I met the Sultans' leader. Besides, I'd been hearing "Motor City Mama" since I was a tad. It would be interesting to finally meet the face behind the voice.

I've acquired a modest reputation in music circles for tracing skips and collecting debts. The sign on my office door says private investigations, but the truth is I don't have to do much Sherlocking. The people in this business aren't very good at hiding. And since he wasn't hiding, Horace DeWitt was easier to find than most.

Mack mentioned DeWitt had only been in the home for a few months, so he was still listed in the phone book at his old address on Montcalm, and a quick call to the post office gave me his forwarding address. Riverine Heights, in Troy.

The funk from in some welfare-case warehouses will drop you to your knees a half a block away, but Riverine Heights appeared to be better than most, a modern, ten-story cinderblock tower on Wattles Road. It even had a view of River Rouge.

At the front desk, a cheery, plump blonde in nurse's whites had me sign the visitor's log, and told me I'd probably find Mr. DeWitt in the fourth-floor residents' lounge. Fourth floor. A relief. The higher you go in these places, the less mobile the patients are. The top floors are reserved for the bedridden, only a last gasp from heaven. A fourth-floor resident should be ambulatory, more or less.

It was less. The residents' lounge was a small reading room with French doors that opened out onto a balcony. Institutional green plastic chairs lined the walls, a few well-thumbed magazines lay forgotten on the bookshelves. An elderly woman in street clothes was sitting on the sofa with a patient in a robe. The woman was knitting a scarf. Her date was asleep, his mouth open, his head resting on her shoulder.

Horace DeWitt was awake at least, sitting in a wheelchair in the sunlight by the French doors. A folding card table was pulled up to his knees. He was playing solitaire.

I'd seen his picture only hours before, but I barely recognized him. The singer on the Sultans' album had been a macho stud. The old man in the chair looked like a picture from Dorian Gray's attic. The conked hair had thinned and his slacks and sports shirt hung on his shrunken frame like death-camp pajamas. The stroke had melted the right side of his face like wax in a fire, one eyelid drooped nearly closed and the corner of his mouth was turned down in a permanent scowl.

His left arm lay in his lap like deadwood, palm up, fingers curled into a claw. Still, he seemed to be dealing the cards accurately, even one-handed. And he was cheating.

"Mr. DeWitt?" I said. "My name's Axton. I've been a big fan of yours for years. Got a minute to talk?"

"I guess I can fit you into my dance card," he said, peering up at me with his good eye. "But if you want me to headline one o' them soul revues, I'll have to pass."

His words were slurred by the twisted corner of his mouth. But his voice carried me back to steamy Mississippi nights, blowing down backroads in my daddy's pickup, WLAC Nashville blaring clear and righteous on the radio. The Sultans of Soul. "I'm comin' home, Motown Mama, I just can't live without ya . . ." I think I could've picked Horace DeWitt's voice out of a Silverdome crowd howling after a Lions' touchdown.

"Fact is, in a way I'm already working for you, Mr. DeWitt," I said, squatting beside his chair. "Varnell Mack hired me to try to collect some back royalties for the Sultans."

"Did he now?" DeWitt said, cocking his head, looking me over. "What's he got against you?"

"Nothing I know of, why?"

" 'Cause the last guy I heard of tried to squeeze a nickel outa Sol Katz wound up tryna backstroke 'cross Lake St. Clair draggin' a hunert pounds o' loggin' chain."

"Maybe I'll have better luck. I can't promise anything, but I think there's a fair chance we'll shake a few bucks loose."

"Uh-huh," he said, turning to his game. "The check's in the mail, right? So what you want from me?"

"Not much. I was hoping you could tell me a little about Mr. Mack."

"Varnell? Fair bass singer, better songwriter. Wrote 'Motor City Mama,' only song Sol didn't screw us out of, and he only missed that one 'cause he blew town in a hurry. That why Sol sent you around? Hell, I signed over my rights to that jam years ago."

"I'm not working for Sol Katz, Mr. DeWitt, I'm working for Varnell Mack."

"So you said." He nodded. "But if you workin' for him, why ask me about him?"

"Because I think he may be in some kind of trouble. Would you know a reason why anyone would be videotaping his movements? Police maybe?"

"Videotape?" the old man echoed, glancing up at me again, exasperated. "Sweet Jesus, what is this crap? The damn stroke messed up my arm some, but my brains ain't Alpo yet. At least the last dude Sol sent around askin' about Varnell came at me straight on. I don't know what kind of a scam you're tryna pull, but take your show on the road."

"I'm not pulling a scam, Mr. DeWitt."

"Hell you ain't," DeWitt snapped. "Look, I let you run your mouth to pass the time, but I'm tired of listenin' to jive 'bout friends of mine. Varnell Mack never hired you for a damn thing, sonny, so tell your story walkin' or I'm liable to get out' this chair and throw your jive ass outa here."

"Mr. DeWitt, why don't you think Varnell Mack hired me?"

"I don't think he didn't, boy, I know. Hell, he ain't even *been* Varnell for more'n twenty years. He went Muslim after the sixty-seven riots, changed his name to Raheem somethin' or other. Wouldn't hardly speak to a white man after that, say nothin' of hirin' one."

"Maybe he's mellowed."

"Musta mellowed one helluva lot. Musta mellowed hisself right outa the ground."

"What are you saying?"

"The man's dead, boy. Died back in eighty-three. Lung cancer. Wasn't but a dozen people at his funeral and most of them was Farrakhan Muslims. So you trot back an' tell Sol if he wants to use that jam, go ahead on. I won't give him no trouble, and Varnell sure as hell won't neither. You got what you came for, now get on away from me." He turned back to his game, shutting me out as effectively as if he'd slammed a door.

I rose slowly, trying to think of something to say. It wouldn't matter. He wasn't going to buy anything I was selling now. And maybe he was wrong, had Varnell and this Raheem whatever mixed up somehow. Maybe.

I stopped at the front desk on my way out and asked the Dresden milkmaid on duty if DeWitt had regular visitors.

"I wouldn't know offhand," she said, frowning. "We have

so many patients. Why do you ask?"

"He seems to be a little confused. About who's alive, and who isn't."

"That happens quite a lot." She smiled, scanning the visitor's log.

"Let's see, a Mr. Rothstein visited a few weeks ago. And a Mr. Jaquette. A Mr. and Mrs. Robinson. Does that help?"

"No one named Mack?"

"Apparently not, not recently anyway. I wouldn't be too concerned about it though," she added. "Residents often get confused about friends who've passed on. They even talk to them sometimes. It can give you shivers."

"Yeah," I said. "I know the feeling."

I found my steps quickening as I made my way out of the rest home, and when I hit the sidewalk I was sprinting for my car. I scrambled in and peeled out of the lot, pedal down, headed back to the heart of Motown.

And Rock 'n Soul Recollections. I barely made it. It was after five and the blinds were drawn, but I could still see movement inside. I hammered on the door. "Open up, Cal! It's an emergency."

"An emergency?" he said quizzically, letting me in. "At a record store?"

"You don't know the half of it," I said, stalking to the golden soul bin, riffling through the S's. The Sultans. Horace DeWitt grinned up at me from the jacket, young and strong. A rock. I scanned the faces of his backup singers. Their images were barely more than grey smears, blurred by the dance step they were doing. I just couldn't be sure.

"Have you got any other pictures of the Sultans?" I asked. "Posters? Anything?"

"The Sultans?" he echoed, eyeing me blankly, while he rapidscanned the computer directory of his memory. "I have two playbills with the Sultans featured, but no pictures. . . ." He crossed to a file of publicity memorabilia, and expertly riffled through it. "Aha. A program for a Warfield Theater revue. Nineteen sixty-two. Sam Cooke, The Olympics, Millie Jump and the Jacks, and . . . the Sultans of Soul. Be careful now, it's a by God cherry original."

I checked the table of contents, then leafed through the program gingerly. And found the Sultans of Soul. A standard publicity shot of Horace DeWitt ringed by four dudes in gleaming lamé jackets. Except for Horace, I didn't recognize any of them. I checked the fine print beneath the photo. Varnell Mack was last on the left. He was tall, and had a Malcolm X goatee. But he definitely was not the man who hired me.

Damn.

"What's with you?" Cal said. "You look like you lost your best friend."

"Worse. I think I may be losing my touch. I'm being conned by a guy who can barely walk across a room."

"Conned out of what?"

"That's the hell of it. I don't know. Cal, why would anybody pretend to be a has-been soul singer? And a dead one at that?"

"Somebody's pretending to be one of the Sultans? But why? Even in their heyday they were strictly small change."

"It can't be for money," I said. "He's already paid me more than he's likely to get from any royalties. So what does he want?"

"You got any idea who this guy is?"

"All I know is that it has to be somebody from the old days who knew the Sultans. I'm guessing he found out Sol was looking for Varnell from Horace DeWitt, so his name could be Robinson, or maybe Jaquette."

"Jaquette?" Cal said, blinking. "First name?"

"I don't know. Why?"

"Because I know a few Jaquettes, but only one who would've known the Sultans," Cal said, taking the program from me and flipping through it. "Could this be your guy? The one in the middle?"

"Yes," I said slowly, "this is him. Or it was thirty years ago. But this pic isn't of the Sultans."

"Nope, it's the Jacks, Millie Jump's old group. Dexter Jaquette was their lead singer. And Millie's husband. She dumped him after he got busted."

"Busted for what?"

"A nickel-dime dope thing, couple of marijuana cigarettes. It'd be nothing now, but it was a hard fall back then. I think he did five years."

"All that was a lifetime ago. What could he possibly want now?"

"I don't know. Why don't you ask him?"

"Maybe I will," I said slowly, still staring at the smiling photo of Dexter Jaquette. "Can I take this with me?"

"Absolutely," Cal said. "That'll be twenty-four bucks plus tax, an extra ten for opening late, call it thirty-five even."

I raised an eyebrow, but paid without carping. He'd been a huge help and we both knew it.

I left the program open on the seat as I drove back to my apartment, and my eye kept straying to it. It was a jolting contrast, the faded photo of Dexter Jaquette the singer, and the broken man who'd hired me. My God, he was so young then. Younger than I am now. But there was more to it than that. Something about that picture that I was missing.

Pictures. The guy with the videocam. What was that all about? The only thing I was sure of was that Jaquette had gone to a lot of trouble to set this up. If I confronted him, he'd probably just back off and try again later. Assuming he lived long enough.

Should I warn Sol? A double conundrum. Sol wasn't my client, Dexter was. And if I warned Sol, he'd sic Roddy Rothstein on Jaquette. The fact that he was a cripple wouldn't bother Roddy. He'd rough him up, run him off, or worse, and I'd still never know what I'd bought into.

Unless I played it out. Seemed to me this show had been in rehearsal for thirty years. It would be a shame to close it before the last act.

The Cadillac rolled up in front of Papa Henry's a little after nine. I climbed out of my Buick and trotted over just as Mack's chauffeur opened the back door.

"There's been a change in plans," I said. "We'll take my car. Give your man the night off."

Mack/Jaquette eyed me a moment, then shrugged. "My car, your car, I guess it doesn't matter."

"Good. And Mr. Mack, I mean give him the night off. I don't want to see him in my rearview mirror, or the meet's canceled. Understood?"

"Yeah," he said, smiling faintly. "I think I understand." He spoke briefly to the chauffeur, who started to argue, then gave it up. He looked me over slowly, memorizing my features, then helped Jaquette out of the car, and drove off.

Jaquette made his way slowly to my car. He'd changed into a tux, with a gleaming ebony cane to match. The suit was an immaculate fit, and broken and bent as he was, he looked elegant. Dressed to kill.

After he'd eased into my car, I leaned in and snapped his seat belt, fussing over his suit to make sure the belt didn't muss it. And gave him a none-too-subtle frisk at the same time. I expected him to object, but he didn't. He seemed amused, energized. Wired up and ready.

Costa Del Sol is one of the hottest discotheques in Detroit. Tucked away on the fifteenth floor of the Renaissance Center, it's trendy, expensive, and *very* exclusive, with memberships available only to the very chic, and the very rich. I'd been there a few times as Desiree's bodyguard, but the bouncers working the front door still wouldn't admit us until Roddy Rothstein bopped out to okay it.

The Costa is on two levels, a huge, lighted dance floor below, a Plexiglas-shielded balcony above, with a deejay suspended in a pod between them, cranking out power jams loud enough to give the Statue of Liberty an earache. A state-of-the-art laser system plays on the dance floor, psychedelic starbursts competing with the camera flashes of the paparazzi shooting the celebrities at play from the press section of the balcony.

We followed Roddy up the escalator to the second floor, the dining, observing, deal-making area. Shielded from the blare of the sound-system, the music from below is reduced to a pulse up here, a thump you feel through your soles like a heartbeat.

Roddy threaded his way slowly through the tables, adjusting his pace to Jaquette's limp, leading us to the head table, where Sol and Millie were chatting up the entertainment editor of the *Detroit Free Press*. Sol had changed jackets, black, with a black shirt, to highlight a heavy gold Jerusalem cross. Millie was dazzling in a white sequined jumpsuit, a spray of diamonds in her hair. Desi was her usual fashionably frumpy self, street-person chic. In the bustle, nobody noticed us, until Jaquette spoke.

"Hello, Sol," he said quietly. "How's the leech business?"

Sol glanced up, annoyed, and the color bled from his face. "My God. Dexter." He glanced quickly around, but Roddy had already moved off into the crowd. "What do you want?"

"To settle up. To close out my account."

"There's nothing to close out," Millie said, glaring furiously at me. "It was all settled a long time ago."

"Maybe not," Jaquette said, glancing at Desi. "What do you think, girl? You know who I am?"

"You're nobody," Sol snapped. "History."

"Maybe it's history to you," Jaquette said. "It's not for me. You got any idea what it's like to see a girl's face on a billboard, have it nag at you? Knowin' there's somethin' familiar about her? Bugged me so much I went to a shop to buy her album, and as soon as I saw her picture up close I knew. I mean *I knew*. It was like bein' struck by lightning. She looks like you, Millie, even sounds like you. But she looks like me, too. And like my mama. The record jacket said she was only twenty-five, but I knew it was a damn lie. She's mine. You were pregnant when you quit me, hid it from me so you could cop yourself a honky meal ticket."

"That's enough," Sol snapped. "I don't know what you think you got comin', Dex, but if it's trouble, you're at the right place. Roddy!" Rothstein hurried toward us, bulling his way through the crowd, signaling to another security type standing near the balcony rail. Beyond him, I glimpsed a familiar silhouette, the man I'd seen on the rooftop that afternoon. He was in the press gallery now, with a camera, or a weapon, I couldn't be sure.

"Too late, Sol," Jaquette said, reaching under his coat. "You took everything, the music, my woman, even my child. It's time to pay up."

"Roddy!" Sol screamed, backing away, stumbling over his chair. Rothstein broke through the crowd and jerked his piece from under his coat, aiming at Dexter's belly, two-hand hold.

"No!" I yelled, stepping between them. "Don't. It's what he wants!"

"Kill him!" Katz shouted. "Do it! Axton, get out of the way!"

"For godsake Sol, he's unarmed! He didn't come here to kill you, he came here to die! To take you with him! He's got a guy in the balcony filming the whole thing!" Nobody was listening. Rothstein was circling to get a clear shot, and he was going to do it, I could read it in his eyes. Dammit!

I shoved Jaquette down out of the line of fire and threw myself at Roddy, tackling him chest high, the two of us crashing over a table. He hacked at me with his pistol, slamming me hard over the ear. I clutched desperately at his arm, but I was too dazed to hold it. He wrenched free, aiming his automatic past me at Dexter.

"Stop it!" Desi screamed, freezing us all for a split second, long enough for me to grab Rothstein's wrist and clamp onto it with my teeth. He roared, and dropped his weapon, hammering my face with his free hand. Sol scrambled after Roddy's piece, grabbed it, and swung it to cover Dexter.

"The balcony, Sol," I managed. "Look at the press box."

He risked a quick glance, spotted the guy with the camera. Then slowly got to his feet. He stood there, in a killing rage, his weapon centered on Jaquette's chest, and if I've ever seen one man ready to kill another, it was Sol at that moment. The moment passed.

"Get up and get him out of here, Axton," he said, lowering the pistol slightly. "But by God, if I ever see either of you again, I'll be the last thing you ever see."

I shook my head trying to clear it. Rothstein was still clutching his bloodied wrist. His eyes met mine for a moment, and I knew that it wasn't finished between us. It was personal now. I'd be seeing him again. Terrific.

I lurched to my feet, and hauled Jaquette to his. He was spent, ashen, barely able to stand. I got an arm around him, picked up his cane, and helped him walk out, one slow step at a time. He hesitated at the escalator and I let him. He'd paid the price of admission.

He turned to look back a moment; God only knows what he was thinking. Sol and Millie were trying to calm Desi, all of them shaken to the core. Jaquette swallowed, and I thought he was going to say something, but he didn't. Maybe he couldn't. I walked him out to the car.

We drove in silence for twenty minutes, the only sound the rumble of the Buick's big V-8 and the rasp of Jaquette's breathing. He rolled down the window, letting the rain sprinkle his face and trickle down his goatee and his collar. It seemed to help.

"I thought it'd be easier," he said softly, more to himself than to me.

"What would be?"

"Dying. I thought it through, thought I was ready. But at the last second there, I thought, maybe it's not worth it. *He's* not worth it. Not even after . . . everything. That, ah, that was a bold thing you did back there. I'm sorry I dragged you into my trouble."

"Why did you?" I asked.

"I needed somebody to walk me through Sol's security. Went to the concert at the Palace to . . . to see the girl. Couldn't even get close. Spotted you. Asked around, found out who you were, what you do. Took me a month to figure this thing out, set it up. The guy with the camera's a film student from U of Detroit. Thinks he's makin' a documentary about an old-time singer tryin' to collect some back royalties from a rip-off record company. Would've worked too. I figured everything but you."

"How so?"

"Willis told me you were honest. He never said you were

crazy. When it come down to it, I thought you'd stand aside, let it happen. And the whole thing'd be on film. No way Sol could duck the rap for takin' me out."

"And that'd be worth dying for?"

"Hell, I'm dyin' anyway, boy, slow and hard. I was lucky to see Christmas. I won't see another. I figured if I could just take Sol down with me . . . Maybe you shoulda let it happen. Hate's all I had left," he said, sagging back in his seat, closing his eyes. "Ain't even got that now. I'm tired. To my bones. I wish I could just . . . be gone."

"You can't though. It's not over."

"No? Why not?"

"You hired me to collect some money, Mr. Jaquette. I haven't done it yet. How would you like to meet your daughter? One on one? I think I can arrange it."

His eyes blinked open. "Meet her? Why? To say goodbye?"

"Or hello. You might have more to talk about than you think. Business, for instance."

"What business I got with her?"

"None. But the Sultans have business. With Sol."

"Man, that was all smoke. A way to get to him is all. He screwed 'em for true, but it was all legal."

"That doesn't make it right. And Desi might not think so either. She's got a good heart, and a hard nose. I think if you asked her right, you bein' a dyin' man and all, she'd talk Sol into doin' the right thing by the Sultans."

"It's too late for that. The Sultans are gone, all but Horace. And he ain't got long."

"Then do it for the others. The Sultans weren't the only group who got ripped off. Maybe you could establish a legal precedent other old-timers can use to get a fairer shake. It might not amount to much. But it's better than nothing."

"Maybe so, I don't know, I'm too tired to think now. Drop me off at the corner. I wanna walk awhile."

"It's raining."

"I know," he said. "Stop the car."

I watched him limp away, step, lean, step, lean. An old man in a tuxedo, in the rain. I wasn't worried about him. His Cadillac had been tailing us since we left the Costa Del Sol.

I think he's wrong about wanting to give up. A man who worked as hard as Jaquette to settle a score would find enough juice to talk to his daughter.

And he's wrong about the Sultans, too. They aren't gone. Not really. Nor are the hundreds of others who sang their souls out in warehouses and storefronts for pocket change. And altered the musical culture of the world. Shysters like Sol were so intent on cheating them out of every last nickel's worth of rights and royalties that they let one minor asset slip past.

Immortality.

When Sol and his ilk are gone, who will remember? But the Sultans? And Sam Cooke? Otis Redding? As long as anyone's left to listen, they'll sing. Forever young.

I slid the worn cassette into the Buick's player, felt the pulse of the kick drum in the pit of my stomach, then the thump of the bass. And Horace DeWitt sang to me. Not the stroke-shattered hulk in Riverine Heights, but the big-shouldered, brown-eyed, handsome man with conked hair, grinning up from the Warfield Theater program. And he was young again.

And so was I.

"I'm comin' home, Motown Mama, I just can't live without ya . . ."

The Taxi Dancer

The woman weighed two twenty if she was an ounce, and she'd never see seventy again. Still, the old darlin' could foxtrot, by God. She followed Toby's lead like a shadow, swaying when he did, gliding over the recreation room's tiled floor, graceful as a swan.

They made a striking couple, Toby tall and slim in his good gray suit, his silver pompadour and mustache a sharp contrast with his deep chocolate complexion. His partner was a lot less chic in a thin cotton robe over her shapeless hospital gown. Her gray hair was cropped boyishly short for easy shampooing.

Toby glanced down and smiled, but her eyes were lifeless as a potato slice. She probably couldn't remember her children or the name of this rest home, or even who she was. Her feet still remembered the steps, though. She'd been young once, and she'd learned to foxtrot. Probably when it was new.

The old swing tune had another chorus to run, and Toby used the time to scan the room. They'd brought down two dozen elderly patients for today's show. A few couples were dancing to the golden oldie on Toby's boombox, shuffling around like trained bears. The rest watched in varying states of stupor, strapped into wheelchairs or reclining on wheeled hospital beds.

Two male attendants and three nurses were clustered near the coffee urn shooting the breeze, paying only nominal attention to Toby and their charges. It was time.

Toby escorted his partner to a chair near the CD player, then casually strolled out into the corridor. Empty. Good.

Walking briskly to the stairwell, he trotted up to the fifth floor and peered through the safety glass of the fire door.

A beefy nurse was on duty at the station at the end of the hall, but she was facing the other way, taking it easy, reading a romance novel. Well, why not? The Riverside Rest Home had no ambulatory patients above the third floor.

Toby sidled out of the stairwell and around the corner, silent as a ghost. If anyone asked, he was looking for the men's room. But no one did. Most of the attendants were at the tea dance four floors below.

He ducked into the first room. Two patients, male, one asleep, the other staring sightlessly at the window. Toby quickly scanned the medical tray on the nightstand. The usual: Soma, Valium, and Talwin. He took four pills from each container, dropping them in separate jacket pockets, then checked the nightstand drawer. No pills, only a comb and a toothbrush.

As he crossed to the second bed, the patient turned and stared at him, but there was no recognition. Toby copped a few Ativan from the nightstand but didn't rifle the drawer. The old dude might be more alert than he looked.

He checked the corridor, then went into the next room. A woman patient, dozing. Valium, Soma, and, bingo, some Demerol, fifteen bucks a hit on the street. Her drawer held some extra Talwin, plus a Lady Bulova wristwatch. The band looked like real gold. He took two pills, thought about the watch, but left it. He was down on his luck but not quite that far gone yet.

Next room, two males, both out of it. Valium and Talwin from the first tray, nothing in the nightstand. Second guy'd spilled some pills from his tray on the floor. Toby scooped them up and sorted through them, Ativan, Soma, and . . . he hesitated. A tooth? It looked like a broken tooth.

He glanced sharply at the guy in the bed. Eyes staring, mouth agape, a smear of blood trickling down his chin. The veins in his temple were as thick as blue worms beneath his transparent skin. They were utterly still. Not even a quiver. Instinctively Toby backed away from the corpse.

"What are you doing in here?"

Toby whirled, thrusting the pills into his pocket. A heavyset, suet-faced nurse with a mole on her check was in the doorway.

"I, um, I was looking for the men's room," Toby stammered.

"There's no men's room in here. Why didn't you check in at the desk?"

"Sorry, ma'am, I guess I'm on the wrong floor."

"I think there's more wrong about you than the floor, mister."

She seized his elbow as he tried to sidle past her. Twenty years ago Toby would have pulled free, dumped her on her wide butt, and sprinted for the stairwell. Maybe even ten years ago. He could almost see himself doing it as she hauled him back to the nurse's station like a naughty child and dialed security.

The cops stashed him in an interrogation room for three or four hours. He had to guess at the time; they took his watch along with the pills they found when they searched him. The room had no clock, only the two-way mirror on the wall, a table, and two metal chairs. He sat quietly at the table, waiting. Trying not to think about having to do jail time again. After a hundred years the door opened.

Mutt and Jeff, Toby thought. The lady cop was short, five five or so, with a pert Irish mug and coarse blonde hair that framed her face. Her plain white blouse, navy skirt, and pumps weren't a uniform exactly, but close enough.

Her partner was tall and gaunt with acne-pitted cheeks and a suit from the bargain rack at Goodwill. He folded his arms and leaned against the door of the interrogation room, looking surly. Toby guessed the woman would play good cop. Stretch would be the heavy.

"Mr. McCann? I'm Lieutenant Erin Maher-Wilkes. The gentleman by the door is Sergeant Nowalski." She placed a tape recorder and a manila folder on the table, switched on the machine, gave the date, time, her name and his, then read Toby his rights.

There was something familiar in her voice, a lilt, an accent? Toby couldn't place it. Maybe he'd just heard his rights read once too often.

"Do you wish to have an attorney present?" Erin asked.

"I can't afford a lawyer, and the free ones ain't worth what you pay 'em. Look, we both know the drill, lieutenant. Suppose you knock the pills you found on me down to one count of possession, I'll cop to it, and we can wrap this up with no fuss?"

"Possession?" Nowalski said, raising one eyebrow. "You're a real piece of work, McCann. You rip off sick, elderly people and expect us to just let you walk?"

"I won't walk, pal. Possession's five hundred bucks and costs or forty-five days in jail. If I had five bills, do you think I'd be taxi dancin' in rest homes?"

"What's taxi dancing?" Maher-Wilkes asked.

"Are you kidding? No, I guess you'd be too young to know. Years ago you could buy tickets to dance with girls at a hall, like hirin' a taxi. Now it's what I'm down to. Taxi dancer."

"Like a gigolo, you mean?"

"Nah, these ladies got no use for a gigolo, they just need somebody to waltz 'em around the floor for the exercise. I'm no spring chicken myself, but I still got my teeth and I move okay so they book me into rest homes to dance with the patients. Ten bucks an hour, couple of times a week. Tough to live on."

"So you steal drugs from the patients?"

"No, I steal drugs from the homes, they pass pills out like popcorn in those places, dope those folks up like zombies. A few pills more or less don't matter. They don't miss 'em."

"A shroud has no pockets, as the Irish say. Is that how you see it, Mr. McCann?"

No pockets? Again, something wriggled in the back of Toby's memory. He'd heard that saying . . . and that voice.

"And you're just a poor old codger of a petty thief, trying to scrape by," Erin continued. "What about the dead man? Did he wake up and catch you rifling his nightstand?"

"What are you talking about? He didn't wake up at all."

"Then why did you smother him with that pillow? For kicks?"

"I didn't smother anybody! Honest to God I didn't!"

"Give it up, McCann," Nowalski put in. "One of his teeth broke off in the struggle. It was in your pocket, forgodsake."

"It was mixed in with some spilled pills I found on the floor," Toby said desperately. "I just scooped 'em up."

"Did you now?" Erin said. "Toby, Toby, Toby, do you have any idea how deep a hole you're in?"

And there it was. He remembered where he'd heard her voice. No, not her voice, her tone and phrasing. He squinted, trying to read her nametag.

"What are you doing?" she snapped. "I asked you a question."

"Sorry. Look, lady, you've got my record there in that folder. I been in the joint three times, but always for bunco or petty theft. I ain't the strongarm type. I never hurt anybody in my life."

"Maybe no one paid you enough before," Nowalski said.

"Paid me?" Toby echoed. "For what? I only get paid to dance nowadays, and not much at that."

The lady cop was eyeing him oddly. "Know something, Nowalski? I don't think he knows who he killed. You don't, do you, Toby? Yeah, yeah, I know—" she waved off his objections "—since you didn't kill anybody, you couldn't know who the dead man was. Right. Tell me, does the name Carlo Zuccone ring a bell?"

A fist closed around Toby's heart. "Zuccone? I've heard of Charlie Zuccone. He's a . . . he lends money to people."

"Charlie Zuccone's a lot more than a loanshark and we both know it. He's a local Mafia boss. The man you claim you found in that room was old Carlo Zuccone, Charlie's grandfather, the original mob godfather in this town. Still think you can cut a deal with us for possession, Mr. McCann?"

"I don't know," Toby said, swallowing. "Maybe not. Look, I want to talk to you, lady. In private. No tape. Okay?"

"Forget it," Nowalski began, but the lady cop waved him off.

"It's all right, Chet. Take five, get us both some coffee, please." She said it mildly, but there was a definite edge of command in her tone. Nowalski started to object, then shrugged and stalked out.

"Well, Mr. McCann?" Erin said. "What's on your mind?"

Reaching across the table, Toby switched off the recorder. "Maher-Wilkes," he said slowly. "Maher was your maiden name, right? Was Mickey Maher your dad? Irish cop? Big guy?"

"My father's name was Mickey, and he was a cop," she admitted.

"Thought so. What you said about the shroud with no pockets rang a bell. Mickey used to say that. We knew each other back in the sixties. I used to work at a club on the river. Motown Underground. Your dad was a beat cop then. Check my file, he busted us once for selling booze after hours."

"So my dad arrested you," Erin said. "So what?"

"He busted me once," Toby said carefully. "Never again. And we stayed open all night for a good ten years after that one time. Do I have to draw you a picture?"

"Are you hinting that my dear old dad was on the take? And you expect me to give you a break or you'll blacken the family name? Dream on, McCann. I know what kind of a cop my father was, and so does everybody else on the force. You can't threaten me."

"I wasn't trying to."

"What then? You're hoping I'll cut you some slack for auld lang syne because you used to bribe my old man?"

"It wasn't like that, lady. I liked your dad. He was a good cop. Nobody begrudged him a little street tax. You couldn't expect a man to put his ass on the line for what the city paid in them days. He knew everybody in that neighborhood, who belonged and who didn't. He looked out for us. He was one of us."

"Maybe that was because he had a piece of the action."

"Maybe, but I could dance on corners for money at three in the mornin'. You can't walk those streets in daylight nowadays."

"Is there a point to this little history lesson?"

"All I'm sayin' is, if you ask your dad about me he'll tell you I couldn't have done this thing at the Riverside. Toby McCann, the dancin' man. He'll remember me."

"Sorry," she said, shaking her head slowly. "I'm afraid my dad's not giving any character references these days. He's in a rest home himself. Parkview, across the river. Sometimes he knows who I am, sometimes not. Mostly he thinks I'm my mother. Sometimes he even asks me to dance."

"A box step."

"What?"

"An old fashioned step, like this." Toby rose and did a graceful sashay in a square. "It's a dance even a bigfoot Irishman could do. I taught it to him myself, for his anniversary . . . fifteenth, I think. Learned it to 'String of Pearls,' the old Glenn Miller tune. Wanted to surprise his missus. I guess it was their song or somethin'."

Erin eyed him thoughtfully for what seemed like a very long time. " 'String of Pearls' was their favorite song," she conceded at last. "I found them dancing in the kitchen at two in the morning once. The music woke me . . ." She shook her head. "Okay, so maybe you really knew my dad. So what?"

"So since I told you the truth about that, you know you can believe the rest of it. I didn't hurt nobody in that rest home. It ain't my style. Your dad would know that."

"It wouldn't matter if he did. The sixties have been over a long time, Toby. You can't walk away from a murder beef just because somebody puts in a good word for you."

"I'm not askin' to walk. The way I see it, it don't matter whether I go inside or hit the street. Either way I'll end up coolin' on a slab in the morgue if word gets out I was mixed up in the old don's death. I been thinkin' on that, though. Maybe you and me can work a deal after all."

"How do you mean?"

"Look, I swear to you I didn't kill Zuccone. For openers, I had no reason to. Maybe his grandson does, though. Word on the street is, Charlie's real short on bread these days. He's got a gambling jones, they say. He's even been borrowin' money from his own shylocks."

"I've heard that," Erin nodded. "So?"

"So you've gotta figure he stands to inherit serious bucks with the old man gone. But doin' his grandfather isn't somethin' he could ask one of his goons to do. Killin' a don's a heavy thing with them mob types. I figure Charlie must've done the job himself."

"Security at Riverside didn't report seeing anyone."

"Maybe not, but I got in there, didn't I? Charlie could have found a way in, too, and maybe I can show you how."

"How do you mean?"

"I been runnin' scams all my life, lady. Charlie's mean, but he's no genius. Suppose I call him and say I'm a patient at Riverside? Tell him I saw what went down and I want a payoff."

"Pretty thin."

"Maybe, but if he did it, he can't risk leaving a witness alive. He'll have to come after me. You can nail Charlie for his grandfather's killing and get his mob on a plate at the same time. If you're half the cop your father was, you can squeeze Charlie like a lemon for everything he knows."

"Maybe," Erin conceded. "And what do you want in return?"

"Get the D.A. to cut me a walk on the rest home bust and front me some travelin' money. I'll have to boogie on down the road after this."

"Unless Charlie doesn't show up," Erin said evenly. "In which case you'll probably be doing life in prison for murder. And a short life at that."

They smuggled him into the home in a linen delivery van after midnight and moved him into a suite on the fifth floor across the hall from the late Don Carlo's room. He phoned Charlie from the hospital so the number would check out if he verified it. Zuccone listened to Toby's pitch in silence, then told him to wait. Was he coming? Who knew? So Toby waited. Alone.

He was dressed like a patient, loose cotton pajamas, blue bathrobe, and slippers. The slippers were the worst. Soft-soled and floppy, they forced the wearer to shuffle like an invalid.

Toby startled himself when he glanced in the bathroom mirror. In his rest home duds with his hair awry, he looked like he actually belonged in this zombie warehouse, as if donning the institutional clothing had mutated him into a resident.

Hell, maybe he was. Maybe this sterile room was reality, and his life on the street was a dream. Sometimes when he danced with his elderly partners they'd murmur to themselves, talking with departed loved ones or reliving scenes from their lives. Perhaps he was doing that now, pacing the room in his slippers and robe, waiting for a visitor who only existed in his mind.

The bed, with its clean sheets and pillowcase, looked inviting, but Toby fought the urge to rest. Truth was, he was terrified of the damned thing, afraid that if he dozed off he might awaken as just another drifty patient.

He was no kid, hadn't been since Jackie Robinson signed with the Dodgers, but he wasn't done living yet, not as long as he could dance a little and enjoy a song and a sip of wine and a woman's smile. And even if his time was up, he didn't want to end in a place like this. Better to take a midwinter walk on the Detroit River and do a buck and wing till the ice gave way.

The door opened, and a familiar figure stepped in, the beefy nurse with the mole on her cheek who'd caught him before. "You?" she said, scowling. "I thought the police arrested you for murdering one of my patients."

"It's okay, the cops brought me back," Toby said. "Check

with the chief of security. He knows about it."

"He said they put somebody in here, he didn't tell me it was you."

"Look, I didn't kill anybody, lady. I was just in the wrong place at the wrong time."

"You still are, sport." Without warning she drove a meaty fist into his midsection and spun him around into a choke hold.

"Hey, ease off," Toby gasped. "You're making a mistake."

"Not as big as the one you made when you told Charlie you saw something. He's holding up my money until I settle your hash." She jerked his robe down around his waist, pinning his arms at his sides.

"Your money?" Toby stammered. "You mean—"

"Save your breath, pops, you're about to learn how to fly." She hauled him to the casement window and began cranking it open.

"You'll never get away with this! The cops know I'm here!"

"Yeah, but right now they're all down in the lobby watching the doors and elevators. This way they'll figure you really killed the old don, you were overcome by guilt and jumped. It's not neat, but it'll have to do."

"Help! Somebody—" Her forearm slammed into the side of his head, wobbling his knees. Dazed, he felt himself hoisted up on the sill, felt the bite of the icy night wind through his thin pajamas. The chill shocked him back to awareness, and he caught a blurred glimpse of the parking lot five stories below. With a last despairing lunge, Toby vaulted backward with all the force his wiry thighs could muster.

His thrust sent them both crashing onto the bed. Toby tumbled off the far side, but the door was closed and his arms were still tangled in the robe. No escape. Kicking off his slippers, he staggered to his feet as the nurse came charging around the bed after him.

"Help! Somebody!" Pirouetting like a toreador to avoid her rush, he kicked the door, hard. He could hear noise from the hallway now, patients yelling. He dodged aside a second time, but the room was too damned small. She clutched his dressing gown as he whirled past, hammered the wind out of him, then dragged him back to the windowsill and lifted him up.

She had him halfway out the window when Nowalski and Erin burst through the door.

"It's about time," Toby said as Erin Maher-Wilkes stepped into the interrogation room. "I been goin' nuts in here."

"Sorry," Erin said, placing the tape recorder on the table. "It took me awhile to convince Florence Nightingale to give Charlie up. She's a stubborn woman."

"A mighty tough one, too. She bounced me around like a beanbag. So what about our deal? I held up my end."

"Not quite. You promised to deliver Charlie Zuccone; instead I had to save your butt from the Dragon Lady."

"Hey, how was I supposed to know Charlie hired somebody on the inside? I did my part and damned near got killed for my trouble!"

"Relax, Toby, I was just jerking your chain." Smiling, Erin tossed a brown envelope on the table beside the recorder. "There's five grand in there, the department's snitch fund for the month. You earned it. The prosecutor agreed to let you off with probation for your rest home scam, but I'd steer clear of them from now on if I were you."

"Don't worry about that, I'm never goin' inside one of

them places again as long as I live. Am I free to go now?"

"Not just yet," she said, fitting a cassette into the tape recorder. "I've been thinking about what you said, about my dad and the way things were in this town thirty years ago compared to how they are now. I know he was on the take in those days, hell, most of the force was. Some of that money probably paid my way through college. Maybe that's why I resented it so much." She took a deep breath and pressed the PLAY button on the recorder.

"Anyway, before you go, Mr. McCann, I'd like to ask you for a favor. If you wouldn't mind?"

When Nowalski passed the interrogation room a little later, he froze dead in his tracks. Lieutenant Maher-Wilkes and Toby were dancing together, gliding gracefully around the barren room to a tinny old song on the tape machine.

The Glen Miller Band playing "String of Pearls."

Sleeper

Cass shot the street sign first, held it in close-up for five seconds to give the location, then two seconds longer to give viewers time to cope with the Polish name. Kosciusko Street. He softened the focus on the sign a bit, bringing in the maple leaves above it, grey-green in the August heat, then panned the minicam slowly to the tickytack split-level tract house midway up the block. The house was a white clapboard box with faux-brick facing exactly like its neighbors, a row of baby boomers fading quietly into middle age. A white picket fence minus a slat here and there encircled the front yard, sorry as a gap-toothed grin.

Cass walked cautiously up the driveway, filming all the way, the shoulder-held Panasonic Steadycam smoothing his movements. Keeping the waning afternoon light at his back so he wouldn't need a sun gun, he zoomed through the open garage door, did a swooping pass over the battered old Chevy four-door parked inside, panned down to the hydraulic jack jammed under the front wheel hub, then followed the rusty rocker panels to the splayed, denim-clad legs protruding from beneath the car.

He zoomed a little closer, focusing the shot the way a human eye would see it but without blinking. He slid down the legs, tracing the pant seams past the frayed knees to the scuffed brown work shoes, then pulled the shot in even tighter, dropping it to the trickle of blood crawling away from the body, inching along a wayward crack down the concrete driveway. Beautiful.

Great stuff. He felt his breathing go shallow, the familiar

sensual tightness in his chest, as he tracked the blood trail all the way out to the street. The blood gleamed black as oil in the Steadycam's viewfinder, but it would glow bright crimson on the Six O'Clock News. Lingering on it would crowd the borderline of airtime standards-and-practices guidelines for early evening, but he didn't give a damn. It was dynamite film. Still, in TV news there's no such thing as too much footage, so he reshot the car and the legs beneath it from three more perspectives, shifting the shot every five to fifteen seconds, attention span of Mr. and Mrs. Average American tube spud.

He was filming the house from the driveway when the front door opened and Stephanie Hawkins came out with a stunned, chubby blonde in nurse's whites. The widow? Definitely was if she was married to the poor sonovabitch pancaked under the car. He shifted the lens back toward the garage, watching Hawk out of the corner of his eye for a signal that the woman had given permission to film, sure she'd get it. She nearly always did. Sympathy, empathy, anger, whatever it took, Hawk had it. She was the best newswoman Cass had worked with since he came back to Motown from the Coast, possibly the best in the Metro Detroit media market. Tall, slender, articulate, clear cafe-au-lait skin, great cheekbones, cool under fire. Too good, really, to stay at WVLT much longer. A pity. Welcome to show biz, check your heart at the door. Hawk tapped the side of her purse as she took out her portable recorder mike. Okay to shoot.

Cass casually swung the Steadycam lens, following the neatly trimmed hedge to the small front porch, keeping his distance to avoid spooking the woman. No need to move closer, Hawk had positioned herself in good light, he could shoot them from the driveway. He zoomed in, centering the shot on Hawk first, then widening to the woman, trembling, haggard—Sweet Jesus!

The pallid, tear-streaked face in the viewfinder flashed from black-and-white to color, filling the lens. Sonya! It was Sonya! And the guy under the car, Stan? It must've been! Holy Mary Mother of God—The lens started to blur.

Shoot it. It's not real, damn it, it's just TV. A photo op. Shoot it. Get the footage. His mouth was cotton-dry, blood pounding at his temples. But the lens never wavered, never blinked. And gradually Sonya's face reverted to being another image in the viewfinder again, losing her color, her reality, fading to black-and-white. She was mumbling responses to Stephanie Hawkins' professionally empathetic questions, but Cass could see she was in shock, out on her feet, dabbing helplessly at her streaming eyes, some snot on her upper lip. Running on empty. He kept shooting her, following the conversation with the camera's eye, hearing sirens in the distance now.

Hawk heard them, too, switched off her mike, said something to Sonya, and helped her stumble back inside, leaving the front door ajar for Cass. He finished the shot, hesitated, wondering whether he should go into the garage to check the body. No—whoever was under that car was dead. No question. And he already had all the footage he needed. He trotted up the sidewalk to the porch.

The living room was cramped and dim after the afternoon glare, too much stuff in it, a worn turquoise Sears sofa and matching easy chairs, sagging Lazyboy in front of the tube, knickknacks, figurines cluttering the end tables, cheap reproductions and family photos on the walls. He'd never been here, but the room was familiar, like the home he'd grown up in, or his friends' houses.

His friend. Stan. He didn't have to ask. A wedding picture of Stan and Sonya on the coffee table told him more than he wanted to know. Cass stood silent, invisible as his own ghost in an old friend's home. Half hiding behind his minicam, feeling the subsonic vibration of its gyro against his cheek, the comforting heartbeat hum of the machine. Not shooting, just watching. Cool, detached, untouched. Until he noticed the car.

He'd been idly scanning the junk on the mantel over the gas-log fireplace: postcards, a bowling trophy, a framed snapshot of Stan, Sonya, and her younger brother—what was his name? Billy? No, Bobby. That was it. Twelve or thirteen when Cass last saw him, early twenties in the picture. The car was half hidden behind the snapshot. A plastic-and-steel model of a '57 Ford Skyliner hardtop convertible. My God.

He walked to the mantel, picked up the car, half hearing Sonya tell Hawk how she'd come home from work, found Stan in the garage, called 911. Mint condition. The Ford's wheels still spun, perfectly balanced. The headlights worked. The hardtop retracted invisibly into the trunk better than the original ever had, thanks to Stan.

Months. He and Stan had handcrafted every single part of the little Ford in high-school machine shop. After school, between classes, whenever. Copped second prize at the Michigan State Fair. A phony silver cup and a fifty-buck savings bond. Cass had long since lost the cup somewhere. But Stan had kept—

"Cass?" He glanced up. Both Sonya and Hawk were staring at him. Sonya looked bloodless, ready to fall. "Cass? I don't understand. How did you get here? How did you know?"

"Sonya, I—didn't know. I'm a cameraman, WVLT News. We monitor police and EMS bands, we just heard the call. I'm sorry, I can't tell you how sorry I am—"

An EMS van howled to a halt in the driveway, doors slamming, men charging into the garage.

"Oh," Sonya said, "seeing you there I thought I must be asleep, that—Oh, God. Stan—" Sonya lost it, broke down completely, dropped her face to her knees, wailing, covering her head with her forearms like a child trying to avoid a beating.

"Mrs. Sliwa? Sonya?" One of the EMS attendants rapped on the door once, stepped in without waiting, knelt awkwardly beside her, took her hand. "Sonya? You okay?" He was tall, rangy, reddish thinning hair, freckled face, thick wrists. He kept swallowing hard, eyes misty, struggling to keep himself together. He glanced vaguely at Hawk, blinking in confusion as he tried to place her. And he noticed Cass. And the WVLT logo on the minicam.

"Hey, what the hell is this?" he said slowly, rising. "What are you people doing in here?"

"Mrs. Sliwa invited us in. I'm Stephanie Hawkins—"

"I know who you are. I asked what the hell you're doing here. Christ, the cops aren't even here yet and you're already tryna get a goddamn interview? You get the hell outa here, the botha ya!"

"Charlie, please," Sonya quavered, "it's all right. I—"

"No, it ain't all right! Goddamn vultures! Damn it, clear out, lady, now or I'll kick your black ass all the way back to Motown where you belong. Now move it!"

"Hey," Cass said, setting the camera aside, "just cool down, buddy, that's enough!"

"It's all right, Cass," Stephanie said, rising. "The gentleman's upset and it's time to go, anyway. Mrs. Sliwa, I'm very sorry about your loss—"

"Keep your sympathy, lady," Charlie said. "Stan was nothin' to you but a couple minutes on TV. G'wan, get outa here."

"Okay, okay," Cass said, shouldering the camera, opening the front door. "Miss Hawkins, ma'am?"

Hawk hesitated, standing her ground in front of Mister Charlie for a moment, then stalked out past Cass without a word.

"Sonya?" Cass said. "I'm sorry as hell, you know that. I'll call you later." He glanced back from the doorway. Charlie was on his knees again, holding Sonya's hands. He wasn't crying, but he wasn't far from it.

A blue-and-white patrol car, flashers on, pulled in and parked beside the EMS van. Local Warsaw Heights cops. A salt-and-pepper team, Misiak and Jackson. Big and Bigger. Cass knew them from other crime scenes in the Heights—a shooting, a dope bust.

"*Jak sie mas, bracia, Meesh,*" Cass said, "how you doin'?"

"Don't gimme that homeboy stuff, Novak," Misiak said, "I only speak Polish to my mother. You guys already interview the lady who called?"

"Afraid so."

"Damn it, Novak, you know you people been warned about doin' interviews at a crime scene before the police—"

"No offense, officer," Hawk interrupted coldly, "but it's not our fault you can get a pizza delivered in this town faster than you can get a cop. This isn't a crime scene until you tie it off, and we're accredited members of the press with First Amendment rights. If you've got a problem with that, I'd love to hear it. On camera, of course. You feel like an interview?"

Misiak glared at her a moment, then shrugged. "Nah, just lemme do my job, stay outa the way, okay?"

"And is harassing the press part of your job?"

"No, ma'am," Misiak said, "mostly we just hang out at Dunkin' Donuts and snooze in the booths. In between gang fights and driveby shootin's. 'Scuse me, I got next of kin to talk to, assumin' she feels like talkin' to anybody *else*." Misiak stamped off toward the front door. His partner, Walker Jackson, finished talking to the EMS medic in the garage and wandered over.

"Nice work, Miss Hawkins, ma'am," he drawled softly, " 'nother milestone in police/press relations. What's the problem?"

"No problem," Hawk said, "it's just—hell, it's not your fault. Is this situation pretty much how it looks?"

"I'd say so," Jackson nodded. "Guy working under his car, the jack lets go, weight of the car suffocates him. We get two or three a summer. What'd the wife say?"

"That she came home from work, found him like that. They've had some junkie burglaries in the neighborhood, always keep the house locked. Guy was a wonderful husband, everybody liked him. Like that."

"Lady seem straight to you?"

"Absolutely. She's a basket case about it. Cass knows them, though. Anything to add, Novak?"

"No," Cass said. "Straight people. Good people." He coughed, his eyes stinging.

"Right," Jackson nodded. "Well, I guess that covers it. Buy you a drink after work, Miz Hawkins?"

"In your dreams, Jackson," Hawk said. But she smiled a little as he sauntered back into the garage.

"Cass," she said carefully, "you *did* know this guy, right? A friend?"

"Yeah, a friend. A good friend. In high school. About a thousand years ago."

"Well, no offense to your friend, but all we've got here is local interest, two minutes tops, C-bag."

"Maybe not that much. The story'll probably get bumped altogether if anything happens in the Middle East. You want me to try for a better shot when they remove the body?"

"That won't be necessary," Hawk said, eyeing him oddly.

"Look, don't worry about me—you want the footage of the body, I'll get it."

"I believe you. We just don't need it, okay? Let's shoot a stand-up in front of the house and that'll cover it. You ready?"

"Sure." He backed off a few feet and got Hawk focused while she checked her makeup in a hand mirror. She took out her handmike, nodded.

"Take one, Sliwa accident. A tragedy today, a fatal accident in—" She stopped, startled, glancing skyward as a sheet of raindrops suddenly splattered. No, not rain. Somebody was spraying them with a garden hose from behind the garage. Cass had an idea who.

"This is Stephanie Hawkins, WVLT-TV," Hawk continued coolly into the camera, ignoring her wilting hair, the water dripping down her face, "signing off from soggy, scenic Warsaw Heights and getting my butt back to Motown where I belong."

Novak went straight to the fridge when he got back to his apartment, rescued a couple of joints from his stash in a box of frozen waffles. He went into the living room, shucked his shoes, and eased down crosslegged on a futon in front of the tube. Left it dark. Turned himself on instead. Fired up the first doobie, sucked the Lebanese smoke deep into his lungs, holding it, feeling the buzz spread out from his chest, mellowing him out. Better. Not good, but better. By the time Hawk wandered in half an hour later, he was medium mellow, cloud seven, maybe seven and a half.

"What's going on?" Hawk said. She stepped out of her heels at the door, set her briefcase on the dining-room table, then sat on the couch, folding her legs under her.

"Nothing's going on. Bad day."

"I had most of the same day, plus a staff meeting at the end of it. Which you skipped."

"I wasn't in the mood. Anybody notice?"

"Only the assignment editor. I told him you were drunk in a ditch. Seems I wasn't far off. I thought we agreed you were through smoking dope in the apartment."

"Stefania, dark goddess of my soul, you know I would gladly lay me down and die for you," he said, taking another hit, holding the smoke, "but don't get in my face. Please."

"I'll get out of your goddamn life you don't tell me what's up in about thirty seconds, Novak. Make up your mind, while I've still got time to meet Jackson for a drink."

"Since you put it so tactfully. You remember me talking about a friend from high school, the guy who introduced me to the sacred logic of machines, got me my first job on a newspaper?"

"Nope, afraid not."

"That was him today—Stan Sliwa. Under that car."

"I see," she said slowly. "I'm sorry. Wait a minute—best friend? The one who married your high-school sweetheart? Her father was a big shot on the paper or something?"

"He owned the paper, but it was no big deal since it was only a Polish-language weekly. And how come you don't remember Stan, but you remember who he married?"

"I am woman, hear me roar. Only if this guy was such a good friend, why haven't you seen him since you came back? Warsaw Heights is only what, fifteen, twenty minutes out of Motown?"

"Twenty minutes, a dozen years. I guess I should have called him. But you can't go home again, or so I've heard. Maybe I was afraid to find out if it's true."

"Or maybe you were afraid to see the best friend's wife. Old flames burn the brightest, they say."

"Who says? Smokey Robinson?"

"I think it was Waylon Jennings," she said, picking up the remote control, flicking on the tube and the VCR. "Time for the news."

"I'm not sure I want to see this."

"Tough. If you're too stoned to take a walk, close your eyes. I want to see it. Strictly business, okay?"

A-bag, the first segment of the broadcast, was a tenement blaze in Dearborn.

"Damn," Hawk said, "I was hoping the drive-by shooting we covered would cop the first slot."

"Nah, the burn has better footage. Nice lookin' fire. Good color."

The Detroit drive-by was next. Two corpses, one a small boy in a Pistons T-shirt, were sprawled in a doorway off the Corridor while Hawk did the stand-up in front of the crack house. "Damn it, Cass, what the hell is on my face? I look like I've got leprosy."

"Shadows, darlin'—you were standing near a tree. Don't worry, it makes you look even more interesting. It's a good shot."

"For an art gallery, maybe. I'm not a model, Cass, I'm a reporter, and I'll never make anchor looking like Typhoid Mary."

B-bag was a millage vote, a Greek festival in Hart Plaza. Lame stuff. C-bag was a fluff piece on the U of D mascot. And then Stan. Cass sucked down the last of the joint, ground out the roach. Street sign, street, garage, car, body. Hawk talking to Sonya on the porch.

"All due respect, your long-lost love could lose a few pounds," Hawk said.

"So could Liz Taylor. Roll that back, show me the garage. I screwed it up somehow."

"It looks all right to me. Mmm, good shot of the blood. Looks alive."

"No, before that. Hell, take it from the top." Street sign, street, garage. "Freeze it. Right there. The car."

"What about it?"

"I don't know, but something—"

"I don't see anything. It's just a car. Pretty ordinary."

"Yeah, it is, isn't it?" he said, blinking, trying to clear away the fog. "Old Chevy four-door, Michigan cancer holes in the rocker panels. A junker. So what was Stan doing under it?"

"Fixing it. What else?"

"Yeah—" Cass nodded slowly "—only why bother? It's a ten-year-old beater. Stan wasn't just a putzer, he was a master mechanic—hell, he was state certified when he was sixteen. I'm damn handy with machinery, but Stan was an artist. So why is he working on a piece of crap like that? It'd cost more for parts than it's worth. The tires alone are probably worth more than—That's what's wrong with the shot."

"What, the tires? What's wrong with them?"

"Nothing, they look new. And they're not stock, either. Footprint's too wide. Racing tires. Exhaust could be oversize, too."

"Maybe he was turning it into a hot rod or something."

"Not that car. Wrong type. It's a four-door-more weight, weaker frame. Any two-door would be better."

"But don't guys sometimes soup up ordinary-looking cars for street racing?"

"A sleeper, you mean?"

"A what?"

"They're called sleepers. A car that looks normal on the

outside but it's tricked out under the hood. Same problem. Wrong type of car."

"Even so, what difference does it make now?"

"None," Cass said, flicking off the tube, easing to his feet. "But it bothers me. I, ah, I think I'll go over there."

"To see the car?" Hawk said evenly. "Or to comfort the grieving widow?"

"Look, the guy was a friend, okay? They both were. If you're worried, you're welcome to come along."

"No, thanks, I've seen as much of Polish Harlem as I care to for one day. Weather's too damp there. The only thing that worries me is that you've burned a couple of joints and it's bad for your short-term memory."

"What's that supposed to mean?"

"Nothing heavy. Only, while you're checking out this sleeper of yours, try to remember where you sleep, okay?"

"Darlin'," he said, slipping on his sportcoat, "when our thing crashes, you'll be the one who walks away, not me. Anyway, not to worry. You're right, the lady could stand to lose a few pounds."

"Not so many," Hawk said. "She still looked pretty good."

"Yeah—" he nodded "—she did, didn't she?"

A half dozen cars were parked in Stan's driveway when Cass pulled up in the WVLT mini van. Charlie Bennett, the angry EMS attendant, answered the door. He'd traded his uniform for civvies, a dark ready-to-wear suit that looked a size too small for his large frame. "Well, well, if it isn't the rainmaker," Cass said, "you here on a house call?"

"I'm a friend of the family," Bennett said. "Look, about this afternoon—I was upset, I didn't realize you were a buddy of Stan's. I called over to the station there to apologize but you'd already gone. I was outa line, I'm sorry. Fair enough?" He offered his hand.

"I guess so," Cass said, accepting it. "It was a lousy situation, anyway. How's Sonya holding up?"

"Not too bad, considering. It probably hasn't sunk all the way in yet." Bennett stood aside, ushering Cass in. "A few friends and neighbors came over to sit with her, brought a ton of food, some beer. Everybody's down in the family room."

Cass followed him through the cramped living room to the foyer, where the split level divided. A young guy in ragged jeans and a grimy T-shirt was coming down the stairway from the upstairs bedrooms carrying suitcases. He was almost concentration-camp gaunt with the same vacant stare, spiky hair the color of moldy hay, ragged stubble of beard. And vaguely familiar.

"Bobby?" Cass said, but the boy ignored him, brushed past, headed for the front door.

"That was Sonya's little brother, right?" Cass asked Bennett. "God, he was just a kid the last time I saw him. I guess he didn't remember me."

"Don't feel bad, he doesn't remember his own name half the time," Bennett shrugged.

"He moving out?"

"I wouldn't know," Bennett said, and his tone made it clear he didn't care. Cass followed him downstairs into the family room. And twenty years back in time.

The "family room" was a recycled basement, plastic oak-paneling, cheap carpet, Sears washer and drier at one end. A few dozen people were standing around, groups of older men in shirtsleeves, dark slacks, conversing in lowered tones. Housewives in plain print dresses were clustered near a Ping-Pong table laden with enough food for a Polish division, the air delicious with aroma of duck's blood soup, *golumpki*, cabbage rolls, *budyn z szykni*, steaming ham pudding. Two heavyset older women were filling plates, passing them out.

As Cass scanned the room looking for Sonya, he noticed he was catching a lot of stares, a few frowns, and realized he was the only person in the room not dressed somberly. In his white Armani sportcoat, peach shirt, faded jeans, he was a flamingo in a flock of starlings. Terrific. He spotted Sonya in the corner of the room with a few women friends and started over.

"Kazu? Is that you?" An ancient gnome of a man in a rumpled black suit levered himself up from a metal chair against the wall and hobbled toward him, leaning on an aluminum cane. Ignace Filipiak, Sonya's father.

"Mr. Filipiak, how are you?" Cass said, embracing the old man gently, afraid he might shatter him. "You look good."

"I look like a stomped pissant," the old man smiled, "but you, you look good, Kazu. Well and prosperous. Sonya tells me you're working for the TV now."

"That's right. I was here, ah, this afternoon. I'm very sorry about Stan, Mr. Filipiak, he was a good man."

"He was, he was." The old man nodded. "It's a terrible thing what happened. Funny, putting out the paper over the years, you see so many things you think it makes your soul as dried out as leather, tough, invulnerable. Then a thing like this—" His eyes were swimming, but he swallowed the pain, shrugged it off. "It must be hard for you, too, Kazu. You and Stanley were good friends, back when you worked for me."

"Yes, sir, we were."

"But you don't see him since you come back to town. You don't come around the old neighborhood. You ashamed of us, Kazu?"

"No, sir, of course not. But my folks are gone now—you lose touch, you know?"

"Yah, I know. The Heights isn't like it used to be, anyway, so many plants closing, no work. White Harlem they call it now, people on the welfare or moving away or mixed up in the *holjeda*."

"The *holjeda?* The plague? I don't understand."

"You know—the drugs, the crack. It's here, too, like everywhere else where people lose heart. In the war, the Nazis took young people for the slave-labor camps. This crack *holjeda* is like that, except the young people volunteer to die. I don't understand it, Kazu. Maybe I'm just too old."

"I don't think anybody understands it, Mr. Filipiak. And you don't seem older to me."

"I am, though," the old man sighed. "I'm feel like I'll be two hundred my next birthday, maybe more. And I talk too much. You go talk to Sonya, Kazu. She needs her friends now. If this TV job doesn't work out, you come see me. You can have your old job on *Populsku Warsaw Heights* anytime."

"You're still publishing the paper?" Cass asked, surprised.

"Of course. It's only bi-weekly now, not so many people read Polish in the Heights any more, but I'm still in the same building, still spend more time in the coffee shop downstairs than at work. Come by, see me sometime, we'll talk like the old days."

"I will, Mr. Filipiak—soon, I promise."

"You're a good boy, Kazu Novak, you always were. You and Stanley were—" He winced, blinking rapidly, then turned and hobbled back to his chair against the wall. And suddenly the room seemed too close, filled with too many people, memories. Cass forced himself to glance around, bleeding the color out of the picture, seeing everything in black-and-white now, mentally filming the scene, the people. Sonya was surrounded by friends, looking lost, dazed. A pity he didn't have a camera. It would have made a great shot.

He turned away, went back upstairs, through the kitchen to the garage. He switched on the lights and stepped out on the small landing, took a deep, ragged breath, glanced around.

In the cold glare of the overhead fluorescents, the garage seemed doubly empty. No car, no jack. The tools had been returned neatly to the racks above the workbench, the bloodstains washed away. As though nothing had happened here. Nothing.

"What are you doing out here?" Charlie Bennett said, stepping out onto the landing.

"I wanted to see something. What happened to the car?"

"The police took it. The car and the jack both. For testing, I guess."

"I can see why they might want to test the jack, but why take the car?"

"How the hell would I know? I thought you came here to see Sonya, but instead you're out here snoopin' around. What's the matter, you didn't get enough pictures today? Maybe you just better take a hike, mister newsman."

Cass glanced up at him. A big guy, Bennett, half a head taller, forty pounds heavier. Angry. And pushy. But standing with his back to the landing stairs, four steps down to a cement floor. Cass could see himself giving Bennett a stiff jab to the belly, dumping his big ass down the stairs, see how pushy he felt when he got up. If he got up. But the moment passed. Wrong time, wrong place. Or at least that's what Cass told himself, walking out to his car.

The Warsaw Heights police station was nearly new, brick fronted, white-tile floors, built a dozen years ago when G.M. bought the old station and half the downtown area to build a new auto plant, which closed eight years later. Cass inquired at the front desk and was directed to a corner office, glass walled, overlooking the brightly lit parking lot.

"Have a seat, Mr. Novak, what can I do for you?"

Lieutenant Gil Delacruz was balding, moon-faced. Brown suit, black bowtie. His desk was piled with paperwork and the remains of a Chinese takeout supper. He looked like a history teacher from a small college.

"You're the officer in charge of the Sliwa case?" Cass said, easing down on the metal folding-chair facing. "I thought you worked narcotics?"

"Do I know you?"

"I'm a cameraman for WVLT. I've filmed you at crime scenes a couple of times."

"I see," Delacruz nodded, munching the last of an eggroll. "I thought you looked familiar. Anyway, here in the Heights, the department's not divided quite as neatly as in Metro Detroit. The Sliwa death happened on my shift, so I caught it. But there's no case, it's already closed, accidental death. Unless you've got information to volunteer?"

"No, just a couple of questions. Like what happened?"

"The jack apparently let go, the decedent suffocated."

"Apparently?"

"We've impounded it, it'll be shipped to the police lab at Lansing and checked out in case there's a product-liability civil suit, but most likely Mr. Sliwa just mis-set the jack and it slipped."

"Stan was a licensed master mechanic. It's hard for me to believe he'd make a mistake with something as basic as a jack."

"There were a few empties near the body, and I expect the autopsy will show the decedent killed a couple beers, screwed up. Why the interest? I thought you people ran your story on the Six O'Clock News."

"It's personal. Stan was a friend."

"I see. Well, there's not much more I can tell you. The widow said the house was locked, no sign anyone else had been there. Sliwa died around two, while she was still at work. I checked."

"I saw her brother, Bobby Filipiak, tonight. He seemed to be moving out."

"From what I understand, Bobby Flip and his brother-in-law got along fine. You have any reason to think otherwise?"

"No, I just—"

"I didn't think so. Look, Mr. Novak, I cut you some slack because I figure you're upset over the death of a friend, but you're a little out of line here. Your friend had too many beers, made a mental error, end of story. We don't have the manpower or the high-tech goodies in the Heights that Detroit Metro has, but we're not incompetent."

"I didn't say you were."

"No, but you must think so. Otherwise why would you walk into my office with reefer smoke on your clothes and think I wouldn't notice? I'll tell you something, Novak—I don't like newspeople much. They get underfoot, interview witnesses before I get to them, and generally make my job tougher, and I especially don't like yuppie potheads because you contribute to the cash flow of scumbags who are screwin' up the world. Any other questions before you go?"

"Just one," Cass said, rising warily, "do you know what Stan was doing to the car?"

"No. What difference does it make?"

"Probably none. I just wondered. Can I see it?"

"The car? I guess you can try."

"What does that mean?"

"We don't have it. I just had it towed away as a courtesy to the widow. Rostenkowski's Scrapyard took it. I imagine it's the size of a suitcase by now. Anything else, Novak, or should I ask the desk sergeant to shake down your car for your stash?"

"No," Cass said, "don't bother. I'll see myself out."

And that was it. Cass went to Stan's funeral stoned to the bone, overdosed on vodka and memories at the wake afterward, lost his lunch out in the alley behind Dom Polski Hall. A few weeks later, he also lost Hawk. She got a promotion to Morning News anchor and moved back to her own place. They promised to remain friends, to stay in touch, then avoided each other like death. He got a new partner, an earnest kid fresh out of CMU named Metcalf. Cass nicknamed him Cowbell, but worked hard at showing him the ropes. It seemed to help. The pain of loss faded as the weeks passed, and after a month he only thought of Hawk once or twice an hour, and Stan hardly at all. Until Sonya called, said she'd sold the house, thought he might like some of Stan's tools.

He almost didn't go.

It was seven when he arrived. The garage door was closed, a Century 21 Sold sign stood in the overgrown front yard, but otherwise things looked much the same as that first terrible day. He rang the doorbell. Sonya answered, and for a moment neither of them spoke, eyeing each other through the screen door. Across half a lifetime.

"So," he managed at last, "how are you doin'?"

"Better than you were the last time I saw you. Come on in."

"You look terrific," he said, following her in, and she really did. She'd dropped a dozen pounds and seemingly a dozen years. In designer jeans, a T-shirt, and running shoes, her figure firm, her hair lightened and tousled, she looked more like the girl from Pulaski High than the shattered widow of a few months ago. "I called you a couple of times, never caught you."

"I've—been gone a lot," she said, opening the door to the garage and stepping out on the landing. "I didn't want to be here while they were showing the place, you know? As far as I know, everything's the way Stan left it. Take whatever you like."

"Are you sure? Some of these tools are expensive."

"It's all right, I have no use for them, and Charlie—" She coughed. "Anyway, Stan would want you to have them."

"Charlie?" Cass said, walking down the steps to the workbench, pointedly avoiding her eyes. "You and Charlie an item now?"

"I know it might seem like I'm rushing things a little," she said, sitting down on the steps, watching him, "but I'm not. I won't lie to you, Cass, I've been seeing Charlie for—a while."

"I see," he said, sliding open a drawer. Vise grips, a complete set, arranged by size, each one lightly oiled.

"I doubt that you do. You've been away a long time, Cass, people change. God knows I loved Stan, but he wasn't the easiest guy in the world to live with. He was—dull. Maybe not to you, you two could always talk about cars, or cameras, or some damned helicopter motor you read about in *Popular Mechanics*, but what do you think *we* talked about? Machinery was all he really cared about."

"You're wrong. He cared about you." He opened another drawer, Allen wrenches, standard, metric.

"I suppose he cared about me as much as he cared about anything that wasn't gear-driven," she conceded. "Maybe if we'd had kids it would've been different."

"Why didn't you?"

"I can't have children," she said simply, "ever. And Stan would have made a wonderful father. Maybe that's why he stayed so distant. Because I was broken and he couldn't order a part or tune me up to solve the problem."

"You know he didn't feel like that."

"No, the truth is I don't know how he really felt about anything. When things got tense between us, he'd just come out here and crawl under a car, or bury his nose in a manual. The funny thing was, I thought Bobby might help. What a joke."

"How so?"

"Have you seen Bobby lately?"

"I saw him here the, ah, the night of Stan's accident. He was carrying a couple of suitcases."

"Right," she said bitterly. "Know what was in them? Our silverware, a couple of Stan's handguns, anything he could pawn for a few bucks. A real prize, my little brother. Killed our mother being born and he's gone straight downhill ever since, in and out of jail, you name it, he's done it. He's just a damned junkie now, steals to support his habit. The last time he got out of detox my father wouldn't have him in the house, couldn't handle him any more, so Stan and I took him in."

"But it didn't work out?" Another drawer, chromed-steel socket sets, ratchet arms, extensions, silent, gleaming.

"It almost did." She leaned on the rail, resting her chin on her palm. "They spent a lot of time together. Stan taught Bobby about tools, thought if he put a wrench in his hand it might straighten him out. They completely rebuilt Bobby's car, and for a while it seemed to be working. Stan was sure it was—I mean, how could anybody who understands the guts of an engine do dope?"

"What happened?" Cass opened a storage cabinet stacked with large boxes and peered in to read the labels. Street Dominator intake manifolds for big block Chevys, six sets of them. Six Holley dual-feed carburetors to match.

"Bobby drove it around till the kick of having the fastest wheels on the street wore off, then he traded it for dope money, got so trashed he almost died, wound up in the hospital, and then in jail.

"And when he got out, Stan let him come back. Just didn't

103

believe there was anything he couldn't fix. What's wrong?"

Cass didn't answer for a moment, trying to make sense of what he was seeing, then realized Sonya was eyeing him, shaking her head. "Sorry," he said. "Where were we?"

"I was talking about Bobby—I don't know where you were. Stan used to do that to me all the time, drift away. I'd be talking to him and realize he wasn't hearing a word, he was off inside a transmission or something. I forgot how much alike you two were."

"Yeah, well maybe he wasn't perfect, who is? But not many guys would've bothered trying to straighten Bobby out. I wouldn't have. I doubt Charlie would, either. Are you, ah, sure you're doing the right thing, being involved with him so soon?"

"Hell no, I'm not sure," she snapped, "how could I be? I've never been in this situation. I think I would have left Stan eventually, but—" she swallowed hard, blinking back tears "—but not before we'd fought it out, gotten things straight between us. Not like this," she said, rising suddenly, her eyes streaming, "not like this." She turned and walked back into the house, slammed the door.

Cass thought about following her, but couldn't think of a damn thing to say. Maybe she was right, he and Stan were too much alike, better with machinery than people. He began opening the boxes in the closet. Four of the Holley dual-feed-carburetor boxes contained used carbs off older cars. What the hell?

"What's goin' on out here?" Charlie Bennett said. "Soni came in bawling her eyes out. What did you say to her?"

"It was a private conversation," Cass said, opening one of the Street Dominator boxes. "If you want to know, you'll have to ask her."

"I asked you, Novak, or Polack, whatever your name is,

but I don't much care. I didn't like you from day one. I want you outa here."

"Sonya invited me here and I'm not quite finished," Cass said, replacing the last Dominator box, "so why don't you cool down a little and back off."

"That's the trouble with you TV guys," Bennett said, stalking angrily down the steps, slamming the cabinet door in Cass's face, "you're outa touch with reality. Like a guy your size tellin' a guy my size to back off. I told you to get steppin', mister. I mean right now."

"You know, Stan Sliwa was a friend of mine once," Cass said, rising, glancing idly around the garage. "Sonya thinks we're a lot alike." He took a twenty-inch crescent wrench out of its drawer, hefted it, checking the balance. "For instance, Stan thought you can fix damn near anything, you use the right tool. How about it, Charlie? You see anything out here needs fixing?"

Bennett hesitated, glancing at the wrench, then at Cass, then the wrench again. "Maybe not now," he said evenly. "No need to disturb the lady."

"Good point," Cass nodded. "Now why don't you just go back in the house? I'd like to be alone."

"I'll let it pass this time, Novak," Bennett said from the safety of the landing, "but when you leave, you'd better not come back."

"Not to worry," Cass said, taking a last look around the empty, immaculate garage, "nobody lives here any more."

The Jury's Inn was busy and dim, the usual mix of cops, bailiffs, and bondsmen from the Heights Hall of Justice down the street. The air was thick with smoke and the din of a dozen simultaneous conversations, dishes clattering, a jukebox thumping Motown goodies against one wall. Cass found Lieutenant Gil Delacruz sitting alone at a corner table cluttered with empty beer mugs, an overflowing ashtray.

"They told me at the desk you might be over here. Got a minute?" Cass asked. "It's important."

Delacruz frowned up at him blearily, trying to place the face. "Hey, I know you," he said at last. "Novak the pothead cameraman, right? Hate to be rude, but since I'm off duty, whyn't you just go away, okay?"

"Thanks, I appreciate it," Cass said, pulling up a chair facing Delacruz. "You remember the Stan Sliwa case."

"I vaguely remember a Sliwa accident," Delacruz slurred. "The case of the Polish pancake, no?" He grinned, then sobered a little as his eyes met Cass's. "Sorry, forgot he was a friend of yours. Okay, what about it?"

"I was in Stan's garage earlier tonight, and I came across something odd. I found sixty-grand worth of bolt-on racing gear for Chevy engines there—enough equipment to trick out a half dozen cars like the one that killed him."

"So I guess your buddy was heavy into hotrods, so what?"

"Damn it, Delacruz, I said sixty thousand dollars' worth of equipment. Stan was a blue-collar guy, he didn't have that kind of money. And nobody builds six cars at once."

"Did I miss somethin' here? I thought you just said that's what he was doin'. What's your point?"

"It's one that I don't like much," Cass said, taking a deep breath. "You said you know Bobby Filipiak, Stan's brother-in-law. A while back Stan tried to straighten Bobby out, built a car for him. Bobby dumped it for dope money, wound up back in jail."

"Sounds like Bobby. So?"

"So I think maybe that car impressed some of the people Bobby did business with. And they did a deal with Bobby or Stan to build a half dozen more just like it. But not just hot rods, sleepers."

106

"You're saying your buddy Sliwa was buildin' fast cars for the drug trade, that it? Nice guy, your friend."

"He was, but—damn it, he was having trouble in his marriage, maybe he needed money, I just don't know. But from the spare parts I found, I'd guess Stan had already built at least three cars, was working on the fourth. If you can find the cars—"

"Catch 22," Delacruz grinned, finishing off a beer.

"What?"

"Catch 22. Even if your buddy was buildin' sleepers, we can't prove it because we can't find 'em. 'Cause they're sleepers. Catch 22. Get it?"

"Jesus," Cass sighed, slumping back in his chair, "what I get is you're about half in the bag. Maybe I'd better try you another time."

"Nah, let's settle this now. Look, you're buggin' me because you want me to do something, right? Okay, like what? Let's say I could find the cars your buddy built. Then what? It's not illegal to own a fast car, even if you're a dope dealer. Way I see it, if he was building hot cars for the dope trade and one of 'em fell on him, I got no problem with it. Poetic justice, no?"

"The problem is that I don't think the car did just fall on him."

"No? Why not?"

"It's hard to explain, but being in Stan's workshop tonight, seeing the way he kept his tools, those old carbs cleaned up and reboxed even though they were almost worthless. I could set a jack wrong, or you could. But not Stan. He just couldn't make a dumbass mistake like that. I think maybe somebody dropped that car on him."

"No kidding? And who do you figure did the taxpayers this favor?"

"Maybe the dopers he was working for. Maybe Bobby. Hell, maybe his wife's new boyfriend, I don't know. But neither do you, and you should. It's your job to know, or to find out."

"My job?" Delacruz said, flushing dangerously. "You come in here gettin' in my face after I put in a sixteen-hour day, and now you wanna gimme a lecture on how to do my damn job?"

"Look, all I'm saying is I think—"

"I don't give a damn what you think!" Delacruz roared, staggering to his feet, weaving. "I listened to your sad story, now you listen to mine! I'll try to explain it so even a punkass yuppie pothead can understand." He cleared the table with his forearm, trashing the beer mugs and the ashtray on the hardwood floor, then jerked a handgun out of a shoulder holster and leaned unsteadily on the table, holding the muzzle an inch from the tip of Novak's nose.

"Jesus Christ, Delacruz," somebody said, but otherwise the room fell absolutely silent. Only the jukebox kept pumping. The Temptations. "My Girl."

"You know what this is, Novak?" Delacruz said, blinking, trying to focus. "It's a piece of machinery, a nine-millimeter Taurus Model 92 automatic. It's brand new, but it's not all that complicated. For instance—" he cocked the hammer with an audible snick "—you just pull the trigger, it'll fire sixteen rounds *boom boom boom* fast as you can squeeze 'em off. Twin safeties, safe as houses, you know? But last year a State Police firing-range officer, a twenty-year man who handles guns for his damn living, shot himself in the foot out in Highland Park. We don't know how it happened. Hell, *he* don't know what happened, it just happened. That's why they call 'em accidents. Like what happened to your buddy. Like what could happen to you if you don't get outa my face. Get the picture?"

"I think so," Cass managed.

"Good," Delacruz nodded. "One other thing about this piece of machinery. It locks open automatically—" he jerked the slide back with his left hand, locking it "—when it's empty. See?" His face split in a grin and he dropped back into his chair as the room erupted into a roar of laughter. Cass glanced around, shaken. The other cops were grinning—they'd known all along. Delacruz laid the pistol on the table as an anorexic waitress brought him a fresh beer, bitching him out about the mess on the floor.

"Do you mind?" Cass said, picking up the gun, not waiting for an answer. He touched the magazine release, popping out the clip, then thumbed the slide latch and removed the slide and barrel assembly. "You know about guns, right?" he said. "You must, considering the business you're in." He depressed the spring guide, stripped out the recoil spring. "Did you know the action of your brand-new pistol was designed over a hundred years ago? Guy from Utah named Browning invented it. I don't know the exact date, but Stan would have. Probably could've told you the patent number." He separated the barrel assembly from the slide.

"Hey," Delacruz said, "what the hell are you doing?"

"Same thing you just did," Cass said, "making a point." The gun was now in a half dozen pieces neatly arranged on the table. "Okay, let's say you're in a tight spot in a dark alley. You fall down, get mud in your piece. Can you field-strip it, clean it, and reassemble it in the dark? Stan could. Machinery talked to him. It was all he was good at, all he really cared about. He was too good to screw up with a damn jack. And he didn't. Which you'd know if you'd made any kind of a competent investigation."

"You've made your point, Novak," Delacruz said. "Now take a walk, okay? *After you* put that piece back together."

109

"Nah," Cass said, rising, "a punk like me might blow it. If I were you, I'd get somebody like Stan to fix it for you, so it'll be done right."

"Yeah? You know that alley you mentioned, smartass? I wouldn't take time to clean my gun. No competent cop would. I'd just use my backup." He reached down and pulled a fist-sized automatic out of an ankle holster, displaying it on his palm. "You don't have to be a goddamn gunsmith to be a good cop."

"What would you know about being a good cop?" Cass said, turning away.

"Hey, Novak?" Delacruz called, pointing a wobbly index finger at him. "Boom, boom, boom! Gotcha."

"I've never had to cover the death of a friend," Stephanie Hawkins said carefully, avoiding Cass's eyes. "I'm not sure I could." She was behind her desk in her new office in the newsroom the next morning. Nicer than her old one—award plaques on the wall, autographed celebrity 8 x 10s. She was wearing her navy-blue WVLT anchor blazer and looked even better than Cass remembered. It was the first time they'd been alone together since the split.

"I take it that's your tactful way of saying you think I'm off base?" Cass said.

"I don't know. Look, we're both pros, Novak, let's do this thing by the numbers. One, you think Sliwa was building fast cars—what did you call them?"

"Sleepers."

"Right, sleepers, for the drug trade. And, two, you think he may have been murdered. By who? The dopers?"

"I don't know. Possibly."

"But you said he had enough equipment to build six cars." She checked the notes she'd made as he'd explained. "He'd

110

apparently delivered three and was working on the fourth, correct? So why would they kill him?"

"Maybe to avoid paying him."

"But they'd probably already given him a down payment to buy the equipment, right? So even if they intended to kill him, wouldn't they wait until he'd delivered all six cars to get their money's worth?"

"Maybe it wasn't over money."

"But would your friend have been under the car if someone he distrusted was there, near the jack?"

"No," Cass conceded, "I suppose not."

"All right then, I think we can eliminate the wife, because she apparently cared for the guy even if she was going to leave him. And the boyfriend had no motive. Why buy a cow if the milk is free?"

"Very delicately put," Cass sighed.

"Sorry," Hawk said, "but I call 'em like I see 'em. Okay, who's left? The junkie brother-in-law? Again, what motive? Your friend treated him very well."

"Who can say what's in a doper's head?"

"You might be able to make a better guess than most," Hawk said sweetly, "but let's move on. Okay, I'll grant you it bothers me that Bobby Flip dropped out of sight, and it seems awfully convenient that the car disappeared the way it did. But those are just feelings, Cass, and here's a fact. The Warsaw Heights chief of police called the station manager this morning, complaining that you were harassing his officers."

"Maybe he's worried about something."

"Or maybe he's just annoyed. Look, Cass, we've both worked a lot of stations in a lot of towns. Do you really think the Warsaw Heights force is corrupt? That they'd cover up a murder?"

"No," he said slowly, "I guess not."

"Good, neither do I. And, anyway, why would they bother? Their crime rate isn't as high as Detroit's yet, but the way the crack trade's developing out there an unsolved homicide is no big deal. So let's cut to the chase. You asked me what I think—here it is. One, I don't know if your friend was murdered or not, but I'm inclined to agree with the police that it was an accident. Two, even if it wasn't, I don't see what we can do about it. We're not detectives, we're in TV news and there's nothing to shoot here. What would the pictures be of? An empty garage? A jack? Some boxes of used car parts? Bottom line is, no pictures, no story. I'll tell you what: if the brother-in-law turns up, we can try talking to him on our own time, but that's the best I can do. And that's the news as it looks from here. Sorry."

"Don't be sorry," Cass sighed. "I asked for your opinion, and the truth is, that's about how I figured it myself. I just needed to hear it from somebody I respect. Helluva thing, isn't it? A guy's life, start to finish, is only worth two minutes of airtime?"

"Or less," Hawk said. "We aren't here to change the world, Novak, just report it. And speaking of reporting, how are you and your new partner getting on?"

"His lips aren't as sweet as yours, darlin', but at least he doesn't snore."

"Good God. What did I ever see in you?"

"A Polish Prince Charming. Wit, charisma."

"That must've been it," she said. "It certainly wasn't your kielbasa, my prince."

"Damn," he winced, rising, "you know, I'd forgotten what a surly bitch you are in the morning. Rest of the day, too, for that matter. I, ah, I miss you."

"I miss you, too," she said. "A lot."

"But not enough?"

She shrugged, a five-page letter in the slightest movement of a shoulder. "Are you going to let this Sliwa thing go?" she asked.

"Yeah," he said, "I think so."

And he did.

For the next few weeks, Cass disappeared back into his life, hiding in the whirlwind, an endless reel of crime scenes, fires, strikes, shooting Metcalf talking to stunned victims, witnesses, exhausted firemen, angry strikers. No two days alike, yet as similar as frames on a roll. Same movie, different faces. Motown news.

Then they hit an ugly accident scene just off the Chrysler Freeway.

State Police had high-speed-chased a drug suspect from downtown, Woodward all the way out into the Heights. Edgy scene—three prowl cars, one with its grill caved in, had the road blocked, gumball lights flashing, police-line tapes strung around. The car they'd chased had skidded broadside into the back of a moving van, smashing up both vehicles, the two of them welded together like modernist sculpture. A half dozen Early American sofas from the van strewn around the road added to the surreality.

Two state troopers were leading the ashen van driver away from his truck, dazed, shaken. The runner in the car had been thrown out by the impact, was dead or dying on a stretcher, one EMS attendant giving him mouth-to-mouth, another coolly rigging an IV bottle to the stretcher. Cass filmed them from behind the police tapes, zooming in slowly, gradually tightening the shot, focusing in on the three faces, the desperate urgency of the attendant giving mouth-to-mouth, his buddy's empty expression, knowing it was useless, his eyes as lifeless as the victim's. Good footage, even better when the victim convulsed, breathed on his own for a moment, the two attendants feverishly jacking up the stretcher, rushing it to the EMS van.

Cass filmed them until the doors slammed and the van gunned away, rubber howling, lights and sirens. Somebody jostled him, running, shouting. The truck was on fire, diesel fuel trickling down from the rear tanks, pooling out, flames spreading, panicky gawkers stampeding away from the coming explosion. Novak was getting footage, two state troopers trying to control the blaze with handheld extinguishers, losing the fight, the rear of the van alight now, paint peeling, flames engulfing the car.

The car. A nondescript Chevy junker, rusty, battered. But wearing new rubber. Racing tires. Cass vaulted the police line and sprinted to the car. The hood was sprung half open from the impact. He got his shoulder under it and thrust it farther up, buckling it, metal shrieking. He focused the minicam into the yawning darkness under the hood. Too dim, damn it! He tightened the shot, getting more light from the flicker of the flames. A tricked-out engine, Cyclone headers, Street Dominator manifolds, Holley—

"Get outa here, goddamnit!" one of the troopers screamed at him. "It's goin' up!" Cass ignored him, filming, shifting his position to be sure he got the shot.

"You crazy sonovabitch!" One of the cops hit him shoulder high, knocking him back. Another grabbed his arms, dragging him away from the car. The Chevy's trunk was engulfed, the fire billowing to a thundering inferno, flames towering into the sky. Cass clutched the camera close, struggling to pull away, stumbling to one knee, then getting flattened, hammered down by the fireblast of heated air as the car's tank blew with the deep metallic whoomp of a naval gun.

Cass staggered to his feet. The cop who'd been dragging him was down, stunned, hat blown off, his face a bloody mask from a gash in his scalp. His buddy was leaning over him, trying to get him up, away from the fire. Cass turned, reeled toward the WVLT mini-van. Caught a glimpse of Delacruz coming on the run, two uniforms with him. Tried to run, but his legs went rubbery and he fell, hitting the gravel hard but protecting the steadycam.

"Get him up!" Delacruz snapped. "Somebody read him his damn rights, he's under arrest!" The two cops hauled him like a sack of potatoes to a Heights patrol car. One of them tried to pull the camera away from him but he folded over it, hanging on with all he had left.

"Leave it," Delacruz said, "just get him in the car!"

They pushed him into the back seat still clutching the camera, slammed the door. He sat up slowly—dazed, deafened, head ringing in the sudden silence. Metcalf was arguing with a stonefaced trooper a few yards away, getting noplace. Delacruz climbed into the front seat, closed the door, and swiveled to face him.

"You stupid bastard," he said coldly, "you coulda gotten killed, or gotten my people killed. Well, welcome to shit city, Novak, you're in it up to your eyeballs, crossing a police line, reckless endangerment, interfering with officers in the performance, and a whole lot more. You're gonna do some slam time, my friend, maybe a year. How's that grab ya?"

"It was one of Stan's cars," Cass said numbly.

"Think so?" Delacruz said, glancing back at the wreck. "Kinda hard to tell now, almost nothing left of it."

"I got it on film."

"Hope that's a comfort to you in the joint. Give me the camera."

"No."

"You want me to have it taken from you? I can, you know."

"It won't matter," Cass said, blinking, "it won't work.

You bust me and I'll be news, Delacruz, heavy press coverage. And I'll talk to anybody who'll listen. You can't cover this up."

"No," Delacruz said, eyeing him, reading the set of his mouth, "maybe I can't. So I guess you'll have to cover it up."

"What are you talking about?"

"You were half right," Delacruz said simply. "Your buddy Sliwa was workin' for dopers, a Jamaican named Johnno, moved his operation into the Heights about six months ago. Bobby Flip traded the car Stan built for him to one of Johnno's people, he liked it, did a deal with Stan for six more—seventy grand in front, fifty more on delivery."

"My God," Cass said.

"Lotta money," Delacruz nodded. "More'n he'd made at the plant in five years. Which is why I was kinda surprised when Sliwa contacted me, told me about the deal, and offered to build a special longwave beeper into each car so we could track 'em."

"And you went along with it?"

"You're damn right, it was like a gift from God."

"Except that Stan was no good with people, only machinery. And the Jamaican smelled something wrong and stomped him like a cockroach. Damn it, you should have guessed it would happen, you bastard!"

"No, you're wrong. The Jamaican didn't tumble to anything or he wouldn't still be using the cars. And he is. In the last six weeks or so we've tracked down his whole network, plus his contacts in Detroit. Believe me, Johnno doesn't know. Nobody knew but Stan and me. And now you."

"Not Bobby?"

"Get real, Novak, I wouldn't piss on Bobby Flip if he was on fire. I didn't tell him anything, and I doubt like hell that Stan did, either."

"But you don't believe Stan's death was an accident, do you?"

"I honestly don't know yet. Hell, I didn't like the coincidence any better'n you, but everybody checked out. Johnno had no reason to do it, and the wife and her boyfriend both have solid alibis."

"But you didn't talk to Bobby, did you?"

"No," Delacruz admitted, "I couldn't. He dropped out of sight right after and I was afraid if we beat the bushes for him we'd spook the Jamaican. Besides, he had no reason to do it. Stan loved the kid, God knows why. Hell, Bobby's the reason he came to me in the first place. After seein' what crack had done to him, he wanted to do something."

"And you let him. And now he's dead. And Bobby's still walking around free as the air."

"For now. But as soon as we bust the Jamaican's ring, I'll find Bobby and lean on him, I give you my word. So how about it, you gonna give me the film?"

"No," Cass said, "no chance."

"But damn it—"

"If Metcalf sees me turn over the film he'll know something's up. I'll keep the film, but I promise not to use it until after you bust the Jamaican. Word of honor."

"All right—" Delacruz nodded slowly "—I guess the word of a guy who's willing to risk burnin' to death for a goddamn picture has to be worth somethin'. But you cross me, Novak, I swear to God I'll stick you in a hole so deep you'll have to phone out for sunshine."

"I believe you. Can I go now?"

"Yeah, get out of here," Delacruz said, hitting the release on the dash, opening the rear door. "Just remember, not a word about this until after you hear from me. And stay the hell out of my way."

117

"Funny," Cass said, climbing stiffly out, "I don't remember promising that."

A sunny fall afternoon. Cass was wearing a sleeveless MSU sweatshirt, jeans, tennies, and he was sixteen again. Or could have been. Things hadn't changed much in the Heights. The cars were different, there was a For Lease sign in Woolworth's empty window now, Zerwinski's hardware had gone Ace, but otherwise the street looked much the same as a dozen years ago. When Cass had worked for *Populsku Warsaw Heights*, and most afternoons Ignace Filipiak would be in the window booth of Klima's Coffee Shop.

"Kazu, *jak sie mas*," the old man said, his face lighting up like a winter sunrise, "sit, sit. Zosia, bring *kawa* for my young friend. You want some *babka* rolls, Kazu? Fresh made this morning?"

"No, thank you, coffee will be fine. How are you, Mr. Filipiak?"

"How am I? I sit in the sun in a room breathing the scent of *chelba* bread baking, a well fed woman to bring coffee, a friend stops by to talk. Heaven will be many fine days like this."

"I doubt I'll ever find out," Cass said.

"Nor I," the old man smiled. "So, what business brings you home, Kazu?"

"Business?" Cass said, accepting a mug of steaming coffee from a large, bell-shaped woman.

"Kazu, my legs are bent, not my head. I'm here almost every day since you left, so I know you didn't come just to see me. It's okay, we'll talk, have coffee, but first the business, so I don't sour the cream wondering."

"You haven't changed a damn bit, Ignace, you know that?"

"You have. You're more polite now, and your eyesight's failing. So, how can I help you?"

"I, ah, I need to get in touch with Bobby. Do you know where he is?"

"I can probably guess," the old man nodded, "but I'm not sure I should tell you. He is hiding, Kazu, seeing ghosts. He has one of Stanley's guns. He's very dangerous now."

"It's important."

"To you, maybe, Kazu, but nothing is important to Bobby but the cocaine. There's nothing left of him. He's lost, a victim of the *holjeda,* the plague. He still walks, but he's dead. If you talk to him, only the drug will answer."

"I still need to see him."

The old man looked away, idly stirring his coffee. "Tell me, Kazu, why you want to see Bobby. Does this have to do with your work on the TV?"

"Yes, sir, in a way."

Filipiak glanced at him curiously, then shrugged. "You've changed more than I thought. You never used to lie to me, Kazu Novak. You shouldn't try. You have no talent for it. It only makes me wonder what you're trying to hide. And I think it must be that you've learned about Bobby and Stanley and those damned cars. Is that it?"

"You know about it?"

"I still have the newspaper, Kazu. People talk to me. And I'm not blind, just old. Do you think my son and my son-in-law could hide such a thing from me? Let it be, please. Sonya is all that matters now. If it comes out what her husband was doing—" The old man seized Novak's wrist with a palsied hand. His grip had no more strength than a child's, but his eyes were alight, like staring into a flame. "Let it go, Kazu. Stanley is dead. Bobby and I will join him in hell soon and it will be over—for us and for Sonya, too."

"What do you mean you'll join Stanley in hell? Why? Why should you?"

"It isn't the gun that makes Bobby dangerous, Kazu, it's the *holjeda.* The evil is contagious. Bobby's heart is long dead. But Stanley. To know what happened to my son, then to work for the *psiakref* dogs who poisoned him for *money!* He was even worse than the animals who sell the drugs. He sold his soul. But he paid for it. I hope the bastard is still paying."

"My God, Mr. Filipiak—Stanley?"

"Not the Stanley you knew, Kazu. He was contaminated by the *holjeda. I* did what I had to do. God forgive me, I would do it again."

Cass couldn't speak, could barely breathe, a fist clamped around his heart so tightly he thought he would die. He slid out of the booth and stood staring down at the old man. He seemed so much smaller than he remembered, and he realized he was shrinking, receding, fading to black-and-white. To a still life, an old man dreaming in the afternoon sun. He tried to think of something to say. Nothing came. Mr. Filipiak was a man people talk to. He would learn soon enough.

Outside, the street had changed, too. It wasn't a dozen years ago. The haze had burned away. A few blocks down, a kid was lounging on a corner, scouting traffic, open for business. Bobby? Too far away to tell. Then his eyes misted and he couldn't see the boy any more. He walked to his van, groped blindly under the dash, and pulled out a small cellophane baggie. Five joints. A hundred and fifty bucks' worth. He tore them to pieces and threw them in the gutter. It didn't help. It didn't help a damn bit.

It's true. You can't ever go home again. But sweet Jesus, you can never truly leave it behind, either.

The old man blinked up at him as he slid back into the booth.

"I didn't finish my coffee," Cass said, "and we never did talk about the old times."

"No," the old man said, "we didn't."

The Hessian

Murder Most Confederate

Horsemen drifted out of the dawn mist like wolves, strung out loosely across the hillside in a ragged line. Two outriders on the flanks, seven more in the main body. Polly guessed they'd already put riflemen in position at the stone fence beyond her barn, ready to cut down anyone who tried to run.

Her son was sitting on the corner of the porch, whetting the scythe, daydreaming. "Jason," Polly said quietly. "Riders are coming. Get to the barn. And walk! All the way."

Without a word the ten-year-old rose and sauntered across the yard as he'd been taught, toting a hay blade longer than he was tall. He disappeared inside. A moment later the upper loading loft door opened a crack.

Picking up a besom broom, Polly casually swept her way across the porch to the front door of the farmhouse. She opened it to sweep off the sill, leaving it ajar as she turned to face the riders coming across the stubbled fields to the house.

Federals. Of a sort. Only one rider was in full uniform, a Union cavalry captain, tall, hollow-eyed and gaunt as a vulture, with a thin mustache and goatee. His men were irregulars, dressed in a mix of work clothes and uniform coats or pants. Farmers and tradesmen from the look of them. Definitely Union, though. Their mounts were sleek and well fed. She'd heard Forrest's men were slaughtering their horses for food.

The riders sized her up as they filed into the yard. A farm wife, square as a stump in a man's flannel shirt, canvas trousers and pebble-leg boots, handsome once, but careworn now, auburn hair awry in the November wind, her hands reddened and rough from field work.

Polly scanned their faces, desperately hoping to recognize someone—damn. Aaron Meachum was with them, slouch hat down over his eyes, stubbled cheek distorted by a plug of chaw. Trouble. Casually, she sidled half a step closer to the door.

"Good day to you, ma'am," their leader said softly. "I am Captain Charles Gilliaume, of the Eighth Missouri. My men and I—"

"These men aren't Eighth Missouri," Polly said coldly. "They're militia. Hessians, most likely."

"Hessians?"

"It's what these Rebs call the kraut-heads," Meachum said. "Like them German mercenaries back in the revolution? Most of Sigel's troops was Germans from St. Louis when they raided through here in '62."

"I see," the captain nodded. "You're quite right, ma'am. My men are a militia unit from Jefferson City, and many of them are of German extraction. But they're as American as you or I now. May we step down?"

"Captain, there is a creek on the far side of my garden. You're welcome to water your animals. I have nothing more to offer you. We've been picked clean by both sides. Hospitality in southern Missouri is runnin' a little thin these days, hard to come by as seed corn."

"She'd find grain quick enough if we were wearin' butternut brown," Aaron Meachum said, spitting a stream of tobacco juice onto her porch. "The whole damn McKee family's secesh; everybody 'round here knows it."

"Is that true, ma'am?" the captain asked. "I see no men about. Are they with the rebels?"

"My husband is in Springfield trying to earn a few dollars. His eldest son is with Bedford Forrest up Tennessee way, his second boy's with the Union blockade at Charleston. The two youngest went off with Sterling Price after he whipped y'all at Wilson's Creek in '61."

"Rebels," Meachum spat.

"Three Confederates," Polly corrected, "and one Federal. At least they're real soldiers, Captain."

"As we are, ma'am."

"Real soldiers don't ride with trash. This fella, Aaron Meachum, is a jayhawker who was murdering and burning in Kansas long before the war. He runs easier with coyotes than with men."

"Mr. Meachum isn't actually a member of our unit, ma'am, he was retained as a guide."

"Well, he doubtless knows the trails through these hills. He's used most of them running from the law. If he's your guide, Captain, you're on the road to perdition."

"Armies are like families, ma'am, you can't choose your kin. We're seeking slaves and deserters, Miz McKee. I'm told you have slaves here."

"Who told you that? Meachum? Captain, this ain't no plantation. We raise saddle horses and draft animals and we're only three days from the Illinois line. Even if we held with slavery, and we don't, it's tough enough to keep animals from runnin' off to say nothin' of men. Our stock's been stolen, our crops burned. We had no slaves before the war and we've surely no need of them now. There's only me and my boy here, you have my word."

"In that case a search won't take long," Gilliaume said. At his nod, the troopers and Meachum began to dismount.

"No!" Polly's voice cracked like a whip, freezing them as she snaked the scattergun from inside the open door, leveling it at Gilliaume, earing back both hammers.

"Ma'am, be reasonable, you can't possibly prevail against us."

"It won't matter to you, Captain. Or to Meachum. Or to one or two near you. My boy is covering you from the barn with a ten gauge goose gun loaded with double ought buckshot. If I fire, so will he."

"You'll still die. As will your son."

"No matter. We've only a little flour and some corn meal. My boy's legs are bowing 'cause Rebs butchered our milk cow. Soldier boys have taken all but the gleanings of the fields. For God's sake, sir, your animals are better fed than most folks around here. We have nothing for you. Unless Old Sam Curtis is passing out medals for murdering women and boys."

Gilliaume stared coolly down at Polly, ignoring the shotgun muzzle, taking her measure. She knew that look. Death had pushed past him to kill his friends so often that he was weary of waiting, impatient for his turn.

But not today. "Gentlemen, the lady says she has no slaves and I believe her. And since there's obviously no forage for us here, we'll move on."

"You're lettin' her run us off?" Meachum said, outraged. "Our orders say deserters, slaves and arms. She's armed, ain't she?"

"So she is," Gilliaume said wryly. "Personally, I interpret our orders to mean military arms, not rusty shotguns, but you have my permission to disarm her if you wish, Mr. Meachum. But kindly give me a moment to back my mount away. This is my best coat and bloodstains are damned bothersome to remove."

Clucking to his gelding, Gilliaume backed off a few paces, touched his hat brim to Polly, then turned away. The other riders followed. Leaving her to face Meachum alone. She shifted the shotgun, centering it on his chest.

"You got the edge today, Polly McKee." Meachum spat. "But this ain't over. I'll be back."

"But not by daylight I'll wager, you jayhawk son of a bitch. If you ever set foot on my land again, Aaron Meachum, I'll blow you out of your raggedy-ass boots. Now git! Git!" she roared into the face of his mount, spooking the beast. It shied away, kicking. Meachum sawed at the reins but the brute's manners were no better than its owner's. Bucking and snorting, it sprinted off to rejoin the others with Meachum clinging to the saddle horn, cursing his animal and Polly all the way.

The laughter and catcalls that greeted him echoed off the hills. It wasn't much comfort, but it was something.

She waited on the porch, her old scattergun in the crook of her arm, watching the troop splash through the creek and vanish into the woods beyond. And then she waited a bit longer, until she was dead certain they were gone.

Stepping into the house, she carefully stood the shotgun in its customary place by the door. And then, in the sweet scented silence of her parlor, she released a long, ragged breath. And hugged herself, fiercely, trying to control the trembling.

It was a day for visitors. A little before noon, working in the barn, Polly heard the tlot, tlot of approaching hoofbeats. Meachum? Not likely, not openly. She peeked out through the crack of the door.

A single seat Stanhope buggy was coming up the road from the west, a lone woman at the reins. Turning the rig in at the gate, she guided her animal down the long lane, slowing it to a walk as she approached the farmhouse.

Polly stepped out, shading her eyes, waiting. Her visitor

was dressed warmly for travel, a fine, seal plush cape over a tailored woolen suit, the first new clothes Polly'd seen since . . . she couldn't remember how long.

"Afternoon, ma'am. Can I help you?"

"Pleasse, I'm becomp lost," the woman replied, her accent harsh. Hessian. Polly's eyes narrowed. "I left Corridon this mornink—"

"Just wheel that buggy around and head out the gate, miss. A mile further on, the road splits. The north fork will take you to Centerville."

"I'm not going to Centerville."

"Look, ma'am, I haven't got all day—"

"Pleasse, I'm seeking the McKee place," the Hessian woman said desperately. "Is it far from here?"

Polly stepped closer to the buggy, frowning up at the woman. Younger than she thought, face as pale as buttermilk, nearly invisible eyelashes. A bruise and some swelling along her jaw. Still, all in all, a handsome girl, Hessian or not.

"What do you want with the McKees? Who are you?"

"My name is Birgit Randolph. My hussband is Tyler Randolph. He iss a cousin to Angus McKee. He—"

"I'm Polly McKee, Gus's wife. I've known Tyler since he was a sprout, but I still don't know who the hell you are. Tyler ain't married."

"We married earlier this year. We met when he was with the state militia in St. Louis and became friends. He was very . . . dashing. After the riots he joined General Price. We wrote back and fort' when he was in Arkansas. This past April he came for me and we were married."

"What do you mean he came for you? Came where?"

"To St. Louis. Tyler iss not a soldier anymore. He was wounded at Pea Ridge. He is discharged now."

"Wounded how? How bad?"

"His leg. Shot. It is mostly healed, but he limps. It causes him pain, I think. He never says. He's very . . . stubborn.'"

"That sounds like Tyler. Where have y'all been stayin'?'"

"At his farm near Mountain Grove.'"

"I'll be damned," Polly said, shaking her head. It was too much, first Meachum and his jayhawks, now a half-daft Hessian woman claiming to be kin. The damned war was making the world a madhouse.

"Well, you might as well step in out of the wind, miss—I mean—Mrs. Randolph. I'm afraid we're out of coffee—"

"I haff tea and some sugar," Birgit said, offering Polly a three pound sack. "Tyler said the plundering hass been bad here.'"

"We get hit by both sides," Polly conceded grimly, leading the way. "Come into the kitchen, I'll make us some tea.'"

Birgit hesitated just inside the door. Though the walls hadn't seen paint in years, the small farmhouse was immaculate.

"You have a nice home. Very clean. Even it smells nice.'"

"What did you expect? A pig pen?'"

"No, I—please. I know I don't always say things right but I don't mean to make you angry. I think I've come at a bad time.'"

"There aren't any good times nowadays. And exactly why have you come, ma'am? What do you want here?'"

"Tyler—told me to come to you. He hoped you can drive me to St. Louis then bring the buggy back here. He will send for it later.'"

"Send for the buggy? But not for you? Why? Farm life too rough for your taste?'"

"No, I grew up on farm in Bavaria. I'm not afraid of work.'"

"What then? Ah, the lame dirt farmer isn't a dashing rebel

lieutenant anymore? So you go runnin' home to mama. Sweet Jesus, serves Tyler right for marryin' a Hessian in the first place."

"I'm not Hessian."

"Don't lie to me, I know damned well what you are!"

"I'm not!" Birgit glared, flushing, not backing off an inch. "My family is German, but we are come from Freystadt in Bavaria! Hessians come from Hesse! I'm not Hessian! And I didn't leaf Tyler. He drove me out!"

"What are you talking about?"

"It's true! I tell him our child is growing in me and he got terrible angry. He says I must go back to my family. And I say no, and he says I must obey him. Still I say no. And he . . . struck me!" Her hand strayed to her bruised mouth, her eyes brimming. "And now I am come here, and you are angry with me too—I don't know why—but I don't anymore know what to do. I don't know what to do!"

Polly knew. Wordlessly, she wrapped the younger woman in her massive arms, holding her while she sobbed like a lost child. Which she was, in a way. Good lord, the girl couldn't be more than seventeen or eighteen. Polly was barely forty, but Birgit's age seemed like a fever dream, dimly remembered now. The low moan of the blue enameled teapot broke the spell.

"I'm sorry," Birgit said, pulling away. "This is my own trouble. I shouldn't burden you."

"Don't talk foolish," Polly said, lifting the kettle off the stove lid, filling two vitreous china mugs. "God help you, girl, we're family now. Sit yourself down at the kitchen table, we'll work something out."

"But how?" Birgit asked numbly, sipping the steaming brew. "Tyler doesn't want me. He doesn't want my child."

"That can't be true. He had to snake through half the

damned Union army to marry you. Discharge papers or no, he could have been lynched or thrown in prison any step of the way. Tyler's a stubborn boy; all the Randolphs are, and the McKees too. There's no quit in any of 'em. If he was willing to risk dyin' to marry you in April, he hasn't changed his mind. There must be more to this. How are things between you two? Has he hit you before?"

"No, never, never. It's been good with us. The best. But this last month, he's . . . dark. Far off. He stays up nights, watching. There are fires in the hills near the farm. Deserters, he says. Or jayhawkers. Then a few days ago, men took our plowhorse. Five of them. Came up on Tyler in the field and just took it. He doesn't speak to me since. I thought telling him of the baby would cheer him but . . ." She swallowed, shaking her head.

Polly sipped her tea, mulling it over. "He's afraid," she said simply.

"Afraid? Tyler?"

"Oh, not of dyin'. After all the warrin' that boy's seen, death's less troublesome than a drunken uncle. It's you he's afraid for. Afraid he can't protect you. Or your child. That's a terrible fear for a man to face, especially a soldier like Tyler. He's seen the killing, knows what can happen. And in his heart, he's afraid of failing you, though I doubt he realizes it."

"So he drives me away?"

"Looks like it."

"What do I do?"

"Depends. Maybe he's right. God knows there's trouble in the wind around here."

"You stay."

"This place is all we've got. You'll be safer in St. Louis, Birgit. Maybe you should go home."

"No. Tyler is my home."

"You sure about that? You seem awful young to me."

"It's true, I am, maybe. But I know. When I met Tyler, St. Louis is full of young soldiers. Thousands. And I am at a cotillion, and Tyler is laughing with friends when he sees me. And he walks over and we talk a minute. No more. And I already know."

"Know what?"

Birgit eyed Polly's wind-weathered face a moment, then shrugged. "Laugh if you want, but I look at Tyler and I see . . . our children. I see my life. With him. But maybe you're right, maybe I am just . . . Hessian."

"No. I was wrong about that. And about you. I'm sorry for that. And Tyler was dead wrong to treat you like he done, though I can't fault his reasons."

"I don't care about his reasons. He's wrong to push me away. And I was wrong to leaf. I want to go back."

"It's not that simple. These are dangerous times, he's got good cause to fear for you."

"I know. I am afraid too. But I'm more afraid to lose him, to lose what we have together."

"Havin' a stout heart's all well and good, darlin,' but it ain't hardly enough. There are men in these hills who'd kill you for your horse or a dollar. Or no reason at all. And the truth is, Tyler can't always be there to protect you. You'll have to protect one another. Do you know about guns?"

"A little. Tyler bought me a pocket pistol. He tried to teach me but I'm terrible with it."

"Just like a man," Polly said dryly. "Give the little lady a little gun. Know the trouble with pistols? Men won't believe women can shoot. You have to kill 'em to prove it. Or die tryin'. That there's a woman's gun," she said, indicating a coach shotgun beside the back door. "No skill required, only sand enough to touch it off. You still have to watch out for border trash, but they'd better watch out too. I can teach all you need to know in twenty minutes. If you'd like."

"Yes, I would. Thank you."

"We'll finish our tea first, talk a little. These days I seldom see other women. I work like a man, dress like one. Sometimes I think I'm turning into one."

"I think you are very much woman, Mrs. McKee. And your home—now don't be mad with me—is very clean. It even smells clean. What is that scent?"

"Eau de Lilac. Lilac water. Before the war, with the boys home and their clothes and boots and such, sometimes it'd get to smellin' like a horse barn in here. Lilac water helps. I'm surprised you can smell it atall; I've watered it down somethin' fierce tryin' to make it last. The boys each promised to bring me a fresh bottle when they went off soldierin'."

"You say boys. How many?"

"Angus had the four older boys by his first wife, Sarah. She died of the consumption, quite young. It wasn't like you and Tyler with us, me and Gus didn't meet at no dance. I was orphaned, livin' with kin and Angus needed a mother for his boys. I was only fifteen when we married. We've got a boy of our own now, Jason, and I lost a girl at childbirth. It ain't always been easy but we've built ourselves a life here. It was a good place before the war. We'll make it so again."

"But you . . . care for him? Your husband?"

"Oh, surely. But Gus is . . . a bit older, set in his ways. But we're a good match, mostly we pull together like a yoked team. But I can't say I've ever had a moment like you talked about, no . . . special feeling like that. We just make the best we can of whatever comes. To be honest, he's been gone so long I wonder sometimes if things will be the same with us . . . afterward."

"Gone to where?"

"The hills. I tell folks he's in Springfield but he's not. After Price's troops got drove down to Arkansas, both sides were raidin' the border, runnin' off our stock. So Angus took the last of our horses up into the hills. Been movin' around with 'em since, hidin' 'em away so us and the boys can start over when the war ends. If it ever does. When he left we thought it'd be a few months, a year at most. Seems like forever now."

"Maybe not much longer. Tyler says it will end soon."

"Darlin', I've been hearin' that ole song since '61."

"No, it is true. Tyler saw a paper. The Federals have all the Shenandoah Valley. Price's men are scattered. Hood is retreating from Atlanta and the city is burning."

"Atlanta burning? But why?"

Birgit shrugged helplessly. Even in faultless English, no words could explain the madness on the land.

"Dear God," Polly said, slumping back in her chair. "This war may stop someday, but it won't be finished for a hundred years. No wonder the hills are fillin' with deserters and the jayhawkers are on the prowl. Both sides smell blood. You need to get home, girl, if that's what you mean to do. But first I'm gonna teach you a little about killin'. In a ladylike fashion, of course."

In half an hour, Polly instructed Birgit in the basics of the short-barreled coach gun. Pointed and fired at close range, the stunted scattergun would erase anything in its path from a poplar stump to three men standing abreast.

The girl took to the gun as a practical matter, learning to dispense death in defense of herself and her own with no more compunction that killing a coyote after chickens. Or a child.

Neither woman derived the pleasure men take from slaughter. It was a chore to be done, perhaps more dangerous than some, but also more necessary. At the lesson's end Birgit could manage the coach gun competently. And as she seated herself in the buggy to leave, Polly placed the stubby weapon on her lap.

"You take this with you, I've got another. And if there's trouble on the road, don't hesitate. These boys been killin' each other regular for a long time, they're damned quick at it. Surprise and that gun are all you have."

"I'll manage. If nothing else, I think Tyler will hear me out when I explain how things will be with us now."

"I expect he will at that," Polly grinned. "You can make Corridon before dusk. Stay the night there, move on in the morning. You'll be home before supper."

"And in spring, when my time comes for the baby, can I send for you?"

"Of course, darlin', surely. I'll come runnin' and we'll haul that child into this world together. I'll see you then, Mrs. Randolph, maybe sooner if this madness ends and our boys come home. Meantime, you take care, hear?"

Jason brought in a load of kindling he gathered in the woods and after feeding him, Polly sent him down the valley to stay over with a cousin, as was customary during the nights of a new moon.

But instead of finishing her work in the barn, Polly spent the last of the afternoon cleaning the house, absurdly pleased that Birgit noted how well she kept it. Only women's opinions matter. Men wouldn't notice a slaughtered hog on the sofa unless they had to shift it to sit down.

With the house immaculate, Polly hauled the copper bathtub into the kitchen and put water on to boil. And for a moment, she glimpsed herself in the hall mirror. And couldn't help thinking how fresh and young Birgit looked. Her own face was growing leathery, weathered by the wind and the work. She wondered how Angus saw her now, and wondered if she'd ever truly feel like a woman again. . . .

Gunshot. A single blast, echoing down the valley like distant thunder. Polly froze, listening for another. Nothing. Which might be good. Because she was sure she'd recognized the bark of a coach gun. And not many used them. Banking the fire in the kitchen stove, she took her own gun and eased out onto the shaded porch. To wait.

An hour crept by. Half of another. Dusk settled over the hills and still she waited, standing in the shadows. A sliver of silver moon was inching above the trees when she heard the distant drum of hoofbeats nearing, then the clatter of a wagon as the Stanhope buggy burst over the crest of a hill, hurtling madly down the moonlit road toward the farm.

Polly was up and running as the buggy skidded through the gate into the yard. Birgit sawed on the reins, yanking her lathered, gasping animal to a halt. Her face and clothing were mudsmeared and filthy, hair awry, eyes wild.

"What happened?"

"A man came out of the woods, grabbed the horse. I warned him off but he won't let go. I struck him with the buggy whip and he rushed at me, grabbed me, tried to drag me down and," she swallowed, "and I shot him!"

"He pulled me from the buggy as he fell and I ran into the woods. Lost. Couldn't find my way. After awhile I came out on the road. And I see the buggy. He's laying by it."

"Dead?"

"I—think so," Birgit said, gulping down a sob. "I'm pretty sure. His head—oh God. Yes, he's dead. He must be."

"It's all right, girl. You did right. But we're not out of this. Is the body in the road?"

"By the side, yes."

"And the gun? Where is it?"

"I—lost it when I fell. I don't know what happened to it."

"All right, now listen here to me," Polly said, seizing the girl's shoulders. "We have to go back. Now."

"I can't!"

"We have to! Don't matter if he was Federal or Reb, if his friends find him kilt they'll come after us, 'specially if that gun's nearby. Too many people know it. I'd go alone but I might go past him in the dark. Can you find that place again?"

Birgit nodded mutely.

"Good. Wait here. I'll get a shovel."

They nearly missed him. Moonlit, dappled with shadows, the road was a slender ribbon threading through the darkness of the hills. Birgit wasn't sure how far she'd traveled or how long she'd been lost. But she recognized the spot. And the crumpled form beside the road.

"Wait here," Polly hissed, stepping down from the buggy, her shotgun leveled. No need. The blast had shredded his upper body. She could smell the reek of death from ten feet away. Not just the stench of blood and voided bowels, but the sickly sweet odor of gangrene as well. Couldn't tell if he was Reb or Federal. Linsey-woolsey shirt drenched with blood, canvas pants, brokendown boots. The strays of both sides had been living off the land so long they much resembled each other. Especially in death.

"Is he . . . ?" Birgit whispered.

"Oh yes. Dead as a stone. He was dyin' anyway. Got a bandaged wound on his thigh and it was mortifyin'. Gangrene. You probably did the poor bastard a favor, girl. Let's get him underground."

Straining, stumbling, the two women tried to drag the reeking corpse into the trees, but he kept snagging on the underbrush. In the end, Polly lifted him by the shoulders while Birgit took his legs, and they carried him bodily into the forest.

Spotting a natural trench at the base of a fallen sycamore, Polly widened it with her shovel, then they rolled the corpse in and covered it over with dirt and forest debris.

"Leaves are already fallin'," Polly panted, straightening. "A day or two, it'll be like we was never here."

"We should say words for him," Birgit said.

"Pray? For a damn' road agent?"

"We can't just leave him like this. It's wrong." Her voice was shaking.

"All right, girl, all right. Do you know what to say?"

"Not—in English."

"Then say it in Hessian. Or whatever that place is you're from."

"Bavaria. But the language is the same."

"Well, I expect the good lord understands 'em all, and this poor devil's beyond carin'. Go ahead."

Kneeling silently in the moist forest mould beside Birgit while she prayed, Polly didn't understand a word of it. Yet somehow she felt better as they made their way back to the road. The girl was right. A proper buryin' was the decent thing to do, even for no account border trash.

They found the gun in the brush beside the road where Birgit dropped it. After reloading, Polly handed it up to the girl in the buggy.

"You drive on now. Corridon's less than an hour away and you'll be safer travelin' this time of night than in daylight. You shouldn't have no more trouble, but if you do, well, God help 'em."

"But what will you do?"

"Walk home. I been in these hills my whole life; moonlight's as bright as a lantern for me. Don't worry. You just take care of yourself and that baby. I'll see you come spring, girl. I promise."

136

Polly watched until the buggy disappeared, then set off for home, a long, weary march. It was well after midnight when she finally trudged up the lane to her home.

She'd thought Angus might be waiting. He usually came down from the hill for provisions on the first night of the new moon. But he wasn't there, at least not yet.

Exhausted, she relit the kitchen woodstove to warm the water, then stumbled into her bedroom. By the light of a lone candle, she filled the basin from the pitcher on the washstand, then stripped off her shirt, hanging it carefully on the doorknob to avoid getting bloodstains on the bedspread.

But as she plunged her arms in the basin to rinse off the gore, the scent of it came roiling up, suffusing the air, a powerful sweet-sour blend of gangrene and . . .

Lilacs. Stunned, Polly stared down at the basin, already reddening with blood. Leaning down, her face just above the water, she drew a long, ragged breath. Dear God. It was Eau de Lilac. Full strength, undiluted.

Her throat closed so tightly she could hardly breathe. Still, she forced herself to take her shirt from the doorknob to sniff a bloodstained sleeve. It was drenched with lilac water. No doubt about it.

The person Birgit killed must have been carrying the bottle in his shirt pocket. The shotgun blast splattered it all over his chest.

With a low moan, Polly sank to the bed, burying her face in her hands, rocking. No tears, her agony was soundless and soul deep, a pain so savage she thought she might die. And wished she could.

Which boy had they buried? She'd never looked into his face, hadn't wanted to. He was just another lost scarecrow of war, another starving, walking corpse, looking for a place to die.

Or to kill. Why had he attacked Birgit on the road? Too sick to walk any further? Or had the war bled the pity from him, made him into another Meachum? Taken his soul?

Wasn't sure how long she sat there. Must have fallen asleep. Because she woke with a start. Someone was moving in the kitchen. And for a wild moment she thought she'd been mistaken, the boy hadn't been dead, somehow he'd clawed his way out of the earth . . . but no.

In the kitchen Angus was fumbling with a lantern.

"Don't light that," Polly said, carrying her candle to the table. "Cavalry was here today. They might be watching the house."

"Whose cavalry?"

"Federals, out of Jefferson City."

"Oh." In the flickering shadows, her husband's seamed face was hewn from granite, his beard unkempt, his graying hair wild. She wanted to hold him, to feel his strength. But it wasn't their custom. And she wanted no questions.

"You're late," she said, her voice quiet, controlled. "It's nearly three."

"I walked in. Took longer than I figured."

"You walked? Why?"

He avoided her eyes, almost sheepishly. "I loaned out my horse."

"The mare? Loaned it to who?"

"Some kid. Union deserter from Curtis's outfit. Came stumblin' into my camp yesterday. Seemed decent. Family's got a farm up near Cairo, Illinois. He needed to get home. So I put him on my mare and set him on an old jayhawk trail. Figured I'd be better off with him gone than hangin' around the hills tellin' his pals about the crazy old man hidin' in the pineywoods with his raggedy-ass horses. Told him I'd send one of the boys for the animal after the war."

"Might not be too much longer. Had a visitor today, Tyler Randolph's new wife. She said the Federals burned Atlanta. Hood's retreating."

"Might be," he nodded. "I've been seein' a lot of strays in the hills, mostly Rebs but some Union. Federals are shootin' deserters now. Huntin' 'em down like coyotes. Is that why the cavalry came?"

"That, and to steal anything that wasn't nailed down. Aaron Meachum was with them. Gave me some mouth, nothing I couldn't handle."

"Meachum," Angus rasped, his eyes narrowing. "That bloodsuckin' scum's ridin' high now, got the Hessians around him, thinks he's safe. But when this is over and the boys are home, we'll be payin' a visit to that jayhawker sonofabitch—"

Polly slapped him, hard! Snapping his head around. He stared at her in stunned disbelief.

"No! By God Angus, when this is over, it's truly gonna be over for us. We've given enough, bled enough. Let the dead bury the dead. No more killing, no more burning, not for revenge nor anything else!"

"What the hell's got into you, Pol?"

"I met Tyler Randolph's wife! And she's Hessian, except she's not—she's from some other place in Germany. But she's a fine girl! And God willing, she and Tyler will have children. I can midwife for her, and they can come visit of a Sunday, stay at Christmas, maybe. But so help me God, Angus, if you ever say any more about killin' or use that word Hessian to me again, I'll leave you! I'll take our boy and go! Do you understand?"

Tears were streaming now, she couldn't stop them and didn't care. Angus eyed her like a stranger, utterly baffled. He touched his lip and his fingertip came away bloody.

139

"No," he said slowly, "I don't understand. But I think it's a damn sight more than we can talk through tonight. I better go. Need to be in the hills before sunup anyhow."

"No! Not yet. You came in for warm food and a bath and you're damned well gonna have 'em!"

"I came in for a kind word too. But I guess I'll settle for a bath."

"Good!" Polly carried the steaming buckets from the woodstove to the tub, filling it with practiced ease as Angus warily unbuttoned his shirt, watching her all the while.

When the tub was full, he turned his back and so did she, giving him privacy, as was their habit.

But not tonight. Instead, she turned and watched him strip off his frayed shirt and the tattered union suit beneath. Saw his pale, scrawny frame, the lump on his shoulder where a horse had broken his collarbone years ago, his flat butt, the hipbones showing through.

My God. He'd been up in those hills for nearly three years, living with their animals, living like an animal. Freezing and going hungry. For her. For their boys. With no complaints.

As he turned to climb in the bath, he saw her watching and colored with embarrassment. But he said nothing. Just eased his aching bones down in the steaming water with a groan.

But in that briefest of moments, when their eyes met, she'd seen her life. With him. And nothing else mattered. Nothing. Not the hunger, not the war, not even the boy lost in the forest. Somehow they'd get through this. They would.

Ordinarily she left him alone to bathe. Instead she knelt behind the tub and wrapped her arms around his narrow shoulders, holding him. "I'm sorry," she said, after a time.

"No need. Up in them hills I forget how hard it must be for you holdin' on here alone. Comin' home feels so good to me that . . . well, I forget, that's all. Are you all right?"

"I will be. When all this is over."

"Soon, maybe. And you're right. When it's finished we'll get back to some kind of life. Make up for these sorry times. All of us. I miss you, Polly, miss our boys, our home. Even miss the way it smells, like now. What's that stuff again?"

"Eau de Lilac," she said. "Lilac water."

Déjà Vu

Something about the corpse was getting on Maxwell's nerves. As he moved around the nude body on the table, methodically spritzing it down with Dis-Spray disinfectant, Max's glance kept straying to the guy's face. The corpse had been male-model-handsome, distinguished, a guy who'd pitch custom tailored suits in a TV commercial. Square features, curly brown hair showing a little gray at the temples, glazed gray eyes gazing vacantly up at the flyspecked fluorescent tube dangling from the ceiling. Somebody hadn't been too taken with his looks, though; they'd roughed him up pretty thoroughly and made a fair start at cutting out his heart.

His face was bloodied and battered, his bridgework was broken, collarbone appeared to be broken, too, and there were a couple of deep, ugly gashes amid the salt and pepper thatch on his chest. Straight razor, Max guessed, or a honed linoleum blade. Still, it wasn't the way the guy'd checked out that was nibbling at him, he'd worked on murder victims before, more than he could count. It was something . . .

"Mr. Kerabatsos, do you know this guy?" Max asked. "Is he from around here?"

The Greek shook his head without looking up from the shriveled crone with blue-rinsed hair he was soaping down on the mortuary lab's other table. He did solid, competent work, the Greek. When he finished pumping the old woman full of Permaglo and doing her makeup, she'd look like she'd dozed off in the middle of a Lawrence Welk rerun. "Don't know nothing 'bout him," he grunted. "Got a call around six from guy's boss, ax me to pick him up at

142

Wayne County morgue. Why?"

"I don't know," Max said, "something about him . . ."

"A relative maybe? He look a little bit like you, you know."

"I never had a relative that looked this good."

"Then somebody you seen around? Maybe in a bar?" the Greek added pointedly.

"I—don't think so," Maxwell said, frowning, "can't recall him offhand anyway." But maybe the Greek was right. It happens sometimes, even in a town the size of Detroit. You work long enough as a gypsy mortician, occasionally you get somebody you know on the table. Max had seen a few over the years, a woman from his apartment building, a baseball player from his high school class. And when it happens, it makes you think. How long before it's your turn on the stainless steel slab with the Porti-Boy pumping your precious bodilies into a plastic bag? And then what?

Max examined the dead man's face carefully, taking his time, trying to place him. Nothing. And yet . . . he seemed familiar. Or something.

The hell with it. Max peeled off his latex gloves, dropped them on the guy's lap, and sauntered over to the coat rack for a taste. He tugged the pint bottle of Absolut out of his sportcoat pocket and checked the level on it. Half empty. Or was it half full? Either way it was half gone, and it had to last him until the next afternoon when he'd get paid. Kerabatsos glanced up at him, but made no comment. The Greek knew he liked a belt now and then. But he also knew Max looked good in a black suit, could make a train wreck victim presentable, and, most important, worked cheap.

Max glanced around the room as he nipped at the vodka. A dump, no doubt about it. Paint peeling off the cinder block walls, two dingy stainless steel tables smudged with a bouillabaisse of body fluids, the kind of a place where they expect you to wipe down your disposable apron and leave it for the next guy. Nothing like the upscale funeral homes he'd worked when he got out of the army back in '72. He . . .

Something clicked in a corner of his memory. The army. Was the corpse somebody he'd known back then? He wandered over to the counter and picked up the death certificate. Bronfman. Edgar L. The name didn't ring a bell. Date of birth: 10 June 52. Cause of death: cardial trauma/edged weapon, which in parts of Detroit is almost death due to natural causes. With luck, the guy was so high he didn't feel much pain. He was obviously heavy into coke, the inside of his nose looked like he'd been snorting Drano. Still, there were worse ways to go. The last time it was—

Max froze, the bottle halfway to his lips. The last time . . . the guy'd died from a broken neck. In an auto accident.

He stalked back to the table, stared down at the corpse, then back at the death certificate. Bronfman. Edgar L. The name didn't seem right, but it was the same man, he was sure of it. He'd worked half the night reassembling that face. The last time. The guy was one of the first jobs he'd ever done by himself. Back in '72.

"Hey," Kerabatsos said, "you gonna do some work? I wanna get home sometime tonight."

Max ignored him, trying to make sense of the situation. Could he be a son, maybe? No, this guy was too old to be the son of the other one. Or his brother? Maybe a twin brother? That had to be it. Except that he was getting a glimmer of the first guy's name in the back of his mind. Connolly? Connery? Something like that. Definitely not Bronfman, though. Not even close. He'd been working at Esperanza's in Highland Park, his first job after the army. And you don't forget your first love, or your first car. Or your first client. And if Connolly or Bronfman or whatever wasn't his first body, he was close enough to it so he remembered

"Come on, Maxwell," the Greek sighed, "how about—"

"Get off my back!" Max snapped.

The Greek scowled, but let it pass. It was late, and sometimes the work made people edgy, even a pro like Max. "Whatsamatta with you?" Kerabatsos said. "You got a problem?"

Max glanced involuntarily at the corpse again, then took a deep breath. "No," he said, swallowing, "no problem. Sorry."

"You wrong, Max," the Greek said, "your problem's in that bottle there." He turned his back on Max as he moved around the table aspirating the old woman's vital organs, working off his irritation on her.

Maxwell studied the half-empty pint of vodka. Maybe the Greek was right. Maybe it was finally happening. God knows he'd been juicing long enough. Isn't this how it begins? First the memory plays tricks, then you wake up in strange places and can't remember how you got there, then—

Nuts. No way. He'd been boozing off and on since his first wife took a walk. He could handle it, and he knew damn well he was still playing with a full deck. And he was just as sure he remembered the man on the table. He took a quick nip out of the bottle. And got nothing. It was empty. Max stared at it stupidly for a moment, then at the corpse. And then he hurled the bottle at the wall.

"Hey!" Kerabatsos yelled, ducking away from the hail of broken glass. "What the hell's with you?"

"Is something wrong?" Linda asked. "Something going on I should know about?" She was dressed for work, wearing a prim navy outfit that only needed medals to make it a uniform. Her blonde hair was pulled back in a taut chignon, and

145

she looked scrubbed and serious and grim, without a trace of makeup. There'd been a time when she'd touched up her face first thing in the morning. But not lately. A bad omen, and a familiar one.

"No," he lied, sipping the scalding black instant from a quivering cup, "I'm fine."

"You don't look fine. I—waited up for you until midnight or so. Did you stop off at Flynn's after work?"

"As a matter of fact, I didn't," he said. "I ah, ran into a guy I used to know at the Greek's. And I went for a walk afterwards. Did some thinking."

"A guy?" she echoed skeptically. "Are you sure it was a guy?"

"It wouldn't have mattered either way, Lin," he sighed, "since the person in question was a client."

"A client? You mean you had to—work on someone you knew? Max, that must've been awful."

"You don't know the half of it."

"Look, I'm sorry if I seemed, well, you know," she said, glancing at her watch. "I've gotta run, it's my turn to open the shop today. Are you going to be all right?"

"Damned if I know," he said honestly.

"You will be," she said, giving him a sisterly peck on the forehead. "I'll call you on my lunch hour. We'll talk. Okay?" She snatched her purse from the kitchen counter and started for the door.

"I may not be here," he called after her. "I ah, I've got something to take care of."

She hesitated in the doorway, sympathy and suspicion dueling in her eyes. Suspicion won. "Max, I know your work is hard on you sometimes, but don't use whatever happened last night as an excuse to go on a bender okay? Because if you do . . ."

She swallowed.

"Go to work, Lin," Max said, "I'll be all right."

"You promise?"

"My word as a gentleman."

"Sure," she said doubtfully. "Right."

After she'd gone Maxwell took a long, thoughtful shower, finishing it off with an icy needle spray. He slipped on a T-shirt, jeans, and New Balance joggers. And then he called Detroit P.D. and asked to speak to the detective handling the Bronfman case.

"Sergeant Pilarski, Homicide."

"Hi, my name's Maxwell, I'm calling about Bronfman, Edgar L."

"Yessir. Do you have information to offer?"

"I'm not sure. I was hoping you could tell me what happened to him."

"I'm afraid I can't discuss an investigation in progress, Mr. Maxwell, but anything you can tell us . . ."

"Did you ah—know he was probably doing cocaine? A lot of it?"

"Yessir, we're aware of that. Would you mind telling me how you happen to know it?"

"Look, this may sound a bit strange to you, but I embalmed Mr. Bronfman last night, at the Kerabatsos Funeral Home. And ah—" Max coughed "—and I used to know him. So if you could tell me what happened I'd really appreciate it."

There was a long silence on the other end. Max could hear office noises in the background, typewriters, telephones.

"How well did you know the victim, Mr. Maxwell?"

"Not well. I haven't seen him in years."

"And then you had to lay him out, hunh?" Pilarski said, not unsympathetically. "Musta been a helluva jolt. Well, I guess I can give you the basics, they're public record. Mr.

147

Bronfman was spotted by a prowl car in an alley off West Lafayette around two A.M. night before last. He was already dead, apparently mugged, beaten pretty badly, and then stabbed to death. Probably cruising the area looking to score some crack and somebody took him off. We get about three cases a week just like it. We found his car this morning, or what was left of it, in a vacant lot down on the Corridor, stripped. That's about it."

"Do you have any idea who might have killed him?"

"Sure. The alley's on turf claimed by both the Pharoahs and the B.T.'s. That narrows the suspect list down to about six hundred gang members. Unless maybe you've got somebody more specific in mind?" Pilarski added hopefully.

"No, I'm afraid not. Like I said, it's been a long time."

"Well, if you think of anything that might help, give us a call, okay?"

"Just one last thing, sergeant. Does Bronfman have any family in the area?"

"I don't think so, no. We I.D.'d him from his driver's license. His assailants tossed his wallet after they lifted his cash and credit cards, but they missed his license. He apparently lived with the people he worked for. His boss came down and identified the body. Some English guy. Why do you ask?"

"I don't know, I guess I was hoping it wasn't—hell, I don't know what I was hoping. Thanks for your help, sergeant."

Max eased the receiver into its cradle before Pilarski could ask him anything else. He stared at the phone for what seemed like a very long time, mulling over what he'd been told. But the only thing he was certain of was that he was developing a major thirst. His eyes kept straying to the small wet bar beside Linda's stereo. Not yet. First he'd better find out if he was cracking up. Esperanza's, the mortuary where he'd met Bronfman or whoever in '72, was a used car lot now, sooo . . . He grabbed the phone book, flipped through the Yellow Pages, called the Detroit *News,* and asked for the library.

But the *News* librarian had no record of a Bronfman killed in an auto accident in the spring of '72, nor a Connolly or Connery either.

"Look, I know the man died in a car crash in Highland Park roughly fifteen years ago," Max said. "Shouldn't you have something about it?"

"The computer shows nothing under that name, sir. If he died accidentally, though, his name might have been withheld from the story pending notification of next of kin, and unless there was a follow-up on it for some reason, it wouldn't have been entered."

"You mean you don't even rate a footnote or something for getting killed in this town?"

"Not in Detroit, no sir, or at least not in the *News.*"

"What about an obituary?"

"We run obits if the family requests one, or if the deceased was a public figure, but I show no record of one under the names you gave me. You might try the *Free Press,*" she added, "they may have something."

She didn't sound optimistic about it, though, and she was right. The *Freep* had no record of a Connolly or Connery either. Only Bronfman, Edgar L., crime victim, two days ago.

Which left Max with two options: accept the idea that he was losing his grip, or . . .

He picked up his car keys and grabbed a corduroy jacket from the hall closet on his way out.

The suburb of Grosse Pointe Farms is only a few miles from downtown Motown, facing Lake St. Clair, but it's light years removed from the urban jungle. Wide, elm shaded streets, multi-storied upper class homes guarded by sculptured hedges and wrought-iron fencing, set amid green velvet lawns broad enough for polo. Max followed Lake Shore Drive past the Crescent Sail Yacht Club, then turned inland toward the golf course. When he finally found the address he'd copied from Bronfman's death certificate, he doublechecked it. The estate was immense, even by Grosse Pointe standards. It was surrounded by a fieldstone wall eight feet high which seemed to stretch unbroken to the back links of the Country Club of Detroit. The gate was wrought iron, with the name HELFORD set in large bronze letters in the center.

Max pulled his rust-spotted blue Camaro up to the gate and climbed out. A call button and speaker were set into one of the gateposts on a brass plate. He pressed the buzzer and waited, wondering what the hell he thought he was doing, wishing he'd worn a tie.

"Yes?" A man's voice. British accent. Probably an honest to God butler, Max thought.

"Uh, hi, was this the ah, residence of Edgar Bronfman?"

A moment's hesitation. "Yes. What is it?"

"My name's Maxwell, from the Kerabatsos Funeral Home? I'd like to talk to someone about Mr. Bronfman, please."

Again a pause. "Very well. Drive around to the parking area, and wait in your car. Someone will come for you."

The voice clicked off, and the massive gates hummed slowly open. Max fired up his Camaro and drove through. He followed a wide cobblestone drive along the outer wall, occasionally glimpsing what appeared to be a good-sized office building through the maze of shrubs and razor-trimmed cedars that lined the drive.

Close up, the house was even bigger than he'd expected, a huge modernist structure, stacked on a hillside on four levels, slab-roofed, glass-walled, with long, swooping concrete ramps linking the sections of the house. The parking area was in the rear, a half-acre of concrete facing a six-car garage. There were several cars parked along the edge of the apron, a Rolls limo, a couple of Benzes, and one small red Sunbird convertible. Max backed his Camaro into a slot beside the 'Bird and waited. But not for long.

Two huge wolf-size dogs loped around the corner of the garage, black, with tan markings, and wearing seriously spiked collars, the biggest Dobermans he'd ever seen. They trotted up to the Camaro and began circling it warily, eyeing Max through the windows as they passed. A small, blocky, Oriental man in a gray business suit followed them. He snapped his fingers twice and the dogs instantly responded, taking up positions beside him. He smiled tentatively at Max and motioned him out of the car. Max hesitated, then sighed and climbed out. Even with two hundred pounds of guard dogs beside him, the little guy seemed friendly enough.

The Oriental turned and walked toward the house without a word, the dogs pacing obediently on either side. Max followed the trio up one of the long, gradually sloped concrete ramps to the second level. In the distance, Lake St. Clair rimmed the horizon like a ring of indigo smoke. On the second level, the Oriental led him across a broad flagstone terrace to a set of french doors inset in the full-width smoked glass wall, motioned him inside, and left him, trailed by the dogs.

Max paused just inside the door, waiting for his eyes to adjust to the dimness after the glare of the autumn afternoon. The room was a long, rectangular office/library, with booklined walls, hardwood parquet floors, translucent ceiling panels overhead. A portly type seated at an ornate rosewood desk in the center of the room glanced up as he entered, then pointedly went back to scanning some paperwork. He looked sour and sixtyish, with thinning reddish-blond hair and a beefy, florid face, freckled and pocked like a pimiento loaf. He was dressed casually, a Harris tweed jacket with elbow patches over a dark turtleneck.

"Mr. Maxwell, is it?" he said brusquely, without looking up. "I'm Mr. Sutliffe. What seems to be the problem?" His accent was British, the voice from the driveway speaker.

"I am," Max swallowed. "It's a little difficult—"

"Then perhaps I can save you some trouble," Sutliffe interrupted. "You people don't have the coffin we agreed upon in stock, but you just happen to have a similar model for only a wee bit more money, et cetera, et cetera. Is that roughly how your little spiel goes? Well, you can forget it. I informed Mr. Kerabatsos—"

"That isn't what I wanted," Max interjected.

"—of Mrs. Helford's wishes in the matter, and—"

"*Hey!*" Max said sharply.

Sutliffe broke off, startled.

"I didn't come about a coffin," Max said. "I don't give a damn what you bury the guy in and you obviously don't either, since just one of those dogs outside probably cost more than you paid the Greek for the whole package."

"What is it you want then?" Sutliffe said stiffly, a rose flush of irritation creeping above his collar.

"I—look, I take it Bronfman worked for you or something. Do you know if he has any other family?"

"None that I'm aware of," Sutliffe snapped. "Why?"

"I just wanted to ask." Max took a deep breath. "I was wondering if he had any brothers? A twin brother or something?"

"Why should Mr. Bronfman's relatives be any concern of yours?"

"It's a little complicated. Are you sure he didn't—"

Sutliffe rose slowly from behind the desk, his eyes narrowing. "I repeat," he said coldly, "Mr. Bronfman had no family that I'm aware of, twin or otherwise, and we check the backgrounds of our employees very thoroughly. See here, I don't know what you think you're playing at, Maxwell, but you've picked the wrong party to meddle with. This interview is concluded and if you are not off the grounds in five minutes, I'll have Lee set the dogs on you. Now, was there anything else?"

"Ah, no," Max said. "I think that covers it."

"The smarmy bastard got me fired," Max said, sipping his vodka/rocks. "Called up Kerabatsos and rained all over him, and when I stopped for my check the Greek came down on me like World War III."

"Helluva shame," Flynn nodded, polishing a brandy snifter with a towel while keeping a weather eye on the two drunks arguing sports at the end of the bar. "So whaddya gonna do now, Max?"

"Ahh, no big deal," Max said blearily, "I've been canned by a lot better places than the Greek's. You know what he wanted me to do once?"

"No, and I don't wanna know," Flynn said, paling. "I've told ya not to talk shop in here, Max, roons my lunch. Hey, you clowns cool it, okay?"

Flynn waddled off to separate the two rummies who'd escalated from name-calling to push-and-shove. Max knocked back the last of the vodka and pushed the empty glass forward for a refill.

"Mr. Maxwell?"

Max swung slowly around on his stool. Another familiar face, but not from fifteen years ago. The Oriental dog handler from the Helford mansion. Mr. Lee?

"Sorry to bother you," Lee said softly, "Mr. Carbasso gave me your address and your ladyfriend say you're probably here."

"So I am," Max said.

"She also said you should not come back. Evah again."

"Terrific," Max said. "You know, this isn't turning out to be a day I'll wanna relive during my golden years. Still, no fault of yours, Mr. Lee, sit down. Can I buy you a drink?"

"No drink," Lee said, "you come with me. Mrs. Helford want to talk with you."

"Who?"

"Mrs. Helford. Lady I work for. Lady who own house."

"Why does she want to see me? You running low on dog food?"

"She don't tell me," Lee said. "She just say to bring you."

"Did she say anything about Bronfman?" Max asked, sobering a little.

"No. Mr. Bronfman dead. You come?"

Max eyed Lee a moment, trying to read him. Nothing. It wasn't that Lee was inscrutable. Max just couldn't manage to bring the little guy's face into focus. "What the hell," he shrugged, "why not?"

"Mr. Maxwell, wake up. Come on, wake up."

Max grunted, and managed to open his eyes. He was piled in the back seat of a Rolls Royce stretch limo, and Lee was shaking him, none too gently. "Okay, okay already. I'm awake."

Max eased out of the Rolls, nearly toppling over as an icy gust caught him. Darkness had fallen, taking the temperature with it, and the wind off Lake St. Clair was bitter. He glanced around, only half awake, trying to get his bearings. He was in front of the Helford mansion, and not altogether sure what he was doing there.

"Come on," Lee said, taking him firmly by the arm, guiding him up the concrete ramp to the front door, "we go now."

The entrance hall was in shadow, and seemed to be several miles long. A museum, Max thought groggily, as Lee led him along, their footsteps echoing hollowly on the gleaming tiled floor. Sculpture, incomprehensibly modern, each in its own setting, paintings hung at regular intervals, the mansion had more art in it than a M.O.M.A. rummage sale. He tried to keep track of where they were going, but lost his sense of direction after a couple of turns. And then he heard voices ahead, arguing, and recognized Sutliffe's baritone bark. Terrific.

Lee paused in front of an exquisitely carved door and listened for a moment, shaking his head. Then he rapped twice sharply. Sutliffe broke off in mid-tirade. Lee opened the door, nudged Maxwell through it, and abandoned him, closing the door softly as he left.

The room might have been a sun room in daylight. It was sparsely furnished in oak and canvas, Scandinavian Moderne, and its tinted glass walls offered a stunning view of the mercury-lit grounds. Sutliffe was standing in the center of the room at parade rest, his hands clasped firmly behind his back. He was dressed almost formally, in an immaculate dark suit and regimental tie. The woman beside him was seated in a wheelchair. Max guessed her to be mid-fiftyish, and while it was apparent from the pallor of her skin and the dark smudges under her eyes that her health was frail, nonetheless she was a striking figure. Ebon hair dusted with silver, fine boned patrician features, alabaster skin, eyes large and dark as a mystery. She was wearing a black suede blouse and slacks, and calfskin boots. An intricately embroidered shawl was draped loosely across her lap.

It didn't quite camouflage her withered legs.

"Mrs. Charlotte Helford," Sutliffe said dourly, not bothering to conceal his distaste. "This is—Mr. Maxwell."

"Ma'am," Max nodded, swaying slightly. The woman eyed him with impersonal curiosity, but said nothing.

"Mr. Maxwell, Mrs. Helford feels that I may have ah, overreacted this afternoon," Sutliffe said. "I understand that you've lost your job because of it. I apologize for that, it was not my intention."

"Wasn't it?" Max said mildly. "Gee, you sure fooled the Greek."

"Well, perhaps it was," Sutliffe said, flushing, "but the strain of Mr. Bronfman's passing—"

"Turned you into a basket case, right," Max interrupted. "Look, Mr. Sutliffe, I've already invested a fair amount of my severance pay in a perfectly good bender and I'd hate to see it go to waste, so can you cut the smoke and get down to it?"

"As you wish," Sutliffe said stiffly. "Mrs. Helford feels that we may have done you an injustice, inadvertently you understand, and she wishes to put it right."

"I see," Max said. "And just how right does she wish to put it?"

"We thought compensation in the area of five thousand dollars would be equitable."

"Five thousand?" Max blinked. "In ah, in return for what?"

"Nothing, really, an agreement absolving us of legal liability, in effect, putting the matter behind us. Permanently."

Max glanced from Sutliffe to the woman, then back again, "I'll be damned," he said softly.

"I might point out," Sutliffe continued, "that if you choose not to accept our offer, which, by the way, I feel is more than generous, we have the financial resources to—"

"I learned my trade in Vietnam," Max interrupted.

"I beg your pardon?" Sutliffe said.

"I worked in a funeral home when I was in high school, just sweeping up, you know? So when I got drafted in '69, I was assigned to graves registration, which in 'Nam meant chasing around the countryside in 6-bys and cargo planes, bagging and I.D.ing bodies, and pieces of bodies, and—" He took a deep, ragged breath.

"I don't see how this is relev—"

"Let me finish," Max said quietly. "The point is, after the things I saw there, I never thought I'd be afraid of anything again. Ever. But I was afraid last night, and all day long today. Afraid I was finally coming unglued, losing it. But I'm not, am I?"

"If you think you can get more money by—"

"I don't want your money, Sutliffe. I've never cared much about money one way or the other. But you shouldn't have jerked my chain. I don't know what's going on out here, but something is. And since I'm temporarily between jobs, I may just pass the time by finding out what. Nice meeting you, Mrs. Helford. Sorry to abandon you in your hour of grief, but I've gotta get back to my guests." He turned toward the door.

"Not so fast, you two-penny ponce," Sutliffe snarled, grabbing Max's arm, spinning him around. "Who the hell—"

Max jerked free harder than he'd intended, and caught Sutliffe sharply across the bridge of the nose with his elbow. The older man stared at him a moment, stunned; then his knees buckled and he sat down. Hard.

"Jesus," Max said, trying clumsily to help him up, "I'm really sorry—didn't mean to—"

"Bugger off, damn you," Sutliffe mumbled, pushing Max away.

"I think you'd better leave, Mr. Maxwell," Mrs. Helford

said quietly, her voice husky, dark velvet.

"Look, I'm sorry, really—"

"Get out!" she said.

"Right," Max said.

Easier said than done. Max made his way unsteadily down the hallway, trying to find the front door, expecting to hear the hounds of the Baskervilles in full cry with every step. No luck. The place was a maze of dead end passages, each with its own gallery. He tried a dozen different doors, giving the priceless displays of art and antiques no more than a glance before pushing hurriedly on to the next. He opened yet another door, glanced into the deserted room, and had the door half closed again before the scene registered. Bronfman. Edgar L. He opened the door slowly and stepped in.

The room was a den of sorts, with natural walnut paneling, a gun rack, and a well stocked bar against one wall, a large fieldstone fireplace with a gas log hissing in the grate, leather easy chairs arranged facing the fire. A fully decorated Christmas tree in the corner flickered to life when Max flipped the light switch next to the door, and soft music filled the room. Nat King Cole. "Stardust."

Edgar L. Bronfman was hanging above the fireplace mantel, gazing calmly from a half-length portrait, much younger than when Max saw him last, early twenties perhaps. He was wearing a double-breasted gray suit, and perhaps the artist had idealized him a bit, but not much. In life, Bronfman had been a handsome man.

The portrait was surrounded by framed photographs, Bronfman as a teenager sitting behind the wheel of a vintage Caddy convertible, Bronfman on horseback in polo gear, and as a bridegroom standing at the altar with a heartbreakingly young and lovely Charlotte Helford beside him. Max lingered over that one a moment, mentally comparing the girl in the white silk wedding dress with the woman in the chrome and leather wheelchair. He shook his head slowly. Life and time. Damn them to hell.

The picture beside it was of Bronfman in uniform, U.S.A.F. blue, complete with silver wings on his chest and silver bars on his shoulders. The frame below held only a medal, with a brief citation beneath it. Silver Star, Posthumous, awarded to First Lieutenant Jason Helford, U.S.A.F., for gallantry in action—Max skipped over the rest, until the date of the award caught his eye, Inchon, Korea, 15 October 1950. The date seemed to waver, and fade out for a moment, and then flick back into place, in cold black and white. October, 1950. He stared at it for a moment, dazed, then examined the photograph more closely, reading the nametag below the wings. Helford. Not Bronfman. And the man in the portrait was dead before Max was born.

A low, rumbling snarl sounded from behind him. Max turned slowly. One of the Dobermans had slipped into the den through the open door. It was advancing on him cautiously, teeth bared, eyes glowing with the light of combat, growling deep in its chest. Max glanced around frantically for a weapon, anything, but there was nothing within reach. He began sliding cautiously toward the gun rack in the corner . . . The dog planted its paws, preparing to spring.

"Hanover!" Charlotte Helford said sharply from the doorway. *"Nicht! Halten!"* The Doberman froze in place, still poised to attack. Mrs. Helford hummed into the room in her wheelchair, her face livid, a study in barely controlled fury. "What are you doing in here?"

"I ah, I got lost," Max said, swallowing. "I couldn't find my way out."

"Lost?"

"Hey, it's not like you've got street signs posted in here,"

Max said. "Look, would you mind calling off your dog, please? I wasn't going to steal anything."

"Weren't you? Perhaps not, but you're still a dangerous man, Mr. Maxwell, Sutliffe can attest to that."

"Come on, lady, you know that was an accident. He shouldn't have grabbed—dammit, will you call off the dog?"

"Don't worry about the dog, Maxwell. You're safe enough, for the moment. How much do you want?"

"How m—? What are you talking about?" Max said. "How much for what?"

"Don't play games with me, Maxwell. Money is what you really came for, isn't it? So what's your price? How much to forget what you've seen?"

"Mrs. Helford," Max said carefully, "I'm not sure what I have seen, or what it means. But one thing I do know, you haven't got enough money to make me forget it. At least not until I understand it."

She stared at him, hard, her gaze as intense and unwavering as the dog's. "You really don't know, do you," she said at last. "Eddie didn't tell you."

"Eddie? You mean Bronfman? No, he didn't tell me anything. He was dead when I met him. Both times."

"Both? I don't understand."

"Mrs. Helford," Max said, taking a deep breath, "last night I embalmed Mr. Bronfman. But not for the first time. I'm fairly certain I worked on him once before. In July, 1972. Only his name wasn't Bronfman then, and it wasn't Helford either," he added, jerking a thumb at the painting over the fireplace. "It was Connolly, or Connery. Something like that."

"I—see," she said slowly, nodding in comprehension. "Sutliffe is convinced you were one of Eddie's—playmates; but I should have known better. You're not his type. Very well, Mr. Maxwell, under the circumstances perhaps we can work something out, though you should bear in mind your bargaining position isn't strong."

"I'm not following you at all."

"And perhaps you won't be able to 'follow me,' as you put it. How much do you understand about art, for instance?"

"Not much," Max admitted, "but enough to know that you must have a couple of million bucks' worth sitting around out here."

"Not correct. The art that I own is worth more than I'd care to discuss, but the art on display in my home is worth only a few hundred thousand, Mr. Maxwell. The sculpture, the paintings are only reproductions, excellent ones but copies nonetheless. The originals are much too valuable to be kept anywhere but a vault. Now do you understand, Mr. Maxwell?"

"I'm—not sure. What are you saying? That the man—men—I worked on were clones or something?"

"Actors, Mr. Maxwell, of a suitable physical type, willing to undergo minor cosmetic surgery in return for salary and benefits totaling roughly a hundred thousand a year, for three years. Sutliffe recruits them in Los Angeles. Acting is a precarious profession. We have no problem finding volunteers."

"You're right out of your tree, you know that?"

"So I've been told," she said coolly, unoffended. "Morbid obsession is the clinical term. I even put up with analysis for a while. Until I realized I was throwing away perfectly good money to rid myself of one of the few sources of pleasure left open to me. I decided it would be more satisfying to enjoy my obsession than to cure it."

"And what happens to these—actors? When their contracts are up, I mean?"

"They're—remodeled, and move on to other things, with

161

a substantial income guaranteed as long as they remain discreet."

"And what about Bronfman? And the other one? Were they indiscreet?"

"Indiscreet?"

"All right, I'll spell it out. How is it that two of your 'reproductions' wound up dead, Mrs. Helford?"

"Two?" she said, arching her eyebrows. "Actually there have been three, over the years. You see, the kind of person who's willing to take on a job like this tends to be a bit unstable emotionally, I'm afraid. Sutliffe does his best to screen them, but . . ." She shrugged. "Eddie Bronfman had a drug habit. Cocaine, I believe, and Tim Kennelly mixed drinking and driving once too often. I was especially sorry to lose Tim. Drunk or sober, he was good company."

"I . . . see."

"I doubt it," she said. "I know what you're thinking, Mr. Maxwell, it shows. But spare me your contempt. I had a good life once, until war and polio took it away. I've salvaged what I could from the wreckage, and I live as I choose. Is your own life so much better?"

"No," Max admitted, "I guess not. You may live in a glass house here, Mrs. Helford, but I'm in no position to throw stones."

"Fair enough. Which brings us to you, Mr. Maxwell. I value my privacy. I'm willing to pay to protect it. Can we reach an understanding, do you think?" She casually patted the Doberman. Its gaze never wavered from Max's throat.

"You don't have to buy me, Mrs. Helford," Max said, eyeing the dog. "In my business, discretion comes with the territory. Besides, who would I tell? My clients?"

"I'd *prefer* to have a financial arrangement. One that's legal and binding, if you know what I mean. Don't worry about the money, Mr. Maxwell, I can afford it."

"All right," Max shrugged, "if that's what you want. But it's really not necessary."

"Trust me, Mr. Maxwell, it's necessary, if not now, then later. Come back tomorrow, if it's convenient for you, and talk to Mr. Sutliffe. You'll find him quite a reasonable man when you don't knock him about." She touched the joystick on the arm of her wheelchair, swiveling it slowly around. "Lee will see you home. I ah . . ."

"Is something wrong?" She was staring past him, and he glanced over his shoulder, following her gaze. She was frowning at the portrait over the fireplace, her eyes flicking back and forth between Jason Helford's face and his own. He met her gaze, and felt the full force of its hungry intensity.

"You know," she said, "physically you're very near—"

"No," he said softly, shaking his head, "not a chance."

"Are you quite sure? The financial arrangements—"

"I'm sure," he interrupted, gently cutting her off. "The past is like . . . New York City. It's a nice place to visit, but I wouldn't want to live there."

"Wouldn't you?" she said, her eyes holding him effortlessly, scanning his soul like a secondhand magazine. "Wouldn't you, really? Well. Perhaps not. Lee will be along directly, Mr. Maxwell. But ah, don't be too hasty. Sleep on the idea. You can give Sutliffe your answer tomorrow. *Raus,* Hanover." The chair hummed her out of the room, the dog trotting obediently after.

And then he was alone again, with Nat King Cole and Jason Helford. Max helped himself to a snifter of brandy from a decanter on the bar, glancing around the room as he poured, absorbing its ambience, its excellence, then eased himself into one of the overstuffed chairs facing the fireplace. And Jason Helford's portrait. A handsome man, Jason, no doubt about it.

He rolled the brandy around on his palate, savoring its smoky aroma, feeling its warmth glide gently down the back of his throat, the soft, slow-motion explosion in the pit of his stomach. The chair was leather, real leather, and comfortable. Very comfortable indeed.

Candles in the Rain

From a distance it looked like a modern-day siege of Rome. A small army of tents and campers were arrayed in a field across from the air-base entrance, and a ragged line of demonstrators were pacing along the shoulder of the road. But as I threaded my battered Chevy van past haphazardly parked cars and strolling protesters, the sense of conflict waned a bit.

The marchers were a mix of scruffy college kids and only slightly less scruffy adults in fashionably frayed denims, working-class duds a la Ralph Lauren. I gave them points for tenacity though. It was a chill, drizzly day but their spirits seemed high and dry.

Their placards were straightforward: No Nukes, No Incinerator. Ban Bombs and Toxic Waste. And on a less enlightened note: Don't Give America Back to the Redskins.

The airfield looked secure enough, protected by a fifteen-foot chain-link fence crowned with coils of bayonet wire. There were air police on duty at the gate, and a county sheriff's black-and-white parked on the shoulder of the road, flashers swirling slowly in the rain. The billboard beside the entrance was as formidable as the fence: lightning bolts clenched in an armored fist. Bullock Air Force Base, Strategic Air Command, Crater Creek, Michigan.

The air-police gate guard, starched and immaculate in white gloves and cap, snapped to attention as I pulled up and gave me a smart salute. I returned it on reflex. Old habits die hard.

"Good afternoon, sir, welcome to Bullock. Can I help you?"

"My name's Delacroix. I have an appointment to see the base Commander, Colonel Webber."

"Yes, sir," the sergeant said. "Could I see some identification, please?" He gave my driver's license a quick once over, then peered into an empty van. "Are you alone, Mr. Delacroix? It was my understanding that the Ojibwa Council was sending a delegation."

"They have," I said. "I'm it."

"I see," he said doubtfully. "A delegation of one?"

"You just have the one air base to give away, right?"

"Yessir," he said, frowning. "Still . . ." A bottle arched high in the air from behind the county black-and-white and smashed in the middle of the road, an explosion of beer foam and splintered glass.

"What's going on across the road, Sergeant?"

"The usual weekend demonstration," he said sourly, handing me a plastic visitor's card. "The local peaceniks have been picketing Bullock for years. Now that it's closing, they're griping about the base incinerator staying open. No pleasing 'em, I guess."

"At least they care enough to get wet," I said.

"Or they ain't got sense enough to get outa the rain," the sergeant said. "You'll find Colonel Webber at the base reception center just up the road. Please keep your pass with you at all times. Enjoy your visit, Mr. Delacroix." He waved me past and saluted. This time I didn't return it.

The base reception center was easy to find. It was the only building with cars parked in front of it. The others I passed were all closed and padlocked. On a field that once supported an entire wing of B-52s, only one solitary plane remained on the tarmac, a transport of some kind, with USAF markings. Beyond it, the runway stretched away endlessly into the silvery drizzle, silent and empty as a parking lot on the moon.

The portico in front of the entrance was draped with a red-white-and-blue banner. Welcome Michigan Ojibwa Council. I brushed the road dust off my corduroy sportcoat, straightened my tie, and walked in.

The reception room was jammed, a cocktail conclave in full swing, mostly civilians, men in suits, women in spring dresses, with a smattering of men in USAF blue uniforms scattered through the crowd. A gaggle of reporters and cameramen were clustered near the door and a refreshment table piled with sandwiches and hors d'oeuvres. Conversation died a slow death as I entered. I had a momentary flash of a half-forgotten dream, walking into high school minus my trousers.

A mid-thirtyish Native American woman in a stylish umber suit, her dark hair cropped boyishly short, left her companions and walked over. She had an open, honest face, and an eager smile. "Hello, I'm Eva Redfern. Are you with the delegation?"

"Not exactly," I said. "I am the delegation. My name's Delacroix, tribal constable from Algoma County. Can we talk somewhere for a moment? Privately?"

"I think we'd better," she said, her smile fading. A pity. I followed her back out under the portico. "Now, what's going on? When are the others arriving? We're running late already."

"We're going to run a little later, I'm afraid. The council voted last night to send me down to inspect the facility. If everything checks out, I've been authorized to accept the base on their behalf. Tomorrow."

"Tomorrow?" she echoed, stunned. "Are they out of their minds? I've spent weeks negotiating this arrangement. The transfer is set for this afternoon, and this is not a done deal, Delacroix. Not until the papers are signed. If we stall—"

"No one's stalling. Anytime somebody wants to cede land back to the tribes we'll take it. They just want me to take a last hard look at it."

"No offense, Mr. Delacroix, but this is hardly a police matter. Why did they send a constable?"

"Because I know a little about military bases. I served on a few. Look, I'm not your enemy, Miss Redfern, but I have my instructions. The sooner I carry them out, the sooner we'll get things back on schedule. Unfortunately, since they only called me in on this last night, I barely had time to scan the paperwork involved. Would you be kind enough to brief me? Please?"

Irritation and professionalism skirmished in her dark eyes for a moment. Professionalism won.

"All right. In a nutshell, Bullock is being closed. There was a government auction, and Kanelos Waste Disposal won the bidding. But since all Mr. Kanelos really wants is the base waste incinerator and a few hundred acres of runway for parking, he's offered to cede the base to the Ojibwa Council in return for a permanent lease on the incinerator and parking area."

"Which sounds almost too good to be true. Why should he give us the base?"

"To avoid taxes," she said simply. "Since the state can't tax tribal land, Mr. Kanelos can operate the waste facility tax free, and we get roughly five thousand acres of land, gratis."

"Most of which is covered with concrete," I said.

"Dammit, it's still a good deal for us, Delacroix. Have you ever heard the old saying about looking a gift horse in the mouth?"

"Yes, ma'am. I also remember one about Greeks bearing gifts. Shall we get on with this?"

"I guess we haven't much choice. But by God, you'd better not blow this deal."

Redfern led me through the crush to a corner where the base commander was holding court. There was no other word for it. In his impeccably tailored blue uniform, close-cropped sandy hair, with just a trace of silver at the temples, Webber cut a striking military figure. The granite-faced black master sergeant standing half a pace behind him added to the effect. Webber was chatting with a gaunt vampire of a man, fortyish, with blue jowls, and fluid-filled pouches under his eyes. He was wearing a dark suit and shirt, a single strand of gold chain nestling in the hollow of his throat.

"Colonel Webber, Mr. Kanelos," Redfern said, "I'd like to introduce Mr. Delacroix, of the Ojibwa Council." She gave them a quick briefing on the situation. I expected annoyance, and got it.

"Mr. Delacroix," Webber said coolly, not bothering to offer his hand, "what's the problem? I was under the impression everything was arranged. Some members of the council having . . . reservations, so to speak?"

"As far as I know, everything's a go, Colonel," I said. "Or it will be as soon as I complete my inspection."

"But what kind of a survey can you do in a few hours?" Kanelos said heatedly. "The base is six thousand acres. Look, I've put myself on the line for you people. I stretched myself to my financial limits to win the bidding and I'm even giving hiring preference to Indians at the incinerator facility. Hell, I should think you people might show a bit more gratitude—"

"Easy, Frank," Webber interrupted, "the constable's just following orders, and as a soldier I can relate to that. Sergeant Jenkins, why don't you give Delacroix a tour of the base, show him whatever he wants to see. Frank, we'd better talk to the newspeople. I don't want any bad press over this." He stalked off without a backward glance, sweeping Kanelos along in his wake.

The sergeant shrugged. "Don't mind the boss. He's used to having people jump when he says frog. What do you want to see, Mr. Delacroix?"

"The major facilities, PX, hangars. As much as I can in the time we have," I said, watching the colonel and Kanelos disappear into the mob scene.

"I'm coming too," Redfern said.

"Then we'd better get started," Jenkins said. "The power's already been shut off to the perimeter lighting. When it gets dark out on the field these days, it really gets dark."

"What happened to the command and electronics bunkers?" I asked. We were in a closed Jeep, humming down a rain-slick runway toward the shadowy mountains of a hangar, Jenkins driving, me riding shotgun, Redfern in the back seat.

"All strategic or classified equipment was dismantled and shipped back to SAC headquarters, or destroyed on site," Jenkins said. "We blew the bunkers, filled 'em in, and laid sod on the graves. How do you know about bunkers? You serve on a base?"

"A few," I said. "U Bon, Thailand, and Tan Son Nhut."

"No kidding? I was U Bon during the war. When were you there?"

"When I was too young to know better."

"I know the feeling." Jenkins smiled, relaxing a little. "Okay, if you know bases, then you know there ain't all that much more I can show you. You've seen most of the buildings, there's really nothin' else to see but a lotta open concrete."

"And trucks," I said. "What are all those trucks doing on the far end of the runway?"

"Toxic waste tankers, waitin' their turn at the incinerator. Must be twenty of 'em down there at any given time. They come from all over the state. It's big business, waste disposal. It's closed for the weekend now, but come Monday they'll be humpin'. Pardon my French, ma'am. Sometimes when the wind's right, it smells a little funky, but mostly you can't hardly tell it's there. You want to drive over, take a closer look?"

"No, what Kanelos does with his end of the base is his business. I think I've seen enough. Let's head back."

"Fine by me," Jenkins said, wheeling the Jeep in a quick U-turn. "I served three tours on Bullock. Hate to see it like this. It's like attendin' your own funeral."

"I should think you'd be happy," Eva said. "No more wars, or a least no big ones."

"Oh, I don't miss war, ma'am. Nobody hates fightin' more'n the people who might have to bleed. But soldierin's an honest trade, and not such a bad life. How 'bout you, Delacroix? You ever miss the life?"

"The people sometimes," I said. "Never the life. What's all the hubbub over by the entrance?"

"Anti-nuke parade." Jenkins grinned, checking his watch. "Right on time, as usual. Wanna check it out? Way the world's goin', it may be the last one."

Redfern sighed. "I certainly hope so."

"Yes ma'am," Jenkins said, his smile fading, "me too."

Jenkins parked the Jeep in the reception-center lot and the three of us trotted briskly to the portico. The rain had started again, a steady, chilly drizzle, driven by the wind. The media people and some of the party-goers had wandered out to watch, but except for the cameramen filming the march through the fence, no one strayed from shelter. There was no reason to do so.

171

The local peace movement seemed to be winding down with a whimper, not a bang. A line of demonstrators formed a lopsided ring in the road opposite the gate. They were carrying candles, but except for a few who had umbrellas as well, most of the flames guttered in the first few moments. Still, I had to admire their persistence. They marched in a circle in the blustery dusk and drizzle for ten minutes or so, singing "Give Peace a Chance," out of tune, and out of step with each other. And with the times.

"Not much of a show, is it?" Colonel Webber said, moving up beside me. "Not like the old days. A few years ago there were a couple of hundred every weekend, blocking the entrance, chaining themselves to the fence, and being a general nuisance. Arrogant fools, the lot of them. They simply didn't see the big picture."

"I served a dozen years, in two wars, and I'm not sure I ever saw it either," I said mildly. "Maybe the picture seems clearer up at forty thousand feet."

"Perhaps it does," Webber said. "Sergeant Jenkins tells me you've finished your tour. I take it you're satisfied?"

"Yes, sir. As far as I'm concerned we can finalize the transfer tomorrow. I'll phone the council tonight, and—"

But Webber wasn't listening. He'd turned, frowning, peering into the drizzle. Even the marchers gradually stumbled to a halt, listening. Out on the tarmac, behind the curtain of rain, there was the sound of drumming. Tom-toms. And the chanting of many voices, instantly recognizable as Native Americans. But not a tribe I knew. Not Ojibwa.

"Sergeant," Webber snapped, "get out there and secure that aircraft. I don't know what's—"

WHOOOMP! Suddenly, far out on the runway, a pillar of fire erupted, a hundred-foot geyser of flame. And then there was an unearthly wail, louder than the drums and chanting.

And a figure came running toward us out of the rain, a human being, ablaze, engulfed in fire, howling like a beast. He staggered, then fell to his knees, crawling like a smashed insect, screaming.

Jenkins was the first to react, sprinting for the Jeep. I followed, scrambling into the passenger's seat as he gunned the Jeep out of the lot and raced down the runway toward the burning man.

He jammed on the brakes a few yards short of the figure on the tarmac, and I banged headfirst into the windshield, hard. Jenkins yanked a portable fire extinguisher from its dash clip and ran to the figure cowering on the concrete. I followed on shaky legs. He quickly fogged the man down, then trotted beyond him and killed two smaller fires as well.

I knelt beside the blackened man, dazed, uncertain. His clothes were still smoldering, and he was moaning, in soul-deep agony. And I didn't know what to do. He smelled smoky sweet, almost . . . I recoiled mentally from the thought.

"Mister," I pleaded softly, "please, just hang on, okay? Help's coming . . ."

The moaning stopped. And the breathing. My God. I tried to roll him onto his back to give mouth-to-mouth, but his body was rigid.

His arms were locked over his face as though they were welded to it and I couldn't pull them away. And then a piece of seared flesh peeled off in my hand, and I lurched to my feet, gagging, and stumbled off down the runway, staggering like a gut-shot bear. Fleeing the smoking body. And the horror.

Jenkins caught me after twenty yards or so, grasping my shoulders, steadying me down to a walk, then stopping me. We stood there for a long time in silence, in the rain.

Behind us, the sheriff's patrol car screeched to a halt

beside the Jeep. Doors slammed. People were shouting. And still Jenkins and I stood there. Holding each other. Like family at a funeral.

"Are you all right?" he asked at last.

"Yeah," I managed. My voice sounded as weak and shaky as I felt. "Is he . . . ?"

"He was dead before we got there," Jenkins said, releasing me cautiously, as if afraid I might fall. "He just didn't know it. There was nothing you could do. Nothing anyone could do."

He turned and trudged slowly back to the crowd gathered around the figure on the field, shrouded now by a blanket.

The sheriff rose slowly from beside the body, carefully unfolding the charred remains of a wallet.

"Buck," he read softly, "Geronimo G. My God, it's Jerry Buck." Eva Redfern paled and turned away, her eyes swimming. I touched her arm.

"You know him?" I said.

"I, ahm, no," she said, swallowing. "Not really. He's Native American but he's not Ojibwa. He's just a side—he came up from Detroit a year or so ago."

"A sidewalk Indian," I said.

"Yes," she nodded. "Lakota, I think. From out West somewhere. Montana maybe. Drank his way out of a line job at Ford. Moved up here, did odd jobs. He was an alcoholic."

"Why would he do this?"

"I . . . don't know. I didn't really know him well."

"When you got to him, did he say anything to you?" the sheriff asked me.

"No, he . . . didn't speak. He couldn't."

"Well, it's apparently a suicide," the sheriff said, glancing around. "Had to be. Nobody else could have been near him

174

out here. Found a gas can back on the tarmac maybe sixty yards away. And what's left of a pile of rags. And a boom box. That's what the Indian music was. Apparently he just turned on the tape, doused himself with gas, and, ahm . . . set himself afire. Crazy. Had to be crazy."

"Maybe not," I said slowly.

"Why not?" Jenkins asked. "You know him?"

"No. But even a crazy wouldn't choose to die like this. It's too . . . horrible."

"But what makes you think—?"

"Dammit, I've seen this before! My first tour in 'Nam, the monks were burning themselves in the damn streets! And people said they were crazy. And nobody listened to them!"

"Easy, bro," Jenkins said quietly. "This ain't no Vietnamese police state. We're in backwoods freakin' Michigan. If the man had a point to make, he didn't have to smoke himself to do it. All he had to do was walk up and speak his piece, right? Nobody woulda stopped him."

"I don't know," I said, swallowing, trying to clear my head. "All I know is, the base was supposed to be transferred to the Ojibwa today. He must have been trying to stop it for some reason."

"You can't be sure of that," Jenkins said.

"You're right, I'm not. But I'm not going to go ahead with the transfer until we know."

"Look, Mr. Delacroix," Colonel Webber said, stiffening, "I know this has been a shock, to all of us. But surely the act of the demented individual—"

"You don't know he was demented," I said.

"But he was crazy, or nearly so," Redfern said. "He was borderline retarded and an alcoholic as well. Who knows what was in his mind? Delacroix, the colonel's right, this is too important to our people to stop now. He was just—"

"A drunk," I finished. "And not even Ojibwa. So forget it? Business as usual?"

"That isn't what I meant," she said, flushing. "It's just that—"

"Mr. Delacroix, I've tried to be patient, but I have my orders," Webber interrupted. "I agreed to delay the proceedings until tomorrow, but that's the best I can do. I must have your decision then, or I'll have to withdraw from our agreement. Since the man's death occurred on the base, it's technically a military matter, so if you wish to make inquiries, I can loan you Sergeant Jenkins to give you some official standing. I assume you'd have no objections, Sheriff Brandon?"

Brandon shrugged. "No, sir. It's a straightforward suicide. The decedent's state of mind isn't really a police matter, and frankly I've got my hands full as it is. As long as you don't harass anybody, make all the inquiries you like."

"You don't seem too happy about this," I said to Jenkins. We were in his Jeep, headed toward the main gate. Eva Redfern had stayed behind to try to pacify the colonel and Kanelos.

"I'm not," Jenkins said bluntly, keeping his eyes on the road. "I put up with these peacenik crazies every weekend for years, picketing the base, blockin' the gate to get themselves arrested. Now I'm one day away from gettin' outa here and . . . I got my own job to do, you know?"

"Maybe if you'd done it better we wouldn't be in this mess."

"What's that supposed to mean?"

"You're in charge of base security, right? So how did this guy manage to get out in the middle of the runway?"

"Wouldn't be hard. He couldn't have climbed the fence carrying the boom box and a gas can, so I'm guessin' he just cut the fence and walked in. The electronic barriers were disconnected last month when the last of the classified equipment was shipped out."

"And the fence isn't patrolled?"

"We inspect the perimeter once a shift, about every eight hours. I've only got six men and I need 'em at the gate."

"What about guard dogs? Most bases use them on the perimeter."

"We, ahm, we haven't used the dogs in a while. To be honest, I haven't worried much about security. Hell, there's nothin' left on Bullock worth stealin'."

"Maybe not," I said grimly, "but apparently there was something worth dying for."

Jenkins eased the Jeep cautiously down the lane between the demonstrators' tents and campers. There were only a few dozen left. He parked beside a battered trailer, covered with bumper stickers: No Nukes, Peace Now. The usual.

"This is Doc Klein's trailer," Jenkins said, switching off the Jeep. "He's been organizing peace marches since the sixties, and bugging me for at least ten years. If anybody knows anything about your guy, the doc will."

"Will he talk to me? With you there I mean?"

"No sweat," Jenkins said drily. "Gettin' the doc to talk isn't a problem. It's gettin' him to shut up. Come on."

We jogged through the downpour to the trailer door. Jenkins rapped and after a moment the door swung open, revealing a squat stump of a man, fiftyish, balding, with a fringe of shoulder-length, baby-fine blond hair, and a neatly trimmed blond beard. A bulldog pipe was clamped in the corner of his jaw. "Well, well," he said evenly, "if it isn't my favorite arresting officer."

"Doc," Jenkins said, "can we see you a minute?"

"Of course, come in, come in. I wouldn't leave a dog out

on a night like this. Or a sergeant.”

Jenkins introduced me to Klein, and we shook hands. The three of us filled the postage-stamp camper like pickles in a jar. I sat on the narrow cot that stretched across one end of the room, Jenkins leaned against the door, while Klein sat in the lone chair at the tiny table for one. A pot was burbling on the small camp stove. The aroma of chili and cherry-blend pipe smoke filled the room like incense in a bazaar.

“Mr. Delacroix, I can’t tell you how sorry I am about what happened today,” Dr. Klein said earnestly. “We’re on opposite sides of this matter politically but, well, I’m sorry. It’s a terrible irony that after a dozen years of peaceful demonstrations, such a thing would happen on the last day.”

“Did you know the man who died, Doctor?” I asked.

He nodded. “A little. As well as anyone, I suppose. He, ahm, he drank, you know.”

“So I understand. You said we’re on opposite sides. Why? What have you got against us?”

“Against the Ojibwa? Nothing. My goodness, your people have been my life’s work.”

“The doc’s an archaeologist, specializin’ in Native American culture,” Jenkins said. “When he’s not playin’ rabble-rouser, that is.”

“I see,” I said. “Then why is your group opposed to our taking over the base?”

“Because of the way it was arranged. We believe you’re being used.”

“Used by whom?”

“By Kanelos, and Webber as well. Kanelos didn’t win the bidding, you know. The high bidder was a salvage company that intended to dismantle the buildings and tear up the runway for the scrap concrete. Colonel Webber awarded the bid to Mr. Kanelos as being least disruptive to the community.”

"Hey, he was right," Jenkins put in. "It'd take a helluva lot of blasting to break up the runway. It's a foot thick, most places."

"More disruptive than flying B-52s loaded with nuclear weapons out of there twenty-four hours a day?" Klein countered. "At least when the blasting was finished, we'd have the land back. As it is, we're trading one hazardous nuisance for another."

"But the incinerator isn't new, is it?" I asked.

"No," Klein said, "but it's never been operated on the scale it is now. And by trading you the land in return for a lifetime lease, Kanelos not only avoids paying taxes, he also avoids federal EPA *inspections*. Did you know that?"

"No," I said, glancing at Jenkins. "I didn't. And Jerry Buck? Was he strongly against the transfer too?"

"Jerry? No, not that I know of," Klein said, puzzled. "He was hardly the political type."

"You mean he wasn't part of your group?"

"No. Not at all."

"But you said you knew him."

"I did, but not from the movement. We're doing an archaeological dig at an old Anishnabeg burial ground just west of the base. Jerry worked for me there, doing manual labor, catch as catch can. For beer money, really."

"Look, I don't understand, Doctor," I said. "If he wasn't political, why on earth would he have done what he did?"

"I honestly don't know. I've been asking myself the same thing since they told me it was Jerry. Joe Gesh might be able to tell you more."

"Joe Gesh?" I noticed that Jenkins stiffened at the mention of the name.

"He's a local character, an Ojibwa, lives in a shack on the edge of Bullock swamp near the burial ground. Jerry was staying with him out there, learning what he could."

"About what?"

"How to live in the past." Klein smiled. "Old Joe's an atavism, a throwback, the last of the wild Indians. He helps me at the dig occasionally, identifying tufts of decorative fur or animal tracks. He's incredibly knowledgeable."

"Oughta be," Jenkins said. "He eats most anything that walks or crawls back there."

"I guess we'd better talk to him," I said, rising. "One last question, Doctor Klein, could Buck's death have anything to do with this burial-ground dig you're doing? Will the transfer affect it in any way?"

"Nothin' to affect," Jenkins snorted. "I been back there, ain't nothin' to see."

"He's right on both counts," Klein said, smiling. "There is very little to see. Cracked stones from fire pits, a few pottery shards, discarded tools. The Anishnabeg lived on this land for nearly fifteen hundred years, and left almost no traces. I wish we could say the same. But the dig won't be affected by the closing of the base. And I doubt that it mattered much to Jerry anyway. He wasn't really serious about the work."

"Maybe not," I said, "but he was damn serious about something."

"Yes," Klein nodded soberly, "I guess he must have been."

"You know this Gesh character, don't you?" I asked. We were in the Jeep, following the narrow track along the outside of the perimeter fence.

"I know him," Jenkins said grimly. "Tangled with him more'n once. And if Buck was livin' with that ol' man, it might explain a lot about him goin' off the deep end."

"Why?"

" 'Cause Gesh is nuts, that's why. Lives back in the

swamp like the last damn Apache or somethin'."

"Or Ojibwa," I said. "Why did you tangle with him?"

"Because base security is my job, and every now and then we hear gunfire back in that swamp. And we have to check it out. And that old man ain't heavy into hospitality, I'll tell ya."

"Maybe he was poaching, thought you might be the law."

"No," Jenkins said positively, "it wasn't that. He knew damn well we were air force. Even recognized my rank. Kept his gun on me the whole time anyway."

"And you just let that pass?"

"Yeah, well, maybe I shouldn't have." Jenkins sighed, peering past the wipers into the downpour. "But I didn't figure it was worth gettin' anybody killed over, and that's what would've happened if we'd tried to disarm him. He was scared to death of us, and crazy as a loon."

"Why do you say he was crazy?"

"He was talkin' crazy. And he kept throwin' tobacco at me."

"Tobacco?"

"That's right. Held his rifle in one hand, aimed at my belly, and kept tossin' bits of loose tobacco at me, little pinches out of a can. Prince Albert, I think it was. And talkin' right out of his head."

"About what?"

"Ghosts," Jenkins said, glancing over at me with a fox's grin. "You know, I'm a black man in a white man's country, and I been called a lotta things in my time, but never a ghost. He kept callin' me a ghost. You sure you want to talk to him?"

"No." I sighed. "But I guess I have to. And maybe I'd better see him alone, if you don't mind."

"Hell no, I don't mind. Best news I've had all day," Jenkins said, easing the Jeep to a halt. He shrugged out of his raincoat and gave it to me. "There's a flashlight in the glove box. See that path up ahead to the left? It'll take you back to old Joe's shack, half a mile or so back in the swamp. Seems like it goes forever, but stay on it. And bro? You watch your ass, hear? If that ol' man wastes you, I'm gonna have to fill out a godawful stack of paperwork."

I didn't bother to reply. The rain was on me in an icy torrent the moment I stepped out of the Jeep, like standing under a waterfall. Jenkins's raincoat was little help. I was soaked to the bone before I'd stumbled fifty yards down the muddy track.

I've hunted all my life, so the trail wasn't all that hard to follow. Rough going though, sodden, slippery with uncertain footing. Tag alders and cedar saplings clawed at me out of the darkness, as if asking me to bide awhile, to share their loneliness. I spotted the faint glow of a lamp ahead.

Gesh's shack wasn't a shack exactly. It was a hogan, a rectangular log hut roofed with sod. It was crude, but not totally primitive. It had glass windows, and tarpaper had been tacked over a patch where the sod had washed away.

"Hello," I shouted. "Mr. Gesh?"

No answer. The lamp in the cabin winked out. "Mr. Gesh, my name's Delacroix. I'd like to talk to you."

"What do you want?" The voice was a low rasp, barely louder than a whisper.

"For openers, to come in out of the rain. I have news for you."

After what seemed like a month, a match flickered in the cabin and the lamp glowed to life. The door swung slowly open on leather hinges. "Come ahead. But move slow."

Even after the darkness of the forest, the hogan was dim, lit by a single kerosene lamp hanging from a sapling rafter. The air was thick with the stench of tallow and rancid suet from the hides stretched over ash hoops hanging on the walls, raccoon, lynx, muskrat. Gesh watched me from the shadows in the far corner of the room. He was smaller than I expected, a wiry little gnome of a man, grey hair tied back in a ratty ponytail, a brown, seamed face, carved from mahogany. He was wearing a green-and-black plaid flannel coat, faded jeans, worn moccasins. Even his rifle was small. A bolt-action Marlin .22. A trapper's gun. After a moment he lowered it, and leaned it in the corner.

"You're from up north someplace, aren't ya?" he said.

"Yes, sir. From Algoma. Bear Clan. How did you know?"

"Because your eyes don't get big. The young ones come out here from town, they always look around like my house is a museum or somethin'. But you know what things are," he said, gesturing at the hides, the hogan.

"I trapped for a few years, after I got out of the army," I said. "Lived with the Cree, up in Ontario."

"What was it like, that country?"

"Empty," I said. "And hungry. Winters last a hundred years."

"Here too, sometimes." He nodded. "Sit. Sorry it's cold in here, I'm outa kerosene for the stove. Here, wrap up in this, you'll be warm after a while." He handed me a frayed army blanket. I draped it over my shoulders and sat on a tree-stump stool that obviously doubled as a chopping block.

"You bring anything to drink?" Gesh asked.

"No," I said. "Sorry. I didn't know I was coming."

"It's okay." He shrugged. "You said you had news. Bad, right?"

"I'm afraid so. They tell me Jerry Buck was staying with you."

"A few months. Tried to dry him out, straighten him out. Didn't work. What happened to him?"

"He, ah, he's dead, Mr. Gesh. Soaked himself with gasoline, and . . . he burned."

"On the base," the old man said. It wasn't a question.

"Yes."

"Sweet Jesus," Gesh said, swallowing hard. "I told him. Stupid bastard."

"What did you tell him?"

"To stay off there. That they'd kill him."

"Who would?"

"The dead pilots, or whatever they are. The ghosts. They kill everything out there. All them planes, loaded with bombs. With death. Death is all they know. They killed themselves, now they kill everything else."

"I don't understand," I said.

"Maybe you can't," he said. "Do you know about ghosts?"

"I'm—not sure. I've never seen one."

"You won't see these either," the old man snorted. "They're dead. A long time ago. Fifteen, twenty years maybe. They died in the spring, in the rain. Now when it rains, they come back."

"Who comes back?" I asked.

"The dead flyers. The ones who died in the plane. Big one. I heard it fall in the night. Shook the ground. Thought it was the end of the damn world. I snuck over by the field, watched from the woods. There were a lotta bodies around, in them rubber bags, you know? Maybe a dozen. Maybe more. Nothing left of the damn plane. Junk. Pieces of it scattered half a mile. It was all gone the next day. The other airmen picked everything up, made it look like nothing happened. Like it had all been a dream. But it wasn't. I saw the dead men all right. And a few years later, their ghosts came back. They killed the dogs first, the ones that guarded the fence. Other animals too sometimes, coons, possums."

"Why do you think ghosts killed them?"

"Because they wasn't touched. No wounds, no blood. They just—take their souls. Leave the bodies behind. Dead all the same. Maybe the flyers weren't buried right. Maybe their souls are trapped out there and need food. I don't know. All I know is, they come back in the rain. And hunt."

"But Jerry Buck didn't just die. He was burned to death."

"Jerry was a man." Gesh shrugged. "Maybe he was harder to kill than the dogs."

"Maybe." I nodded, glancing around the hogan, inhaling the aroma of curing hides, and tobacco, and blood. A primeval scent that evoked a hazy memory of other lodges, in other places, long ago. Before I was born.

"Do you know what Jerry was doing out there?" I asked.

"Celebrating," the old man said. "Someone told him the air force is giving the base to the Ojibwa. Is that true?"

"Something like that," I said.

"But why? We don't have no planes."

"We'll make something out of it," I said. "We're good at that. You said Jerry went there to celebrate?"

"Yeah. He wasn't from here, he was Lakota Sioux from Montana. Knew a dance he learned in reservation school. Buffalo dance. Did it pretty good too. Had a tape of the drums and everything. He said he was gonna dance out on the runway, put on a show for the people. Maybe make a few dollars."

"I see," I said. "Jesus. He, ahm, he had a gas can with him."

"Not gas, kerosene," Gesh said. "He needed a fire for the dance. Took my kerosene and wet down some rags so they'd burn in the rain. Musta screwed it up. He was drinkin'. He was always drinkin'. It's all the young people know these days."

"Not so many," I said. "Not anymore. Are you sure it was

kerosene he took? Not gasoline?"

"I don't keep no gas here. Got no car or nothin'. Just use kerosene for the lamp, the stove."

"Yeah," I said. "Right. Look, there's going to be a ceremony at the base tomorrow. Would you like to come?"

"No," he spat. "No way. It's a bad place. Haunted. I won't go there."

"Suit yourself. Maybe I could come back here, sometime."

"Why?"

"To talk. I'll tell you how the Cree breed wolves. Maybe I'll even bring a couple beers."

The old man stared at me a long time, reading me. Then he shook his head. "I don't think so," he said quietly.

"No? Why not?"

"Because you ain't comin' back, Delacroix. I ain't stupid, just old. You don't believe me about them ghosts. I read it in your eyes. So you're gonna go see for yourself. Ain't you?"

I didn't want to lie to him. So I didn't answer.

"Thought so," he said, not bothering to conceal the contempt in his tone. "You got some education, I can tell by the way you talk. Jerry didn't know nothin'. Just a sidewalk Indian. But if you go out on that field, you'll be as dead as him. As dead as them dogs."

"I can take care of myself," I said. "I'll be back."

"No," he said. "You won't." And he turned his back on me, shutting me out. As though I were dead already.

"Took you long enough," Jenkins said as I climbed into the Jeep. "You find the shack?"

"I found it. The old man said Buck took a can of kerosene to soak some rags and start a small fire out on the runway. He was going to put on a little show. To celebrate the tribe taking over the base."

"But something went wrong?" Jenkins asked, his tone neutral.

"He'd been drinking. My guess is, he spilled some of the kerosene on himself. And when he lit the fire . . . he burned."

"Yeah." Jenkins nodded warily. "That must've been how it happened. It wasn't suicide, then?"

"No. He didn't go out there to die. He went out there to dance."

"So we can go ahead with the transfer ceremony tomorrow?"

"I don't see why not. Do you?"

"No," Jenkins said, visibly relaxing. "What happened was a damn shame. But we have to move on."

"Yeah, I guess we do. The old man said something odd, though. He said the field's haunted. By the ghosts of flyers who cracked up a plane a long time ago. That the ghosts killed Jerry somehow. That they killed your dogs too."

"I told you he was crazy."

"Is he? If the dogs had been patrolling the perimeter, Buck never could have gotten on the field."

"Yeah, well, they weren't. We had no reason to think anyone would try to penetrate the field, so we shipped the dogs out. Transferred 'em back to Offutt. Wish to hell I'd gone with 'em."

"What about the plane? Was there a crash?"

"Bullock was a Strategic Air Command base," Jenkins said warily. "We flew nuclear missions out of here twenty-four hours a day, seven days a week, for nearly thirty years. There was a cold war on, remember? Even if there were crackups, I couldn't tell you about 'em. It'd still be classified information. You were a soldier once. You know how it is, right?"

"Yes," I said. "I think so."

Jenkins dropped me off at my van and drove off to report

187

to his colonel. I trotted to my Chevy through the rain and scrambled in.

And started as a figure sat up in the back seat.

"Hi," Eva Redfern said. "Sorry. I wanted to make sure I didn't miss you. Must've fallen asleep. What did you find out?"

"That Jerry Buck's death was an accident," I said, starting the van. "Sort of."

"I don't understand."

"Neither do I, exactly. Have you got time to take a short ride with me?"

"I suppose so. Where are we going?"

"To the dogs," I said. "Or to where they used to be."

The kennels had been removed, but the chain-link dog runs were still in place, probably more trouble than it was worth to tear down. The concrete runs had been swept clean. But I found what I was looking for in the grass that had grown up beneath the edge of the fence. A chalky white pebble, not much bigger than a marble. I bounced it in my palm a moment, thinking. Then carried it back to the van.

"Well?" Redfern said. "What did you find?"

"A lump of truth," I said, passing her the pebble. "You've got fingernails, see if you can dent that."

"I can . . . scrape it a little," she said, "but I can't dent it. What is it? Chalk?"

"Nope, it's crap. A dog turd, to be specific. Hard as rock. Calcified."

"What?"

"Don't worry, it won't contaminate you. It's old. Probably a dozen years or so. And it was the only one I could find."

"And is this thing—" she tossed the turd into my ashtray and dusted off her hands. "Is this supposed to mean something?"

"Maybe. It might mean that what old Joe Gesh told me about the dogs was true," I said, slipping the van into drive and heading out onto the tarmac. "That they were killed a long time ago. As near as I can tell, no dogs have used those kennels for years."

"But why should that matter?"

"I'm not sure it does, but it makes me wonder if the rest of what he told me is true. About dead flyers. And ghosts that kill in the rain."

"You're not making much sense."

"I'm about to make even less," I said, easing the van to a halt on the runway. "Look, I'm going out there to look around. I'll leave the headlights on, but since I may lose track of them in the rain, I want you to blow the horn in exactly ten minutes. And keep blowing it, once a minute for fifteen minutes or so. If I'm not back by then, go to the air-police barracks, find Sergeant Jenkins and tell him what happened. He'll know what to do. Understand?"

"No. I don't understand any of this."

"Maybe there's nothing to understand," I said. "Maybe the old man really is crazy. It shouldn't take long to find out. One last thing. If I don't come back, whatever you do, don't come looking for me. I want your word on it."

"All right, I promise I won't look for you. But why?"

"Because if I'm not back in half an hour, you can offer tobacco to the spirits who haunt this place. I'll be one of them. The stupid one. The one who wouldn't listen to his elders."

I closed the van door on her objections, turned up the collar of Jenkins's raincoat, and trotted off into the rainy dark. I tried to move in a straight line, keeping the headlights directly behind me, but it was impossible. The third time I glanced over my shoulder to get a fix on the van, I couldn't see the lights anymore.

189

I chose to follow a seam in the concrete instead, hoping it would keep me moving in a more-or-less straight line down the tarmac, away from the van. I didn't meet any ghosts. At least, not at first. There was only the solitary slap of my boots in the puddles, as I trotted along in the sickly glow of the flashlight.

Big airfields have their own special reek, *eau de* exhaust fumes, scorched rubber from rough landings, the acrid stink of wing and windshield de-icer and fuel spills. The stench was strong at first, but seemed to fade as I jogged on. Bullock hadn't been used much for a while, perhaps the rain was rinsing the perfume away. Just as well.

It didn't sound like an airfield either. They're never silent. Always there's the scream of jets, taking off, landing, or just warming up, mingling with the constant rumble of support vehicles. Here there was nothing. Just the whisper of the drizzle. And the occasional whistle of the wind in the wire of the perimeter fencing.

It seemed oddly peaceful, running along in a halo of light, alone, hidden from the world of men by the gunmetal curtain of the rain. No ghosts, no dead dogs, nothing to see. . . . I checked my watch to see how long I'd been running, but the dial was wet and blurry and I couldn't quite make it out.

And then I fell. Hard. I tucked and rolled instinctively, skidding along in the water like an otter on a slide. The flashlight clattered away from me in the dark.

I lay there a few minutes, dazed, trying to catch my breath, gather my wits. God, I was tired, exhausted, heart pounding, head splitting. If I could just rest a bit. . . .

Sweet Jesus. The dogs. They'd died out here. In the rain. Just like this. I forced myself to my hands and knees and crawled toward the faint glow of the flashlight. It was lying beside a puddle, its light diffused, scattered into swirling rainbow bands, by the water, and the nearly invisible turquoise liquid floating on it. I tried to sniff it, but couldn't get a sense of what it was. And realized I couldn't smell anything at all, not the water or the wind. Nothing. And then I recognized the floating slick. Knew it for what it was. It was Death. In the rain. For the guard dogs. And Jerry Buck. And now for me.

I picked up the flashlight, but it was oily, slippery, and I fumbled it away, watched frozen with horror as it tumbled slow-motion down on the tarmac. And winked out.

I turned slowly in a circle, knuckling the rain out of my eyes, trying to get a sense of where I was. It was hopeless. I could only see a few feet. It didn't matter. I had to move, to get away, so I started walking, dazed and aching, stumbling along like a wino, lost in the belly of the beast.

I don't know how long I walked. Years. Then off to the left, I caught a glimpse of a monstrous shape. A ghostly aircraft? It wasn't real. Couldn't be. So I ignored it, and stumbled on. But then I saw a second silhouette, as huge as the first.

I turned and reeled toward them. And found the fence. And the trucks. Toxic-waste tankers, a line of them, a few yards beyond the fence. Waiting their turn at the incinerator. They seemed ugly and misshapen in the rain, foam streaming down their sides like lather, sizzling as the rain reacted to the specks of toxic sludge spatters.

I peered blearily through the fence for a night watchman, anyone. But there was no light, and the exit gate was locked. The tankers might as well have been on the moon. In the shape I was in, there was no way I could climb a fifteen-foot fence and fight through the bayonet wire. And if I got hung up there, I'd die as surely as—

I heard a groan. A low moan from behind me. I turned,

191

trying to place it . . . And realized what it was. The horn. Red-fern had started blowing the horn.

And without thinking, I started running toward it, shambling across the tarmac, a puppet without strings. Veering, stumbling, called on by the horn. And each time it was a little closer. Fifteen. She would blow it once a minute for fifteen minutes. How many had I heard? I couldn't remember. I only knew that to stop running was to die. Like the dogs.

I saw the van. Spotted the faint halo of the headlights ahead, off to the right. I swerved toward them. And fell, tumbling along on the concrete runway, knocking what breath I had out of me. And then Redfern was there, helping me crawl.

I couldn't make it through the van door. I vomited, head down, still on my hands and knees in the rain. I retched and spewed until there was nothing left to give, and then I lost that too.

But it helped. And the drive back toward the gate helped more. I hung my head out the window, drinking the nightwind and the rain, purging my lungs, and my soul.

"Do you have a car here?" I asked. It was the first thing I'd said since she found me.

"We'll leave it. You're going to the hospital in Crater Creek."

"No," I said, coughing. "I can't. If I go there we'll lose everything. And we've already paid too much. Jerry Buck paid for it. We can't back off now. Just stop at your car."

"No. I'm staying with you."

"You can't. There are arrangements you have to make for tomorrow. I want you to talk to Dr. Klein. He'll help us, I think."

"Klein? Why should he help?"

"Because at heart, he's basically a decent man," I said,

managing a weak smile. "But more important, he has a . . . warped sense of humor."

"What are you talking about?"

So I told her, and she said I was crazy. And she was right and I knew it. But I was so coldly enraged that I didn't care. I asked for her promise. And she gave it. Probably just to humor me. But she gave it. And that was enough.

"If you won't go to the hospital, at least come home with me," she said. "You can't stay here."

"I'll be all right. I'll rest. But I have one last bit of business to take care of first."

"This time of night? What kind of business?"

"Private," I said. "And personal. Very personal."

In the end she left me alone. She didn't like it, but she did. And I was sorry she did. I was sick and miserable and exhausted, and the only thing that kept me going was the thought that if I stopped for even a moment, I wouldn't get up for a week.

That, and the anger, of course. It was like a fire in my belly, a cold blaze of killing rage. For what had been done to Jerry Buck, and to me. And what they were trying to do to my people.

So I sat in my van, with the windows open, and the radio on, and waited. And thought. And I must have dozed off. Because the next thing I knew there was a wan hint of grey light on the horizon and the deejay was babbling about breakfast. I checked my watch. A little after four A.M. Time enough.

I fired up the van and drove over to the air-police barracks. There was a light in the day room. No others. I unlocked the van's glove compartment and took out my revolver, a Smith and Wesson .38. I checked it, and slipped it into my waistband.

I'd hoped they were too shorthanded to post a guard, and

there was none, I just walked in. The day room was immaculate, tiled floors gleaming, every magazine aligned. Something clicked in the corner, and I realized the large coffee urn had switched itself on automatically. They'd be up and about soon.

His room was easy to find. It was the largest, and his name was on the door. Chief Master Sergeant Purvis L. Jenkins.

It wasn't locked. I eased the door open, stepped in, and closed it behind me. I waited a moment for my eyes to adjust to the dimness, until I could make out his form on the bed. He was lying on his back, snoring softly, his fingers laced behind his head. I peeled off his sodden raincoat and draped it over him. Then I drew my weapon and switched on the lights.

He blinked instantly awake and alert. I was impressed. He glanced at me, and the gun, and the raincoat. And his eyes widened a fraction. But he didn't flinch.

"Shit," he said softly. "You went out there, didn't you?"

"That's right. I nearly died. Suffocated. Like the dogs."

"What, ahm, what are you going to do?"

"I'm going to ask you some questions. And you're gonna tell me the truth. Because if I even *think* you're lying to me, I'm going to fire this weapon in your general direction. I won't even have to hit you. And your raincoat will explode, and you'll burn. Just like Jerry Buck. Do you understand?"

He nodded, swallowing.

"The plane the old man told me about, the one that crashed. What was it?"

"Look, for God's sake—"

I eased back the hammer of the .38. He read my eyes, and saw his own death there. "It was a tanker," he said, grudgingly, as though each word was an agony. "A KC 135 Stratotanker."

"My God," I said softly. "And it crashed on takeoff?"

"Right. Spilled its whole payload. Nearly twenty thousand gallons of jet fuel. Just dumb luck it didn't explode on impact. But it was raining, and it didn't."

"Why didn't you recover it?"

"Because by morning, most of it was gone," he said simply. "Drained away, soaked into the gravel bed under the runway. It's low land at that end of the field, next to the marsh. There was no way to recover it short of tearing up the whole damn field, and we couldn't do that. Hell, there was a war on and we had to keep B-52s in the air twenty-four hours a day. Anyway, it was gone. So we went on flying missions, and figured we'd got off lucky. Until it showed up again three years later. And the guard dogs all died."

"In the spring," I said. "In the rain. From the fumes. Gasoline, not kerosene. Buck might have burned himself with kerosene, but it wouldn't have exploded the way it did."

"That's right. Basic physics, jet fuel's almost two pounds a gallon lighter than water, so when the water table rises high enough, we get seepage onto the field. More this year than most. Usually we don't get much, and not for long."

"It was long enough for Jerry Buck," I said. "It was forever."

"Yeah." He nodded. "Look, I'm—"

"Don't!" I snapped, cutting him off. "If you say you're sorry I swear to God I'll blow you away just for the hell of it. Now, maybe you couldn't clean up the fuel while the base was operational, but it's closing. Why not do it now?"

"Budget," he said bitterly. "With peace breakin' out, they've cut us to the bone. We've barely got money enough to keep a third of our force active. It'd cost millions to tear up the field to clean up the spill. We just don't have it anymore."

"But why us? Why dump it on the Ojibwa?"

"Two reasons. One, because you're broke, and wouldn't have the money to develop the field. We figured you'd open a gift shop or a bingo hall and that'd be it. You'd probably never come across the spill at all. And if you ever did, you likely wouldn't report it and risk losing the land."

"I see. And where does Kanelos fit in?"

"He's a front. If we'd just ceded the base to you, you might've had it inspected. This way it's maybe not the nicest deal in the world, but at least everybody gets something out of it."

"Everybody but Jerry Buck."

"That was an accident. He shouldn't have been out there."

"Maybe he wouldn't have been, if the area was posted as hazardous. And he sure as hell wouldn't have started that fire. Would he?"

"No, I suppose not. What are you going to do?"

"What I have to. Take the deal. Maybe it's a bad deal, but my people have never gotten any other kind. And as you said, at least there's something for everybody. Even for us."

"Good." He nodded. "You're doing the right thing. I'm sorry—"

I pulled the trigger. A reflex. The hammer clicked on an empty cylinder. Jenkins winced, then his eyes narrowed. "You bastard!"

"Easy," I said. "Maybe I just forgot to load one cylinder. Thanks for your—cooperation, Sergeant."

"Look, please try to understand. I was just doing my damn job. Trying to protect my own people."

"Your people?"

"The air force. It's the only family I've ever had. But for what it's worth, I really am sorry. About Buck. And the rest of it."

"I think you know what that's worth," I said.

"Yeah," he said, "I guess I do."

The rain paused briefly at first light, just long enough to reveal a pallid sun, bled white by the storm. But then the sky darkened and the torrent resumed with a vengeance, an icy, wind-driven drizzle, the kind you only see in northern Michigan, or Seattle, or Nome.

Jenkins had told the colonel about my visit. I could tell by the wariness in his eyes as he greeted Eva Redfern and me at the reception center. None of us spoke of it, still the tension was there, like a fuse smoldering just below the surface. An explosion only a word away.

The gathering was almost a repeat of the day before, reporters, a few cameramen, and a gaggle of local politicians. But there were no hors d'oeuvres, no air of gaiety. It was less a celebration than a wake. A vigil for a sidewalk Indian who'd traded the poverty of the reservation for an ugly death, far from his home and his people. A wake for Jerry Buck.

Another difference was the presence of Dr. Klein and a half dozen of his neo-hippie students. I'd thought Colonel Webber might object when they arrived, but I made it clear they were the honored guests of the Ojibwa Nation. Klein and his raggedy clan of peaceniks had protested the presence of nuclear death on this land for years. They'd been ridiculed, harassed, and arrested. Right or wrong, they'd paid their dues, they'd earned admission to this last matinee.

Jenkins surprised me by greeting Klein warmly, and openly. Shaking his hand. Webber's mouth soured in disapproval, but Jenkins's action seemed to defuse some of the tension in the room. If there was going to be trouble, it would have been between these two old adversaries. But there was no animosity left between them. They were like two fighters who go the distance, savaging each other until the final bell, and then embrace. Gladiators, with more spiritual kinship to each other than to those who never bled, no matter what their politics.

The actual transfer was almost an anticlimax. Colonel Webber made a brief speech of welcome, then introduced Mr. Kanelos and his attorneys, Eva Redfern, and me. He then transferred title to the property formerly known as Bullock Air Force Base, Strategic Air Command, to Mr. Frantzis Kanelos, head of Kanelos Waste Disposal. Kanelos in turn transferred the title to the legal representatives of the Ojibwa Nation in exchange for a permanent lease of the waste incinerator and four hundred acres of land adjacent to it. I'd suggested Redfern change the wording of his lease to read: for as long as the sun shall rise, but she said sarcasm had no place in a legal document.

And she was right. The stakes were too high. Native Americans have been swept into the corners of our continent by a tidal wave of history. Our past is over, we can only press on, and struggle to survive in the present. And sometimes that means eating the dirt of injustice and making the best of it.

But not always.

Kanelos signed the final documents with a grin and a flourish, to a smattering of polite applause. And I met Redfern's eyes and they were brimming, with joy or pain, I couldn't tell. Both, perhaps. But there was steel in her glance too. The land was ours again. We had a done deal.

"Ladies and gentlemen," I said, raising my voice, "on behalf of the Ojibwa Nation and its ruling council, I thank you for coming to witness this historic event. But as all of you know, the proceedings were marred by a tragedy, the accidental death of Geronimo Gall Cobmoosa, known to us as Jerry Buck. To honor Jerry's memory, and to exemplify the brotherhood that now exists between us, we would like to invite Mr. Kanelos to lead a candlelight procession to lay a wreath where Jerry Buck died. Doctor Klein will pass out candles and umbrellas at the door—"

"Wait a minute," Kanelos said, glancing at Webber, "you mean go out there on the runway now? With candles?"

"What's a little rain?" I said. "With a prosperous future—"

"Forget it, Frank," Webber broke in. "Jenkins told me Delacroix was out on the runway last night, damn near got himself killed. This is just his idea of a little joke. He knows it's not safe out there."

"It's not a joke," I said. "It was a fishing expedition. I needed to be sure Mr. Kanelos knew about the fuel spill."

"Even if I did, it won't make any difference to our agreement," Kanelos said uneasily. "My lawyers—"

"Assured you it's rock solid," I finished for him. "I certainly hope so. In any case, since it is a little damp for a candlelight procession, we've arranged alternate entertainment. Ladies and gentlemen, please step to the observation window to view a small display . . ."

Far down the perimeter road, there was a blast of white smoke, and three solitary shafts of light flashed into the gunmetal overcast above the runway. And burst into red flowers of flame, sputtering gamely in the darkness. Candles in the rain.

". . . of fireworks," I finished.

"What?" Webber said, his face going grey. "You can't—"

But it was too late. In slow motion, the flares continued their arc across the sky, and began to fall, raining petals of fire down on the tarmac. There was a deep chuff, like a sharp intake of breath, and the runway burst into flame, in scattered spots at first, but quickly dancing across the surface of the water, until the fires united in an inferno a half mile across, howling into the sky as though the gates of hell had opened.

I moved quietly back and stepped out onto the portico, joining Redfern and Dr. Klein at the railing. Reporters and cameramen streamed past us, drawn like moths to the flames. A few minutes later Jenkins sauntered out and stood behind Dr. Klein. Jenkins's face was a carved, ebon mask. I could read nothing in it.

"Quite a bonfire," he said at last.

"Not so bad," Klein said. "Compared to Kuwait, this one's a marshmallow roast. By my calculations, it should burn between five and six hours, depending on how much fuel has evaporated over the years. And that will be the end of it."

"And of the runway, and the incinerator," Jenkins said. "Ain't you worried Kanelos will sue your tails off?"

"I hope he tries," Redfern said grimly. "I'd love to take his deposition under oath, about what he knew and when, about the fire hazard that killed Jerry Buck."

"Good point," Jenkins conceded. "Doubt the government will bother you either. Might try though. The colonel's in there ravin' about sabotage. Ordered me to arrest all three of you, in fact."

"So?" I said. "Are we under arrest?"

"Hell no," Jenkins said wryly. "It just shows how shaky his grip on reality is. We've got no authority to arrest anybody. This isn't a military base anymore. Won't even look much like one in a few hours. Won't be anything left of that runway but gravel and ash. A couple years, you won't even be able to tell it was there."

"There'll always be traces of it," Klein said. "When you cauterize the earth, it leaves scars. I wonder what archaeologists will make of them a thousand years from now?"

"Maybe if we're real lucky, Doc," Jenkins said quietly, "they'll look around and scratch their heads. And won't even be able to guess what it was used for."

Out on the perimeter of the field, the blaze was already burning low, the concrete sizzling and cracking in the drizzle. But on the tarmac near the spot where Jerry Buck died, the inferno still raged on, furiously roiling plumes of oily smoke into the sky. The flames leapt and twisted and writhed, like a ring of ghostly dancers, carrying candles in the rain.

The Bad Boyz Klub

They drifted in by twos and threes, some carrying coffee cups from the vending machine in the hallway. The classroom's metal chairs were arranged in a semicircle facing the desk and they slouched into them in no particular order. It was only the second meeting for this group, too soon for cliques to form.

The men were a mixed lot, mid-twenties to late thirties, a couple of biker types in denim vests, autoworkers in coveralls or flannel shirts, a few professional men in sport coats and slacks. One man was in uniform: a renta-cop. A typical crew.

"Good evening, gentlemen. Welcome to the Domestic Violence Program, under the aegis of the 14th District Court, city of Flint. I'm Dr. Colleen Mackenzie, Assailants Counselor—"

"Doc, it's only been a week. We haven't forgotten your name. Not yet, anyway." Charlie Weeks. Car salesman, fortyish, tweed sport coat over a maroon turtleneck.

He'd thrown his wife through a screen door into the street. At her interview she told me he was a devoted husband and father. Her medical records showed a long pattern of minor injuries typical of abuse.

"Actually we don't all know it, Mr. Weeks," I countered mildly. "We have a new member tonight, Mr. Florian Woytazek, the gentleman on the end." Woytazek nodded warily at the others. An autoworker, he was wearing dungarees, a brushcut, thick glasses, and an owlish look.

"Welcome to the Bad Boyz Klub, Flory," Jojo Lassiter said. "What's your beef? Goose your old lady in church?"

"We'll deal with specifics later, Mr. Lassiter," I said. "Everyone's specifics." Lassiter was a biker, compactly built with a dark, shaggy mane, a Fu Manchu moustache, jeans, leather vest. He seemed affable enough, but his girlfriend had gone underground, refusing to testify against him. A bad sign.

"Mr. Woytazek will be the last new member of this therapy group, we're at our limit, so from here on—"

"Actually, I think we're already short one, Doc. Vic Manetti won't be coming." The voice was one of the group's two blacks. Martin Cleveland, a TV cameraman for Channel 18, mid-twenties, shaved head, goatee, dressed like a college jock, Dockers, deck shoes, a teal Eddie Bauer sweater. He'd slapped his wife out of her chair in a Taco Bell. "Haven't you heard about Vic?"

"No. Has something come up with him?"

"You might say that," Cleveland said. "He got busted this afternoon. He, um, he murdered his old lady."

Dead silence. I had a quick flash of Linette Manetti, slender, girlish, dishwater blonde hair that hung to her waist. Retro-hippie paisley granny dress. Defiantly barefoot at her interview in my office, daring me to comment. I hadn't.

"He killed her?" Charlie Weeks echoed, straightening in his chair. "You mean that little blonde he showed us? What the hell happened?"

"My station caught the squeal off our police scanner," Cleveland said. "Neighbors reported a domestic dispute. The cop at the scene said the apartment was all smashed to hell, wouldn't let us film inside. They were bringing her body out when Vic showed. He tried some lame-ass alibi but they didn't buy it. He left in handcuffs. Story'll be on the eleven o'clock news, A-bag or maybe B. I got a nice goodbye shot of Vic through the prowl car window. He didn't look too happy."

"And so it goes," I said, hoping I looked less shaken than I felt. "Welcome to the wide world of domestic violence, guys. Let's get to work, beginning with the confidentiality pledge. Read it aloud with me please. *On my honor, whatever I see here, whatever we say here, stays here. I will discuss these sessions only with members of this group.*" Some of them mumbled the words at the top of their work sheets. Most didn't.

"The Bad Boyz Klub's now in session," Weeks added dryly. "Membership nine and shrinking fast."

I couldn't recall which joker named this particular therapy group the Bad Boyz Klub. Someone wisecracked about it in the first meeting and I found it scrawled on the slateboard after the coffee break, underlined, with a cartoon baseball bat for an exclamation point.

No problem. Domestic Violence Assailants Groups are edgy sessions. Anything that bonds the members to each other and hopefully to the therapeutic process is fine by me.

After Cleveland's bombshell, George Falkenburgh, a pudgy, earnest high school teacher related a domestic argument that didn't end in violence. He seemed proud of his new-found self-control. On the other hand, he'd been just as pleased when he'd described knocking his wife around at a family picnic. Family discipline, he'd called it. Right.

Still, it was better than silence. Sometimes in the first weeks domestic assailants are so resentful of court-ordered counseling that they scarcely talk. The Bad Boyz were surly and sarcastic, but at least some of them were talking.

And some weren't. Leroy Gant, a lanky, tousle-haired Tennessee import, hadn't said anything but his name so far. He might not. He'd stabbed his wife in a drunken quarrel and was facing prison time no matter what my counseling evaluation said.

The session fairly flew by, driven mostly by a discussion of Manetti's situation. Murder. An ugly word. I hoped someone would make a connection between Manetti's violence and their own, but I didn't point it out myself. Any chance for real change had to begin with them. So far, we were batting zero.

We closed the final hour with the pledge and they filed out. All but one.

Griswold, Oliver Daniel. He'd asked the group to call him Griz at the first meeting. No one argued. A six-foot, two-hundred sixty pound biker, he'd trashed his ex-wife's car with a Louisville Slugger. There was no testimony he'd ever struck her, but one look at him was enough for the judge. Counseling or jail.

"Can I talk to you a minute, Doc?"

"A minute, but not much more," I cautioned. "What's up?"

"A simple question. Is that pledge we say for openers legal? I mean, are these meetin's really off the record? Or could some of this be used against us in court?"

"Anything you say here is protected by doctor-patient privilege unless it's an overt threat against someone. Why? Is there a problem?"

"I got no problem, Doc, but Vic Manetti does. He couldn't have killed his old lady this afternoon. He was with me all day."

I eyed him a moment. A joke? No, his body language said he was serious. "If that's true, shouldn't you talk to the police?"

"No way. Manetti's a dealer, you know? Coke, crack, weed, speed, whatever. He was pitchin' everybody in the john on the break at our first meeting. I happened to know some people who were lookin' to make a buy so I set up a meet. We were together all afternoon doin' a deal and a few lines of product. That's why he lied to the cops about where he was."

"But surely now that he's been arrested he'll explain."

"The cops won't believe him and the guys he did the deal with are serious people, outlaw Iron Hawgs, both of them. They aren't about to alibi Manetti even if he's crazy enough to rat 'em out. They'd waste him in a New York second and me with him."

"If you're not willing to help him, why are you telling me about this?"

"Because it's . . . wrong, that's all. Manetti ain't no choirboy but he didn't wax his wife. You're a Doc and Docs are supposed to fix things. Okay, how about fixin' this?"

"Without involving you, you mean?"

"Damn straight. It's tough about Vic but I ain't lookin' to get jammed up over it. Push comes to shove, Manetti's nothin' to me. You ain't either, for that matter."

"That almost sounds like a threat, Mr. Griswold."

"No, ma'am, I'm a little crazy but I ain't stupid. I never threaten ladies, especially not officers of the court." He rose, his beard split by a gap-toothed grin. He hesitated at the door. "You know, I got no beef with that affirmative action crap, but there's one big drawback to bein' a lady doctor."

"Such as?"

"You can't use the men's room and a lot of Bad Boyz Klub business goes down there. Last week, Manetti wasn't only dealin' dope, he was tryin' to peddle his old lady's ass for two hundred a bang. Even showed pictures of her around. Beaver shots, you know? I think a couple guys mighta took him up on it. Manetti's scum and his old lady wasn't no better. You seem like a nice lady, passable lookin', educated and all. Why do you even bother about losers like them? I mean, what's the point?"

"I guess the point is that sometimes I can help. Sometimes things can get better."

"Even for trailer trash like Manetti?"

"Sometimes even for a guy like you, Mr. Griswold."

"You're gonna straighten me out, Doc?" He snorted. "You're a real dreamer, you know that?"

"Maybe I'm just an optimist. It comes with the territory. I'll, um, see what I can do about Manetti. See you next week?"

He stalked out without answering. In psychology there's a syndrome called the doorknob effect. A patient will often wait until his hand's on the doorknob to tell you what's really troubling him. Doorknob effect. Griz stayed to tell me about Manetti, but in the end he asked if there was any hope for Manetti. Or maybe for himself? Maybe, maybe not. As Freud said, sometimes a cigar is just a cigar.

"It's a scam, Colleen," Burris said, leaning back in his chair, lacing his fingers behind his head. "The guy's blowin' smoke at you tryin' to help out a buddy." Detective Gene Burris has thinning hair, stooped shoulders, and the gentlest brown eyes this side of a cocker spaniel.

Deceptive eyes. His closure rate for homicide cases is one of the best on the force. And I'd stopped by his office to ask him to reopen one.

"I don't think he was lying," I said. "He had no reason to."

"People don't need reasons to lie, Doc. They do it to get over or because they're scared or just for the hell of it. Sometimes they lie when the truth would serve 'em better and you know it."

"Not this time," I said. "He had nothing to gain by telling me, and a lot to lose."

"He had nothing to lose. You're bound by doctor-patient confidentiality and he knows it."

"But he couldn't be sure I'd honor it. He took a chance."

"I'm telling you, Doc, we've got Manetti dead bang. He's

got a history of violence toward his wife, he was stoked to the gills on crank and his alibi was a total crock."

"My . . . source said Manetti was doing drugs at the deal. He also said he'd been pimping for his wife. If she was earning for him, why would he kill her?"

"Who knows? Maybe he was too wrecked to know what he was doing. The M.O. even fit him to a tee, or maybe an AT&T. He beat her to death with a phone book."

"A phone book?"

"More or less. He used his fists for openers, then finished her off with the book. According to his file he's used it on her before."

"He mentioned that." I nodded. "In the first session some members talked about why they were there. Manetti said he used a phone book to beat his wife because it didn't leave bruises."

"A prince of a guy."

"Okay, he's pond scum. So we just hang him on general principles whether he did it or not?"

He eyed me a moment, then slowly shook his head. "You know, if it was anybody but you, Doc, I'd write you off as a Froot Loop and forget it."

"But you won't."

"Not yet, anyway. I can't promise anything, but I'll keep the investigation active, see what we turn up. Deal?"

"Deal. I owe you one, Gene."

"Actually, I owe you one and we both know it," he said quietly. "Remember a few years ago when I was seeing you for post-traumatic stress after I . . . used my weapon on that kid?"

I nodded.

"I recall coming to one session pretty loaded. I even talked about eating my gun. I've seen your post-treatment evaluation report on me. It didn't mention any of that."

"How did you get that report? They're confidential."

"Hey, I'm an ace detective, Doc, it's what I do. But my career would have been toast if you'd labeled me suicidal."

"I didn't think you were."

"Even so, you stepped over the line to give me a break, so I'll return the favor. Don't step over the line with this Bad Boyz Klub of yours. Dot every i, cross every t. Okay?"

"What are you saying?"

"I've already said more than I should have. Just be sure you do everything by the book with this bunch."

It was my turn to stare. "What's up, Gene? What's special about this group? Are you saying somebody's planted a ringer in it? A narc or something? Is that what you're telling me?"

"I didn't say that, Doc, and you'd better not say it either. In fact, we never had this conversation. Okay?"

"It's a damned good thing," I said, flushing. "Because if you'd actually told me that, I'd have to inform the court and go after somebody's butt."

"There's no need for that, Doc, it's got nothing to do with you. Just be careful is all. Please."

"I'll keep it in mind," I said, hesitating in the doorway. Doorknob effect? "One question, Gene. Was Vic Manetti the guy your undercover type was after?"

"It's always good to see you, Doc. Take care now, hear?"

"Damn it, I won't stand for it," I raged, pacing the worn carpeting. "It's illegal to say nothing of unethical."

"Unethical definitely," Mavis Dellums said placidly. "I'm not so sure about illegal." She was knitting at her desk behind a pile of paperwork, a massive, motherly brown woman with four kids, a fireman husband, and responsibility for the budget and personnel of a multimillion-dollar mental health facility. My boss. My friend.

"But it's crazy, Mavis. They can't use anything they hear in court anyway, it's protected by privilege. But even so, our patients come here for therapy, not to be spied on."

"These particular patients didn't exactly crawl in on their own pleading for help," Mavis countered mildly. "They were sent here by a judge."

"All the more reason to be sure the process won't be used against them. It's just wrong."

"So is domestic violence, Colleen, but you deal with both sides of it every day. So how do you want to deal with this?"

"I'm not sure. Burris went out on a limb to warn me. If I kick up a fuss he could get burned. I don't want that."

"Then maybe you should just take his advice and be careful. Call me silly, but if I was working with a roomful of violent assailants, I think I could live with the idea that one of 'em was an undercover cop."

"And what's next? Do we bug our offices? Turn over our files? No way. I won't have a police spy in my group. I want him gone. I'm just not sure how to go about it. Yet."

"Maybe your problem will solve itself. If this undercover cop was after Manetti, he'll drop out of the group now that Manetti's in custody, right? End of problem."

"And if no one drops out?"

"Then I think you have more to worry about than one of your clients being a cop."

"What do you mean?"

"The thing is, I doubt the police would risk violating doctor-client confidentiality over a simple domestic abuse case. The guy they want must be into something a lot heavier. If I were you, girl, I'd be worrying less about your cop and more about the man he's after."

I opened my mouth to argue, then closed it. Because she

was my boss, and my friend. And as usual, she was dead right.

No one dropped out. The following meeting had a full roster, nine clients. Damn.

"Gentlemen, welcome to the third session of—"

"The Bad Boyz Klub," Charlie Weeks interrupted.

"Minus one," someone added.

"I'm glad you mentioned it," I said. "Since it's on everyone's mind, let's spend this session discussing Mr. Manetti's problems."

"His big problem's life plus twenty years," Martin Cleveland said. "Can we cover that in two hours?"

"We can take up a collection," Jojo Lassiter cracked, giving Griz a nudge. "Send him a pizza with a file in it."

"Maybe you should save that file for yourself, Mr. Lassiter," I said. "Or are Manetti's problems so different from yours?"

"Vic made his own mess," Weeks said. "He was a loser, a degenerate who freaked out and killed his woman. It's got nothing to do with the rest of us."

"No? Let's consider a hypothetical situation a moment. Put yourselves in Manetti's situation, guys. Your wife, ex-wife, or significant other is murdered. Brutally. Whom do you think would be elected the number one suspect? Mr. Falkenburgh?"

The pudgy schoolteacher blinked, frowning. "Well, I suppose we'd be suspects, the husband always is, but—"

"But you're not an average husband, are you, Mr. Falkenburgh? According to your dossier, you slapped your wife around at a picnic in front of witnesses. How do you think the prosecuting attorney would react to that? Or a jury?"

"But it would never go that far," Falkenburgh said. "Maybe the police would suspect me at first, but they'd eventually find the real murderer."

"Wrong," Martin Cleveland said thoughtfully. "Cops quit looking when they think they've got the right guy. And we'd all be that guy, wouldn't we, Doc? That's what you're saying?"

"In Manetti's situation, with a record of violence and no alibi, you're right, Mr. Cleveland, you'd be the prime suspect. And so would every other man here."

"But this is all hypothetical crap," Earl Macklin said the first time he'd spoken in the group. Macklin was a weasel-faced security guard who wore his uniform to meetings either because he was going to work or because he thought epaulets buffed up his skinny frame. "Manetti was an honest-to-God criminal. People in that life attract trouble. But most of us are just workin' slobs. Our wives aren't in danger."

"Mine is," Weeks cracked. "As soon as I get off probation."

"That's perfect, Charlie," I snapped. "You just threatened your wife in front of witnesses. And the fact is, every man in this room is capable of violence toward women. You're all members of the club. The Bad Boyz Klub."

"Hey, anybody wants a shot at my old lady, go for it," Charlie said. "My support payments are killing me." But for once no one laughed. They were still mulling over Manetti's problems. And their own. Good.

"All right, Mr. Macklin. Let's make our hypothetical case a bit more real. Suppose there was compelling evidence that Manetti did not kill his wife."

"Whoa, you're wandering off-base, Doc," Martin Cleveland said. "My cops say the evidence fits Manetti like a glove."

"Like O.J.'s glove maybe," I said. "The police are convinced Vic did it because his wife was beaten with a phone book and Manetti'd used one on her before. But you all knew that, didn't you? He talked about it in the first session. He seemed rather proud of it, as I recall."

"So he used it again," Lassiter groused. "So what?"

"No," I said evenly. "Let's bring our problem totally into reality now. There actually is strong evidence that Vic did not kill his wife, that it must have been someone else."

A rustling through the room, shuffling feet, glances exchanged. "What kind of evidence?" Macklin asked.

"I'm sorry, I can't tell you that. But I can tell you the police haven't closed their investigation. It's ongoing."

"Then why's Manetti still in jail?" asked Charlie Weeks.

"Because, as Martin noted, the evidence fits him. And that's a problem, guys. Because if Manetti didn't do it but the evidence indicates he did, then that evidence must have been fabricated by someone who knew about his previous behavior."

"Like . . . one of us, you mean?" Cleveland said quietly.

"Not necessarily. Manetti mentioned the phone book here but he could have told others as well. But if you're looking for a pool of suspects with the proper knowledge and a history of violence toward women . . . ?"

"Welcome to the Bad Boyz Klub," Griz said darkly. "Jesus."

"You're serious about this Manetti business, aren't you?" Charlie Weeks asked. "This isn't just some schoolhouse game?"

"Most people take murder seriously, Mr. Weeks. Don't you?"

"But you're saying we could be in real trouble here, right?" Falkenburgh said. "Not only could the police suspect one of us of killing Manetti's wife, but if somebody else really did do it, it could happen again. He could stalk one of our wives knowing we'd be blamed for it."

"This is crazy," Jojo Lassiter said. "Nobody's gonna take a run at your old lady, Falkenburgh. Take a look around. We may have a few problems in this room but we ain't psycho killers."

"Looking's not enough, Mr. Lassiter," I said. "I've been a therapist nearly fifteen years. I've worked with troubled kids and hardtime cons, battered women and assailants, but if you put me on the stand and asked me to swear no one here's dysfunctional enough to commit murder, I couldn't do it. More than half of the killings in America stem from domestic violence and we definitely know you're all capable of that, don't we?"

"This ain't right," Cleon Tibbits, the other black in the group, put in. A huge, alcoholic laborer, Tibbits' violence was usually triggered by booze, a resolvable problem. I had hopes for him. "The judge sends us here, now you're sayin' we could be jammed up for doin' what he said?"

"The court didn't put you here, Mr. Tibbits, your behavior did. As for it not being fair, you're right. It might seem like poetic justice to some people, but it's definitely not fair."

"So life ain't fair," Macklin said. "Is this news to anybody? I sure as hell never caught a break and I'm not about to sit around waitin' for this crap to hit the fan either."

"No?" Weeks asked. "What have you got in mind, sport?"

"An alibi, for openers. From here on out I'm gonna make damned sure I'm around other people as much as possible. Mostly I'm covered because I'm at work or bowling or whatever."

"I never bowled in my life," Tibbits growled.

"Then maybe you'd better start, pal," Macklin shot back. "Unless you're lookin' to do natural life in a graybar motel room next to Manetti."

"Maybe we could work out a system," Falkenburgh put in. "If we all made up schedules, we could help cover each other. Meet for dinner instead of eating alone, maybe play cards or something."

"Turn into a real boys club, you mean?" Lassiter snorted, rising, glaring around. "This is a load of crap! It's bad enough I gotta listen to your whinin' about what a fuckup you are, Falkenburgh. I ain't interested in bein' your pal. Screw this, I'm outa here. How 'bout you, Griz?"

"No," Griswold said, shaking his massive head slowly. "I think I'm goin' along. If what the Doc says is true, we could be in somebody's sights already. The law or whoever. Makes sense to gang up, watch each other's backs."

"Like in the army," Tibbits said.

"Somethin' like that," Griswold said. "You in the army?"

"Eight years," Tibbits nodded. "Rangers. You?"

"Marines for five, last one in Leavenworth for sluggin' a captain."

"Hey, I'll buy you a beer behind that," Tibbits chuckled. "Thought about it real hard a few times myself."

"You see?" Falkenburgh said. "Maybe we've got more in common than we think. Maybe we can make it work."

"You're nuts, the lot of ya," Lassiter growled. But he didn't walk out. He eased back down in his chair.

"Okay, we can cover each other some," Weeks said, "but that's only half of it. Maybe we should do a little detective work of our own, check each other's alibis for the Manetti thing."

"Rat each other out, you mean?" Lassiter said. "This is gettin' better and better."

"We wouldn't burn anybody who didn't deserve it, which is more than you can say for what the cops might do to us," Weeks said. "Maybe Falkenburgh can make up a list of where everybody says he was and we can check it out."

"Who checks it out, Weeks?" Lassiter shot back. "You?"

"No, we do it in pairs, that way nobody can pull anything and like our pledge says, anything we find stays in the group. Except for the guy who actually did it. What do you say?"

Nods and a general murmur of assent.

"So how about it Lassiter? Any reason why you don't want us to know where you were at the time?"

"It's nobody's business where I was. You ain't the law, Weeks. But I'll tell you what, if Griz here signs on, I'll go along." He glanced at Griswold, who nodded.

"Okay," Weeks nodded. "So let's get started. Who's first?"

The rest of the meeting was spent working out schedules and cross-referencing same. Technically it wasn't therapy, but since the toughest part of working with an assailants group is getting them to interact, I could live with it. Maybe they were only trying to save their miserable butts, but at least they were talking to each other.

I waited in the classroom after the session in case anyone wanted to see me. Like an undercover cop, perhaps. No such luck. But as I approached my car in the dimly lit underground ramp, a figure stepped out of the shadows. Lassiter, hardbitten and angry in a faded jeans jacket and a two-day stubble.

"Hi, Doc. I need to talk to you."

"Not here you don't and if you take one more step, Mr. Lassiter, you'll get a faceful of pepper spray, industrial strength. Now back off before I call security."

"Chill out, Doc. I didn't mean to spook you."

"The hell you didn't."

"Okay, okay, maybe I did a little. Look, I need to show you something. It's in my vest pocket so don't shoot me or zap me or whatever." With one hand raised, he opened his jacket, lifted out a folder and flipped it open. A gold badge. "I'm a cop."

"Actually, that's a detective's badge," I said. "Who's the secretary of the patrolmen's union?"

"The union? Dan Postlewaite. Why?"

"Because anybody can buy a badge or steal one. Okay, so you're probably a real cop. So?"

"You don't seem surprised."

"Actually I've met enough cops that I don't get all wobbly-kneed when somebody flashes a badge at me, Detective Lassiter. Or isn't that your name?"

"My name's Jack Hutchinson. Hutch, to my friends."

"I'm not one of your friends. I'm more interested in what you're doing in a court-ordered therapy group using a false name."

"My job, just like you are."

"Wrong. I'm doing my job within ethical and legal limits. How do you think the judges who ordered these men into counseling would react to a cop infiltrating the group to spy on them?"

"I'm not here to spy, exactly. Look, Doc, I'll lay it out, straight up. The gang I'm working is super bad news, they're into guns, extortion, drugs, and probably murder. The last guy who tried to infiltrate them wound up dead in the road, hit and run. Almost looked like an accident, except he'd been run over five or six times by somebody who really enjoyed the work.

"He was a good cop and he was my friend and now my butt's on the line. The way you've got the Bad Boyz checking each other out one of those clowns might just stumble over my cover at which point I stand a real good chance of becoming a traffic fatality myself. Please, you've got to get them off this kick."

"I'm sorry, but I can't do that. Ethically, I'm bound to maintain the confidentiality of the group and you're compromising it just by being there."

"The group? The Bad Boyz Klub? For pete's sake, every one of them's a wife beater or worse. I don't understand how an intelligent woman can bear to be in the same room with them let alone try to help them. You don't really believe you're going to turn their heads around in fourteen weeks, do you?"

"Not all of them, no. Maybe one or two."

"One or two?" he echoed in disbelief. "And you're willing to blow a year's investigation and risk my life for that?"

"I'm not putting your life at risk, Detective, you are. I understand you're in a dangerous situation and I don't want to make things tougher for you, but I won't let you spy on my group and that's it."

"Or what? You publish my name in the paper? How many court referrals do you think you'll get when word gets out that you let a cop killer walk so your little club could play detective?"

"Look, Lassiter, I'm not looking for a beef with you. Suppose we compromise? If you drop out now you can walk away with your cover intact. Make up any story you like. I won't lie for you but I won't contradict you either."

"And I'm supposed to bet my life you won't accidentally drop my name in the faculty lounge?"

"I've done counseling for the department and I have friends on the force who'll vouch for me. I can give you a name or two."

"No thanks. After what happened to the last guy, the fewer people who know I'm here, the better."

"Then I guess you're stuck with my word, which is worth at least as much as yours, whatever you said your name was."

"Point taken," he conceded with a wry smile. A good smile. For a moment I glimpsed what he probably looked like minus the rock'n'roll hair and attitude.

"Okay, Doc, I walk away, you keep your mouth shut about me and we're even. Deal?"

"Not quite. I want to know if the man you're after—"

"I can't tell you anything about him."

"I'm not asking you to. I just want to know if he's a threat to the group?"

"Lady, being on the same planet with the guy is risky, but your little club is in no more danger than anyone else."

"Fair enough. And Vic's wife? Could he have had anything to do with her death?"

Lassiter blinked, surprised by the question. "No, I don't see how. I keep pretty close tabs on him."

"All right," I said, beeping my car unlocked with the remote control. "Decide what you want me to say about your leaving, Detective, make a graceful exit and good luck. I hope things work out for you."

"Maybe I'll buy you a beer and tell you about it sometime."

"Sorry, I never socialize with clients," I said, sliding behind the wheel.

"But I'm not a client. You just fired me, didn't you? So how about a beer? Or dinner? Or something? Sometime?"

"Okay, maybe," I nodded, shaking my head at his persistence. "Sometime. Later." He grabbed the corner of the car door as I pulled it closed. "One last question, Doc. Why are you so sure Vic didn't kill his wife? Something he told you?"

"Good night, Detective." I closed the door and fired up the car.

"Psychic hotline?" Lassiter called after me, grinning as I backed out. "Or can you read minds?"

Halfway home, in both senses of the word. With luck, Lassiter/Hutchinson would drop out without a ripple, preferably without badmouthing me to the department. Which still left me with the second half of the problem. If the man he was hunting was as dangerous as he'd said, he didn't belong in a therapy group where the confidences shared by the participants could make them vulnerable to a predatory criminal. The Bad Boyz weren't angels, but they weren't beyond help either. Or at least, not all of them.

Lassiter's parting shot about being a mind reader stung a bit. Psychologist/mind reader/witch doctor. Synonyms. Arggh. And every shrink on TV is either a nebbish or a whiz kid who solves crimes by brilliantly interpreting a dream or a doodle.

I suppose it actually happens but people hit the lotto, too. I'm not one of them. The truth is simpler. The keys to effective clinical work are empathy, insight, and a nose for detail. Most breakthroughs take months, not minutes, and clients heal and reveal themselves in ordinary office interviews, not on ledges forty stories up.

I was so lost in thought I was nearly home before I realized I was being followed. Living in a quiet suburban neighborhood has its plusses. Strange cars stand out. The car was a new Cadillac Seville, burgundy with darkened windows. Lassiter? Unlikely. Cops don't drive Caddies, undercover or otherwise.

Perhaps it was the man he was after. I made a series of left turns in the village of Metcalf and thought I'd lost him, but as I crossed the Genessee Bridge I spotted him again.

I pulled into my driveway, hurried into the house and waited beside the living room window. The Caddy cruised past, made a U-turn at the end of the block and parked across the street. No one got out.

I changed into sweats and tennis shoes, keeping a wary eye on the car the whole time. To hell with this. I slipped out the back door, skulked across a couple of lawns and came out behind the Caddy. I only wanted the plate number, but when I saw it I knew. It was a dealer plate. It figured.

Stepping into the street, I walked up to the Caddy and rapped on the window. It hummed open.

"What are you doing here, Mr. Weeks?"

"Hey, I'm just taking my therapy seriously, Doc, all that stuff about looking out for each other. I mean, suppose Falkenburgh's right and there's a serial killer around?"

"I see. So you're here to protect me?"

"Something like that. And I thought we could get to know each other better. Socially, I mean."

"And your wife? Isn't she part of your social life?"

"Libby's the understanding type, besides she'll never hear about it. Anything between us is privileged information, right Colleen? C'mon, hop in. I'm sittin' in a forty thousand dollar ride here. Let's live a little."

I took a deep breath, then rested my arms on the window ledge, crowding him a little. "You want to know me better? Gee, where should I start? Four years ago I was attacked. I was between sessions at the institute and the husband of a woman I was counseling jumped me and dragged me into a utility room."

Weeks blinked rapidly. "What, um, what happened?"

"I got roughed up pretty badly. I'm not a wuss, I work out, I run, try to stay in shape—"

"I noticed that."

"Yeah, well it didn't matter. The guy outweighed me by a hundred pounds and he was wired on speed. I just couldn't handle him."

"So he—I mean, did he—"

"Rape me? Why? Would that bother you?"

"Well, no—I mean—I just—"

"Oh, don't be embarrassed. A lot of men have trouble dealing with women who've been victimized. Makes them feet inadequate or guilty about their own rape fantasies. I can understand that. I had trouble dealing with it myself."

"What did you do? See a shrink?" He chuckled uneasily.

"No. I bought a gun."

"A gun?"

"That's right. One of my cop friends picked it out. A derringer. Forty-five caliber. The kind Booth used to kill Lincoln only with better ammo. Very effective. I carry it all the time. I love the way it feels in my hand. Hard, you know? Freud thought guns were phallic substitutes. What do you think?"

"I, um—"

"Personally, I think it's more like an un-phallic symbol. If guys think having a penis is power, well, mine's bigger than yours now and it's right here in my pocket. There's a danger to carrying a weapon, though. One I'm sure you can relate to."

"One I can—?"

"Self-control. When somebody makes me angry I have real difficulty controlling my temper. I tend to blow up. The same way you do with your wife, Mr. Weeks. Of course, I'm not big enough to slap people around. But my little friend here is." I patted my pocket. "Do you understand what I'm saying to you, Charlie?"

"You, um, you want me to go, don't you?"

"I'll make it even plainer. If you ever follow me again or if I even see you in my neighborhood I'll rearrange your plumbing so you won't ever harass another woman. Because there'll be no . . . point, if you get my drift. Now take off."

"You're the one who needs a shrink," he muttered as he fired up his Cadillac and roared away. I watched him speed across the Genessee Bridge and disappear into the village, then took a .45 caliber roll of Life Savers out of my pocket and popped off the top one. Cherry. My favorite. I turned and trotted back to my cottage.

I spread the dossiers and interview note files of the Bad Boyz Klub members on the kitchen table, made a cup of cinnamon tea, then settled down for some serious reading. For a change I wasn't looking for hints of repressed homosexuality or substance abuse. A simple connection would do.

As an undercover cop, Lassiter knew he wouldn't be able to use anything he heard in a therapy session in court. So why was he there? I was betting he'd joined the group simply to meet someone and get next to him. But would a domestic assault beef be enough common ground? Probably not. He'd need more.

I scanned Lassiter's records for the minutiae that make up a life, even a false one. Date and place of birth, where you went to high school, college if any, military service, employment record, prior convictions . . . and there it was.

According to the file, Lassiter had served two years for narcotics possession in Jackson Prison. I had no way of knowing which bio facts were false, but no way could a felon be a cop. The prison time had to be a lie, which could make it important.

I quickly scanned the files of the other Bad Boyz and got a hit almost immediately. Griswold had served time in prison too, and he was the only member of the group who had. It made sense. Lassiter said his target was dangerous and as an ex-con in an outlaw biker gang Griz definitely qualified. A prison record would give them a common bond.

Jackson's the biggest, toughest walled prison in the world

with over six thousand hardcore inmates. Properly briefed and with a few yardbirds to vouch for him, Lassiter could make Griz believe he'd been there. As an ex-con he could be introduced to the Iron Hawgs without too many questions. It all fit.

There was no connection between Griswold and Linnette Manetti, but there didn't have to be. Vic had flashed her picture around so any of the Bad Boyz could have paid her a visit, as could anyone else he'd offered her to.

So what did I have? Apparently Griswold had important criminal connections or Lassiter wouldn't be after him. But did that mean I should bounce him out of my therapy group?

My professional experience with bikers has been mixed. Some are career felons, brain-damaged by the amphetamines they gobble like popcorn. Others are just outcasts who drift into the gang life looking for kindred spirits. But even the most sociopathic of them maintain a rudimentary sense of loyalty to their thug brotherhood, like wolves to their packs.

Griz had already demonstrated loyalty by trying to help Vic, and he'd put himself at risk by doing so. He might be a dangerous man, but so were the others. My gut told me he didn't pose a serious threat to the group. Still, I had a nagging feeling I was missing something about him, or someone. Some detail I'd seen in the records.

When in doubt, quit. Do something else, come back to the problem fresh. My Volvo was scheduled for maintenance so I drove over the bridge into Metcalf, parked the car at the dealership and dropped my keys through their mail slot. It was less than a mile home and the evening was warm so I didn't bother trying for a cab. I walked back instead, brooding all the way.

Metcalf is a small village of older homes on rolling hills, separated from Flint's urban sprawl by the Genessee Bridge over the murky Flint River. I paused in the middle of the bridge to stare down at the forty foot drop to the rocks below. The river's fifty yards wide but except for the narrow channel near the center, it's shallow as a freshman's fantasies.

The village lights were winking on and I could hear the roar of a crowd in the distance. Football game? No, not on a Tuesday. Soccer perhaps. Metcalf High had a first class . . . and that was it.

High school. Not Metcalf High, Flint Northern. They'd both gone to Flint Northern High and their birth dates were close enough that they could have been there at roughly the same time. That's the detail that had been bugging me.

I jogged the rest of the way across the bridge and down the narrow lane to my cottage. I hurried into the kitchen, but even before I noticed that the files spread out on the table were disarranged I felt a chill, a subconscious warning that I wasn't alone. Someone was here. I froze, unsnapping my purse just as he stepped out of the shadows.

He was wearing a motorcycle helmet with the visor down and a denim vest blazoned with the Iron Hawgs emblem. It wasn't much of a disguise. To me anyway.

"How the hell did you get in here, Lassiter? What do you want?"

"The truth," he said, taking off the helmet, shaking his shaggy mane free. "Look, I'm really sorry for all this but not knowing could get me killed. You've got to tell me why you think Vic didn't kill his wife. Please."

"You must be awfully desperate to risk a burglary charge trying to find out, but I guess I can understand that. Okay, Detective, I'll tell you what you need to protect yourself but I want to know some things too, to make sure this situation never comes up again. Fair enough?"

"Deal, Doc, whatever you say."

225

"All right. From Vic's record of violence and drug use, he was certainly capable of killing his wife, in fact, since Linette was easily as violent as Vic, it's a wonder they hadn't killed one another long since. But he definitely didn't do it."

"Why not?"

"Your turn. How did you get in here and how much of the bio information in your dossier is accurate?"

He hesitated, then shrugged. "Older home, old locks, piece of cake. You need a new security system, Doc, and a dog, a big one. As for the bio info, most of it's true so I don't trip up on minor points. I was never in prison, though. After the army I went to Michigan State. Police Science major. If Vic had a history of violence, what makes you think he didn't just crank it up a notch and kill her?"

"He has an alibi," I said simply. "A witness was with Vic when it happened. Where were you at the time, by the way?"

"Me? I told you, on stakeout watching my guy. Why?"

"And that's why you didn't want to tell the others where you were?"

"Exactly. So why hasn't this witness of yours come forward?"

"He can't without incriminating himself. He was doing a drug deal with Vic."

"One of the Bad Boyz?"

I nodded. "Is Griswold the man you're after?"

He hesitated, then smiled ruefully. "I asked around the department about you and they said you were sharp. They were right. Griz is an Iron Hawg, not the worst of them but bad enough. I'm hoping to work into the gang through him. I don't suppose you've got a cup of coffee handy?" His mood was easier now. Relaxed. Relieved?

"Sorry, but this hasn't turned into a social visit, Detective, at least not yet."

"No, I guess not. Okay, what you've got is a convicted felon who claims Vic's innocent of one crime because he was committing another one and won't testify to anything, is that about it?"

"Not quite. When Vic showed his wife's picture around in the men's room, you recognized her, didn't you?"

"Recognized her? I don't follow you." His face was blandly immobile. Unreadable. He was good. But then he'd have to be.

"You and Linette were in high school together. If she remembered you she could have gotten you killed. Is that what happened? Did she recognize you?"

"Nothing happened, lady, because I have no idea what you're talking about. I was on stakeout the day she bought it and you're way off base. Look, I'd better go. I'm real sorry about busting in here and all. I won't bother you again." He shook back his hair and put on his helmet.

"Detective? Your story won't fly. Griz is Vic's alibi. They were together that day doing a drug deal. If you'd been watching him you'd know that. You should have known."

His visor was down so I couldn't see his reaction. He didn't move. He stood there, frozen.

"It's not too late to get past this," I continued quietly. "I interviewed Linette and I can testify that she was unstable and violent. But you've got to talk to me now. What the hell happened?"

"Sweet Jesus," he said, turning away. "After my partner was killed I spent months developing a cover identity that could get me access to the gang. Griswold's domestic violence beef gave me an opening, but when Vic flashed a picture of his wife in the john I felt like I'd been kicked in the belly. For all I knew she'd seen me already and ratted me out. I had to know." He turned away, shaking his head.

"So I, um, I went to see her. I offered her five grand just to blow town until this was over. Figured the way Vic was treating her she'd jump at the chance. Instead she freaked out and attacked me. I couldn't believe it. Her old man beats her and sells her ass on the street and I hadn't done a thing to her. Nothing."

"She saw you as a threat to her family," I said simply.

"Family?"

"Or its equivalent. She was pathologically dependent on Vic, for drugs, sex, even violence. He was scum, but he was all she had. She was an emotional time bomb and you tripped her trigger. What happened when she attacked you?"

"I'm still not real clear on that. I've, um, I've been under a lot of pressure with this thing and I must've lost control for a minute. She tried to clobber me with a lamp and I decked her. I . . . hit her a lot harder than I meant to. She banged her head against a table, twisted her neck going down. I thought I'd just cold-cocked her but . . . She wasn't breathing. I tried mouth-to-mouth, seemed like forever. Nothing. She was gone. God." He sagged against the kitchen table, swallowing hard, covering his eyes with his fingertips. Then he steadied himself and took a deep breath.

"I should have called nine-one-one, but it happened so fast I wasn't thinking. Eight years on the force, I've never even drawn my weapon on anybody. I kept getting flashes of prison. Jackson. Like in my bio only for real. My God, Doc, do you know what happens to cops in jail? I thought if I could cover myself somehow . . . There was a little blood by her head so I dropped the phone book in it to make it look like Vic used it on her. I know that was wrong but all I could think about was getting clear. Vic's no loss, you said yourself it was a miracle he hadn't killed her before."

"But he didn't. Maybe he wouldn't have."

228

"That's kind of a moot point now. I'll be honest with you, Doc, I'm sorry as hell about this, but I'm not willing to throw myself away over it. I've spent my whole life trying to do the right thing. But if I'm in jail, there's no way I can ever make things right again. So the question is, what are you gonna do? Can you let this alone? Please. For God's sake, give me a break. I need a chance to redeem myself here. I'm begging you."

"Even if I was willing to go along, it wouldn't work, Hutch. I don't think you can live with this."

"And you're not willing to let me try, are you? Because it wouldn't be . . . ethical? A piece of crap like Vic Manetti gets priority, even if you have to bury me to do it, right? And I'm supposed to just lay down for it? Go to jail? Take it up the ass from bastards I've put away? Wrong, bitch! Wrong fucking answer!"

Without warning he lunged, swinging his helmet at my head like a flail. It bounced off my shoulder, slamming me against the counter and then he was on me, forcing me back, his hands on my throat, cutting off my air.

My spine was ablaze, ready to snap like a twig. My purse! I'd dropped it on the counter! Groping blindly as the room began to fade, I found the strap and dragged it to me.

Felt my car keys . . . the pepper spray on the key ring. Safety release? Couldn't remember how . . . something snapped off. I jammed the plunger down, spraying a full dose into Lassiter's eyes.

He roared, staggering backward into the table, knocking it over, going down. I reeled down the hall to the front door, stumbled down the steps, then I was off, shambling into an unsteady trot, instinctively heading for the lights of the village.

My lungs were on fire from the pepper spray I'd inhaled

but gradually my legs fell into a jogging rhythm, pounding across the bridge, carrying me to safety. I was more than halfway across when I heard the motorcycle roar onto the bridge. Lassiter, his face hidden by his helmet shield, wearing the Iron Hawgs vest . . .

My God, he'd planned to kill me from the beginning. I'd die in a hit and run, Griswold would be blamed and Lassiter could swear his life away.

But not yet. He was coming at me full bore, seventy at least. No way I'd make it across the bridge. Jump? To the rocks forty feet below? No. I only had one chance.

Whirling, I sprinted back the way I'd come, heading directly for Lassiter and the center of the bridge. At the last second I veered off and made a desperate dash for the opposite railing.

Lassiter swerved to follow, so totally focused on running me down that he'd didn't realize the angle of his attack was wrong now. But I'd misjudged the distance too. He was too close, I couldn't wait.

I launched myself toward the railing, slammed into it and managed to scramble over, failing, hoping to God I'd come far enough, hearing the shriek of steel against concrete as Lassiter skidded into the wall behind me and the blast of an explosion—

The river hammered me like a fist, smashing the breath out of me. I gagged, sucking water, stunned, sinking, dying and knowing it, feeling the weeds and muck of the river bottom reaching up to gather me down . . .

And somehow the slimy chill of the muck snapped me back to awareness, a guttering candle of will to live . . . and I made a last despairing thrust with my legs, vaulting myself upward, up toward the village lights glinting on the surface, up toward the air.

★ ★ ★ ★ ★

A smaller group filed in to take their seats. Somber, no joking. Each of them taking a silent head count, as I was. The Klub was three short now.

Vic was still in jail on drug charges, as was Griswold. Not for long though. Griz was going into witness protection in exchange for testimony about gang activities. It was the smart move, and in his wolfish way, Griz was a bright guy.

Lassiter? He lived for three days after the crash on the bridge. To their credit, the police hadn't tried to cover up his guilt in Linette Manetti's murder. Death and dishonor. A bad end. But one he'd earned.

I wasn't in much better shape. I'd broken my left arm at the bridge rail and the clumsy plastic cast was trussed in a sling. I was battered and bruised and weak as a roadkilled rabbit. Still, working was better than brooding, so here I was.

"Gentlemen, I'm sure most of you have heard about what happened last week—"

"Be hard not to," Charlie Weeks interrupted. "You've been all over the news, Doc." Irrepressible. Mentally, I dropped him from my list of potential cures.

"Since you're all here by court order," I continued, "if anyone wants to transfer to another group I'll try to arrange it."

"Why bother?" Macklin snorted. "Way things are going the Bad Boyz Klub's gonna run out of members pretty quick anyway."

"I'm staying," Weeks said. "I haven't had this much fun since my first wife got hit by a train. In fact, I've made a few calls to see about getting on *Geraldo* or *Hard Copy* and—"

"Will you shut the fuck up, Weeks!" Cleon Tibbits stood up, a dark giant towering over the others in his grubby coveralls. "You don't get it, do ya? This ain't some fuckin' joke! It never was. Vic's wife is dead, Lassiter's dead, Vic and Griz are in the slammer, and they got cells waitin' for the rest of us if we screw up one more time. What happened to Vic could have been any fuckin' one of us! Just because we're members of this stupid club.

"Well I'm sick of hearin' how the world's screwed ya'll over, sick of lookin' at your loser faces and seein' myself. I want out of this mess and anybody who can help, Doc or whoever, let's get to it. And any of you Bad Boyz who thinks I'm jokin' go ahead and laugh. But you'd best stand up first. How about you, Weeks? You think I'm funny?"

No one laughed. Not even Charlie Weeks. They eyed each other warily. Strangers again. I had no idea whether Tibbits' tirade made any impact at all, but I knew one speech couldn't change them. They'd spent their whole lives getting into this place. And overnight cures only happen in movies.

Still, it was an opening, a place to start, and we still had eleven weeks to try. Tibbits' rage would fade, men would show up drunk or high or just stop coming, and in the end I'd wind up reaching only one or two of them. As usual.

Or maybe the Bad Boyz really were as special as they pretended to be. Maybe I'd get lucky with them. Maybe this time I could actually reach three.